FOREST OF DOOM

The forest teemed with sounds as I strode along its edge, but I had no other choice—this was the only route possible.

Quite unexpectedly the sky darkened, and within minutes I was being pelted by windblown sheets of rain that drove me back into the dense foliage.

The thick roots around me were fascinating; they sent off a delicious pungent aroma. Innocently I watched as one by one their tactile ends separated and snaked across my arms, my legs—all over my body. When they began to constrict, I realized what was happening: *I was being torn apart!*

Searing bolts of pain assailed me—I cried out in agony, the piercing sound shattering the silence of the black forest. My teeth gnashed together and my body quivered as I struggled against the creeper.

Drawing the knife from by belt, I slashed at the monster, and it began to fall away slowly. Looking down, I saw that I was drenched in a sticky, rust-colored sap—the blood of these silent jungle creatures . . .

Don't Miss These Heroic Fantasy Favorites

RO-LAN #1: MASTER OF BORANGA   (616, $1.95)
by Mike Sirota

Swept into a strange, other dimensional world, Ro-lan is forced to fight for his life and the woman he loves against man, beast, and the all-powerful evil dictator, the MASTER OF BORANGA.

RO-LAN #2: THE SHROUDED WALLS OF BORANGA
by Mike Sirota   (677, $1.95)

Love and loyalty drive fearless and dashing Ro-lan to return to the horrifying isle of Boranga. But even if he succeeds in finding and crossing through the warp again, could he hope to escape that evil place of strange and hostile creatures?

THE TWENTIETH SON OF ORNON   (685, $1.95)
by Mike Sirota

Dulok, the twentieth son of Ornon, is determined to become the Survivor—the sole ruler of the mighty kingdom of Shadzea. But he is also determined to avenge the death of his mother—whose blood was spilled by the great Ornon himself!

THREE-RING PSYCHUS   (674, $1.95)
by John Shirley

The year is 2013 A.D. and the human race is faced with total destruction—or moving into the next stage of psychic development, the Great Unweighting: a partial cancellation of gravity, the destruction of cities, and the death of countless people.

Available wherever paperbacks are sold, or order direct from the Publisher. Send cover price plus 50¢ per copy for mailing and handling to Zebra Books, 21 East 40th Street, New York, N.Y. 10016. DO NOT SEND CASH!

THE SHROUDED WALLS OF BORANGA

RO-LAN #2

BY MIKE SIROTA

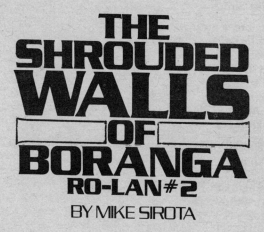

ZEBRA BOOKS

KENSINGTON PUBLISHING CORP.

ZEBRA BOOKS

are published by

KENSINGTON PUBLISHING CORP.
21 East 40th Street
New York, N.Y. 10016

Printed in the United States of America

FORWORD

More than a year had passed since I first became embroiled, however briefly, in the strange events surrounding the life, and presumed death, of Roland Summers. So often has the specter of that tormented young man dominated my thoughts; so often have I blamed myself for his demise. Others have assured me that Roland's apparent inclination toward self-destruction would have seen him accomplish his goal under any circumstance, that my role was nothing more than a matter of ill timing, and I know that they are right. Yet this scarcely lessens the hurt, and consequently I feel that I must shoulder some of the responsibility, for I had been the last to see him, the last among the few who cared.

Why, on this particular morning, did the image of his scarred, unnaturally aging face again haunt me? Doubtless it was because of the poorly wrapped, bulky parcel that had been delivered with the rest of the day's mundane letters and journals, the package that bore a Honolulu postmark. Honolulu, where it had all begun for Roland Summers, and where, unless one's hopes far exceeded the borders of reality, it had ended. For a short time after my return I had corresponded with one of the doctors at the Pacific Hills Medical Center, in the hope of hearing some definite word regarding Roland's fate. But the verdict remained unalterable, and the channel of communication between myself and the gleaming islands far to the west was closed—until now.

Two minor surgeries, the first scheduled in less than an hour at a crosstown hospital, would occupy a considerable portion of the day, and, despite the responsibility I felt toward my patients, I sorely regretted the fact that the contents of the parcel would remain a mystery until later. I locked the shabby bundle in my desk, and I assumed the most professional face that I could muster in embarking upon the busy day—one that, under normal circumstances, would have been relished, but which was soon to seem interminable.

All manner of foul-ups saw the afternoon lengthen into early evening, and not until I had satisfied myself as to the health of my now recovering patients did I set off for home. Only a few traces of daylight remained in the western sky, and the first droplets of a predicted storm clung to the windshield as I mechanically guided my car along a still busy freeway. I paid minimal heed to the vehicles that raced by at questionable speeds as I once again, for perhaps the hundredth time, mulled over the story of Roland Summers, the inexplicable words that he had penned while recovering from his near fatal injuries in the Honolulu hospital. Did I believe what he had related? Often I've asked myself this, and always with the same answer: I don't know, I just don't know!

Honest, intelligent, practical—these adjectives were all applicable to the Roland Summers I had known for so many years. Only because of my past association with him did I so strongly seek to grasp his words, to try and understand, to accept them, though often I wavered. His doctors in Hawaii had assured me that, to Roland, these experiences were quite real, that he had indeed lived every one of them—*in his mind*. Was this possible? Perhaps. But whatever the case, in the fifteen months subsequent to my return I have come to be certain of one thing: the images of the people and places, of the horrors so meticulously described by Roland Summers are as vivid, as familiar in my own mind as they are in his.

By Roland's own account it was late summer of 1953 when he and Denny McVey, his close friend and partner, left Honolulu Harbor on their ill-fated voyage aboard the *Maui Queen*. While in pursuit of a school of porpoises some miles off the Mokapu Peninsula, the unwilling two were borne by a strange, inescapable force to a blindingly luminescent vortex, which rendered them senseless as it pulled the wildly spinning *Maui Queen* downward. They awoke under an alien sky, one that exhibited a pair of moons at night, and worse, a huge, savage orb that turned the daylight hours of this other-dimensional world into a living hell. Such was what Roland and Denny endured as their vessel, long since incapacitated, floated helplessly atop the waves of this uncharted sea.

After six unbearable days an island was sighted, and the relieved pair searched hopefully for a safe place to beach the *Maui Queen*. But a sudden, violent storm destroyed the vessel, and Roland barely managed to reach the sands of a small, cliff-bound cove under the added burden of Denny, then unconscious from a deep gash on the side of the head. Roland carefully tended to this wound, until he was reasonably certain that his friend would live.

A brief separation, during which Roland explored the limited confines of their sanctuary, resulted in the disappearance of Denny. The self-chastising Roland discovered his friend's footprints, as well as those of others, leading down to the shoreline; and he assumed that Denny had accompanied these unexpected strangers, certainly not of his own volition. That they departed the small beach by way of the once more becalmed ocean seemed a certainty to the troubled Roland, though this logic was proved erroneous hours later, when the fully receded tide revealed an opening in the heretofore unyielding sea wall. Roland penetrated the adit, confident that he had found a means of access to the interior of the island that he eventually came to know as Boranga.

The trek along an underground tributary was fraught with hazards, foremost of which was Roland's encounter with the Guardian, a flesh-eating saurian that dwelled in a deep lake. Roland escaped the fate of many before him by fortuitously wounding the creature, and before long he reached the end of the tunnel, where his fatigue, coupled with the rabid bite of a cave rodent, thrust him near death.

Roland soon regained his health with the assistance of Ter-ek, a serious, albeit kindly, young warrior of the Homarus. After they established an early bond of respect, Ter-ek advised Roland that Denny had without a doubt fallen into the hands of the Mogars, a belligerent people who had long been the enemy of the peace-loving Homarus. Ter-ek vowed to aid in his rescue, though not before he had completed his own quest for the head of a satong, one of the savage man-beasts that dwelled in the hills on the far side of the eastern forest.

During the tedious journey eastward Ter-ek willingly satisfied much of Roland's interest regarding the cloud-covered Boranga and its people, but he adamantly drew the line at discussing what he referred to as "holy things." Earlier inadvertent allusions to someone or something called the Master had elicited innocent questions from Roland regarding this entity, and the subsequent wide-eyed, groveling manner of the normally brave, placid warrior was enough to convince him that matters not yet within his realm of understanding did exist upon this mysterious island. Ter-ek, who eventually conceded the fact that Ro-lan (as he called him) was not of Boranga, begged him to speak no more of the Master, and Roland grudgingly acceded; but his curiosity had been whetted, and he vowed to himself that he would some day learn the answer. Those early incidents were but minute precursors of the horrors to come.

The dangerous satong hunt ended successfully, and the pair journeyed to Mogara immediately thereafter. Ill fortune saw them captured by Mogar warriors, who led them before the ruling triumvirate. Ophira, the queen, was cruel and sadistic, albeit no more so than her daughter, the Princess Oleesha. But it was the third member who elicited far greater interest on the part of Roland, for even the gaudy trappings of a Borangan monarch could not conceal the identity of Denny McVey.

Roland's joy over his discovery soon turned to anguish as the truth of his friend's fate was revealed. Denny, his mind vacant due to the severe blow he had received during the sinking of the *Maui Queen*, was found by a small group of Mogars, and he did not question them as they proclaimed him Omogar, lost son of a long-dead king. They returned him in triumph to Mogara, where Oleesha, while tending to his injuries, molded his thoughts to those of herself and her parent. Her success was more than evident as Denny gleefully announced the sentence of death for Ter-ek and Roland.

The Council—a Mogar faction sworn to the destruction of Ophira and her spawn—saved the pair, and they overcame their initial loathing of the false Omogar in light of Roland's explanation. They vowed to safeguard his well-being for forty days, when Ter-ek's people would return to join them in a coup, one that would hopefully achieve a lasting peace. An escape was then detailed, but before the plan could be initiated a bizarre phenomenon occurred. An evil aura enshrouded the city, and the Mogars, stricken by terror, poured into an underground chamber at the base of a towering crimson obelisk. Roland and Ter-ek were able to flee into the jungle, where the latter, himself affected by the inexplicable presence, refused to offer the least detail to the incredulous American.

In Var-Dor, the Homaru city, Roland was welcomed without question, and he trained with the warriors in preparation for the return to Mogara. It was there that he met Adara, and the two soon fell in love. Roland was also stunned to learn that Col-in, Adara's grandfather, was in fact Peter Collins, an Australian who arrived there years earlier in much the same manner as himself. The zestful and intelligent Peter exhibited only marginal hesitancy in answering Roland's questions, and for the first time the young man heard of the Master, of the so-called "holy things" that the inhabitants of Boranga were forbidden to discuss.

Beyond the Vale of Fear far to the north, on the Other Side, dwelled the descendants of Homarus who, nearly two centuries past, had been banished from Var-Dor due to an inherent madness. Their leader, their Master, was one called Ras-ek Varano, himself among the first to come there. This seemingly immortal being was the possessor of bizarre and terrifying powers, which he drew from an enigmatic object discovered by him during the earliest days of his exile. With these powers he established dominion over a cringing Boranga, and with them his reign of terror continued to this day. It was for him that the crimson obelisks of Mogara and Var-Dor were erected; it was the thought or mention of him that drove otherwise brave men to their knees in whining supplication; it was for fear of this devil that Peter Collins, over a decade, had clandestinely constructed a boat in a cave near the satong hills—a vessel in which he hoped to see his granddaughter, with the help of Roland, some day flee the enslaved island.

Adara and Roland were soon wed, though they were to know little more than one night of happiness. The disembodied image of the Master appeared in Var-Dor, and the subservient Homarus retreated to their underground chambers, where they knelt trancelike as the most beautiful of their young women, Ter-ek's mate included, were spirited away to an unknown, unimaginable fate. Roland dared to challenge the malformed Ras-ek, and as punishment for his boldness he stood by helplessly while Adara was taken. Her screams roused Peter from his lethargy, and the old man sought to rescue his granddaughter; but the exertions were more than his already weakened heart could bear, and he died.

The Homarus emerged from their stupor, and Roland berated them for their cowardice. But his erstwhile hosts, stunned by his defiance of the Master, chose not to listen as they imprisoned him. He soon escaped Var-Dor with the help of Ter-ek, who was now regretful of his own timidity. The warrior vowed to follow in the wake of Roland and his mate, though not before he had taken part in the overthrow of Mogara and had seen to the safety of Denny. The relieved American, gratified over his friend's newly found strength of will, set off northward for the mysterious Other Side.

With the mocking Ras-ek cognizant of his every step, Roland reached the dreaded Vale of Fear. This broad valley, enshrouded in darkness, sought to wrest the sanity from the incredulous traveler as it assailed him, taunted him with unspeakable images, both

14

past and present, from the recesses of his mind. Roland survived, though barely, and he pierced the perimeter of the Other Side, where the horrors of his ordeal were multiplied during the days that ensued. The Holy Ones, insane acolytes of the Master, strewed his path with all manner of atrocities and perversions, until his increasing torment—coupled with a strong desire for self-preservation—forced him to indiscriminately destroy scores of the depraved creatures. His body caked with his own blood and that of others, his will all but wrested from him, Roland crawled to the portals of the ominous Sekkator, the Master's house. Here he was welcomed derisively by Ras-ek, and he was afforded a brief reunion with the tearful Adara before darkness seized him.

Days later, Roland was released from his torpor. He found himself alone with Adara, and his love for her again ignited the fires of survival. Together they explored the silent corridors of Sekkator for a means of escape, but their search was unsuccessful. Then, to further stifle their hopes, they were confronted by Ras-ek, and both were driven to their knees by the force of the evil aura that emanated from him. The Master and his servant, a giant subhuman called Willo, urged the pair into the Arena of Joy, where they bore unwilling witness to incomprehensible acts of depravity perpetrated by the fiend. It was near the termination of this bloodletting that Roland noticed the first signs of weakness on the part of Ras-ek Varano, though he feared that the knowledge would not avail him, for he angered Willo, and the creature began to strangle him. But the Master intervened, for his curiosity regarding the American had not yet been satisfied.

Adara and Roland were returned to their cubicle, where they struggled vainly to rid their minds of the horrors they had seen. Once this was marginally accomplished they returned to the corridor, for Roland wished to test his theories. They concealed themselves near the Arena of Joy, and after a while their diligence was rewarded with a puzzling sight. Willo emerged from the torture room, in his arms a helpless, unconscious Ras-ek. As he watched the huge beast ascend a spiraling staircase, Roland realized that his assumption was correct. The Master's powers were short-lived, and they must be renewed—more than likely by exposure to the enigmatic object that, as an ordinary mortal, he discovered in the ground so long ago. During this time he had little defense, and his destruction was more than just a possibility.

Willo returned to the Arena of Joy, and Adara and Roland climbed the stairs to the Master's chamber. They discovered the withered body of Ras-ek Varano upon a stone slab, his malformed head thrust into the maw of a kilnlike structure, from which emanated a throbbing glow. Roland sought to destroy him, but his designs were thwarted by the unexpected entrance of Willo. This time they knew that the subhuman, without the guidance of the one for whom he existed, would surely tear them apart, and they desperately defended themselves. Adara managed to wound the creature, thus further enraging him, and they were forced to flee before his fury to the lower level. There, at the portals to freedom,

Roland paused and, despite the urgings of Adara, he refused to leave, for he was obsessed with the destruction of the Master.

The subhuman soon reached the base of the stairs, and the American stood ready to confront him. But Willo, near death from the wound inflicted by Adara, was barely able to walk. In a final act of blind obedience to Ras-ek the creature destroyed the spiraling stairway that led to the upper level, his feat depriving Roland of the chance he had hoped for. There was no other apparent way to the Master's chamber, and the two could not expend time in a potentially fruitless search for one, since the restoration of Ras-ek's powers might be little more than a matter of hours.

Their emotions mixed, Adara and Roland fled Sekkator. The rapidly flowing Otongo River carried them southward, and at the end of a long day's journey they found themselves far from the Other Side. But their first night of freedom was brief, for the spectral image of Ras-ek appeared, and the fiend's mocking voice chided them for their desertion. He then utilized his powers in transporting them about Boranga: first to the underground lake of the Guardian, next to the tropical forest near the satong hills. Each time they were severely tested, and each time they endured, though their dwindling strength and their feeling of helplessness soon became portents of a less than limited existence.

Seemingly at the mercy of a fierce satong pack in the lower hills, the two were granted a reprieve by the discovery of a cave, one whose narrow walls prevented ingress on the part of the huge man-beasts.

Further exploration led them to believe that this was Peter's cave, a fact that was verified by the presence of his boat in a cavern near the seaward opening. The reality of this unquestionably seaworthy vessel, coupled with the prolonged absence of Ras-ek, seemed to indicate that their luck had turned, that an escape was more than possible. But the shrill, mocking voice of the Master filled the cavern before a launch could be effected, and once again their hopes were crushed.

While Adara watched helplessly, the now paralyzed Roland was lifted by unseen hands and thrust repeatedly against the rock walls. His shattered body was then deposited into the boat, which drifted out to sea. The anguished Adara cried out that she would destroy herself, rather than live without him; but Roland, momentarily denying his own unbearable pain, begged her to await his return, and she agreed. Then, with the screams of his beloved and the derisive laughter of Ras-ek Varano fading behind him, the semiconscious Roland was carried away from Boranga by a strong tide, and he was but vaguely aware of the blinding vortex that returned him to his own world.

The remainder of Roland's story, as well as subsequent events, is well documented. He was discovered floating near Kauai, and the doctors who attended to his abused body all swore that he should not have survived. But soon they came to question his sanity, and his aggressiveness in seeking release was the cause of his confinement.

I flew to Honolulu fifteen months ago, after

18

reading the pages that Roland sent me, and the doctors at Pacific Hills Medical Center were only too happy to release their charge into my custody. Initially he was uncommunicative, almost sedate, as we drove to the hotel, though I believed that he would eventually open up. But how grossly in error I was, for within the first hour he fled the hotel, his brief note of apology stating that the deception was the only way he could find freedom, his only chance of getting *back there*.

An intense search was begun for the boat that Roland had commandeered in Honolulu Harbor. For three days the surrounding sea was combed, but it revealed nothing. Then the islands were pummeled by a series of violent squalls, and the hunt was abandoned. Thereafter no sign of Roland Summers, no identifiable wreckage from the small craft, was ever found. The official verdict: "Missing at sea, presumed drowned." Sufficeit to say that I grieved deeply for the fine young man that I had once known, for the tormented man I had tried in vain to help.

Upon arriving home, I immediately withdrew the parcel from my desk and fumbled with the knotted cord. Why such anxiety over a package from Hawaii? I wondered. Likely it was nothing more than a souvenir sent to me by a vacationing colleague or an appreciative patient; but somehow I thought not.

Wads of paper were torn away before a large, weighty envelope was revealed. On one side was a note, written in bold letters with a red pen. I first glanced at the signature, and I was faintly aware of my increased heartbeat as I read the name of Kim Onaka. Kim! This young islander, whom I had met

19

during my brief stay, was once employed as a deck-hand on the ill-fated *Maui Queen*. I spent no time speculating on his reason for contacting me but instead absorbed the few words:

Dr. Morrison:
Some fishermen find this off the coast of Molokai in a caulked barrel. An attached note say to send it to you through me or one of the doctors at the hospital. I give the captain twenty bucks for his trouble.

Kim Onaka

Making a mental note to reimburse Kim, I carried the envelope over to my armchair. Sheets of rain, propelled by a strong wind, dashed against the window of my study, but I scarcely noticed this as I undid the clasp. My hands trembled as I withdrew the thick sheaf of parchmentlike paper, and I gasped in disbelief as I stared at the handwritten words of the first page, the unmistakable scrawl of *Roland Summers!*

CHAPTER ONE

RETURN

I realize, Dr. Morrison, that the odds against you, or for that matter anyone of my world, ever looking at these words are considerable. But my own occasional disbelief over the inexplicable events that have occurred during the many months since our paths crossed have forced me, however reluctantly, to review them; and so I consign the lingering images to paper during rare moments of solitude. If some minor miracle finds these pages in your hands, then once again please be aware of my regrets for the trouble that I caused you.

My joy at knowing freedom once more, at sensing the touch of the briny spray against my face, was more than overshadowed by the realization that my recapture would end in confinement, likely of infinite duration, in a maximum-security wing. It was the horror of such a living death that saw me forego all caution as I urged the speedy boat that I had stolen past Diamond Head, past Koko Head, and finally beyond Makapuu Point, where I aimed its bow toward the north-northeast. Not until a few hours later, far from the sight of land, did I idle the overworked twin outboards of the aptly named *Winged Messenger*.

A rapid inventory revealed that both fuel tanks were more than three-quarters full, though this proved to be one of the few positive aspects of the vessel that I had acquired with little attention to selectivity. Two pairs of water skis, a tow rope, and a compartment crammed with assorted life vests left no doubt regarding the primary function of the *Winged Messenger*. Those who would have enjoyed their afternoon in the sun had brought along no food, or perhaps they had not yet loaded any aboard, when I commandeered the boat. There was, however, a thermos of steaming coffee and, more importantly, a plasticized half-gallon container of water, its clouded contents, though drinkable, hinting that it had not been refilled for at least a few excursions. An anchor with a lengthy coil of hemp, two oars, a well-equipped tackle box, and a tattered canvas cover completed the limited list of items on board the sleek vessel.

The reality of the situation was clear as I coaxed the engines to half-power: I might chance upon the dimensional vortex in a matter of hours, though more than likely it would take days, weeks, even longer. Ample fuel would be needed during the search, and certainly the basic requirements for sustaining my own life. Sooner or later, though loath to do so, I would have to return to one of the islands to replenish my stores. Perhaps I would seek out a larger, more utilitarian vessel before returning to sea, though the advantages of such a swift, innocuous craft as the *Winged Messenger* rendered this a debatable point. Whatever the case, I would make the decision if and when it arose. But for now, I could think of only one thing: the passageway! Not until forced to do so by necessity would I abandon the quest for the enigmatic passageway to the world that had once shunned me.

No other vessels, save for a southbound tanker far to the west, passed within my sphere of vision during the remainder of the daylight hours as I plied the waves toward my uncertain goal. When darkness fell I lowered the anchor, for an unending pall of dense clouds concealed what would otherwise have been a nearly full moon, and this, coupled with the weariness I felt from the events of the long day, was a more than effective deterrent. I nursed a cup of the still hot coffee for a while, until the gentle bobbing of the *Winged Messenger* atop the calm sea drew me within the folds of a dreamless slumber on this, my first night in an eternity as a free man.

I resumed the search not long after sunrise, the quarter speed that I grudgingly maintained making the day seem interminable. Only once was the stillness of the surrounding sea broken—this toward the latter part of the afternoon by the drone of an airplane's engine. I saw the low-flying craft more than a mile to the southeast, and I verged on panic as I realized that it was headed in my direction. But a sudden arc altered its path, and within moments it was gone. Silently I thanked the fates that had seen it pass at such an altitude, rather than many thousands of feet higher, where it could not have helped but notice me.

Thus did the second night descend, though as yet I was far from dejected, for even having the opportunity to pursue my goal was more than I could have hoped for only days earlier. If I did exhibit some frustration it was because of the fuel that, despite my measures of conservation, had been reduced considerably during the efforts of the day. By tomorrow evening I would have to return to the islands, for if I extended my time beyond that deadline I might find myself cast helplessly adrift, and this was something I could not allow to happen, not here, at least.

The nature of the sea was marginally altered during the night, and I was roused from a light sleep by the more vigorous rocking of the *Winged Messenger* amidst a sporadic parade of heightened swells. I sensed a storm in the offing, though past experience led me to believe that its full effects would not be felt for twenty-four hours or more. Nonetheless, to challenge the potential fury even in its early stages aboard a vessel such as this would at best be foolhardy, at worst suicidal; and while loath to do so I knew that I must depart for a safe port with little delay. As I raised the anchor I swore disgustedly at being deprived of the additional day that I would otherwise have had to continue the search, and I vowed that my eventual return to the moody sea would be aboard a craft far more substantial than this harbor-bred ski boat.

I dissected the waves for more than an hour, until

the dual outboards, which heretofore had functioned perfectly, sputtered and died simultaneously. Try as I might I could not coax them to life again, and once during my frantic efforts I was nearly tossed from the stern of the now helpless *Winged Messenger* by an especially turbulent swell. And yet, in the midst of this potentially dangerous situation I found myself wearing a tight-lipped smile, for I now sensed the portent of what was happening to me. Minutes later, I knew that I was right.

All around me the dark sea churned vigorously; but the *Winged Messenger* seemed unaffected by the engulfing upheaval, as though it stood detached in the foreground of a three-dimensional portrait. I found that I could stand on its deck without fear of losing my balance, though for a brief moment I was overwhelmed by a dizzying sensation as its bow was suddenly twisted toward the north. Then it began to move, albeit slowly at first, while I peered downward into the water off the leeward side with a demeanor that approached smug familiarity. There, just below the surface, was a narrow, luminescent strand, the radiance that it emitted something other than brilliant. This was by far one of the less significant spokes emanating from the blinding hub that was the vortex; but it was enough.

Despite the reality of what I would soon encounter, I calmly went about the business of securing the few items of possible value aboard the small craft. I then stood near the bow and watched the streak of light widen, until it was nearly half the breadth of the hull. It appeared to rise to the surface during the indeterminate amount of time that passed, its glow eventually becoming impossible to gaze at directly. Not far ahead was an even brighter light, and the sight of this, coupled with the now breathtaking speed of the seemingly airborne *Winged Messenger*, saw me drop to the deck, my arms and legs spread-eagled against the sides of the vessel. Thus firmly braced, I awaited the inevitable.

The fiery luminescence rose all about me as the *Winged Messenger* began to spin, first slowly, then with unnerving speed. I struggled vainly against losing consciousness, and soon the white blur had altered to Stygian blackness.

It was all the same: the early euphoria, then the unbearable thirst, which I quenched intelligently with limited sips of the clouded water. The sun that only minutes earlier had begun to rise was an immense crimson ball and, even before it had broken free of the horizon, its intense rays were rapidly dispelling the chill of night. Though there were no landmarks within my view to further assure me, I had no doubts that this was the world into which Denny McVey and I had once been thrust unwillingly, the other-dimensional orb upon which sat the enigmatic island that had victimized my friend—as well as one of its own daughters, my beloved Adara.

The glassy sea, barely nicked by a ripple, began to reflect the savage rays of the daytime monarch as I hastily broke out the canvas cover. In an exercise of futility I attempted to start the engine, the resultant silence as I turned the key advising me to quicken my actions with the bulky roll of cloth. By the time most of the snaps were in place I perspired freely; and no additional urging was needed as—after a last brief pause to glance at the now hovering killer sun that those of Boranga called Ama—I reclined on the deck beneath the prefabricated shelter.

I did not know in which direction the *Winged Messenger,* adrift within the perimeters of sluggish currents, was carrying me, nor did I care. Even had this world been charted, even had I possessed those maps, I could not have begun to guess where the capricious vortex had chosen to deposit me. As before I would have to rely on luck, or perhaps a more powerful entity, to guide me toward the rugged outcropping that was Boranga.

Before long I fell asleep, for in addition to the necessity of conserving my strength I was still greatly fatigued from the effects of the passage. This time the nightmares came, as they had so often in the months past, and for the remainder of the day I was assailed by the terrible images of my first sojourn upon this world.

I awakened shortly before dusk, my body sore and stiff from the less than comfortable bed upon which I had rested. It did not seem as scorchingly hot as I thought it should be, and the reason for this was apparent as, after stretching languorously, I peered out from beneath the canvas. Ama, now dipping toward the western rim, was but marginally visible between layers of dense clouds, which absorbed the brunt of its searing rays. These white nimbi did not appear to be storm clouds, a fact enhanced by the still relative calm of the sea.

The giant orb vanished entirely behind the thickening formations, and a refreshing breeze sliced through the warm, heavy air as dusk descended upon the silent sea. After unfastening the canvas cover, which I planned on utilizing as a more comfortable cot, I watched the darkening sky for the appearance of Zil and Dal. The latter, this world's distant moon, rose first, followed shortly thereafter by the more imposing Zil, which was nearly full. As they commenced their nearly inverse arcs I shook my head, for despite the length of my earlier stay upon this world I still found it difficult to accept the reality of two moons overhead.

The reign of the nighttime pair was short-lived, for soon the thick clouds blotted the heavens, and the *Winged Messenger* was encircled by blackness. My thoughts now turned to my own survival, and I became aware of the intense pangs of hunger that gnawed at me. When was the last time I had eaten? Doubtless on the morning prior to my flight, though I could hardly remember, for it seemed ages ago. I sipped a small portion of water from the plastic container, but this did little to satisfy me; and for the first time I wondered if I would reach my destination or, at the least, another body of land, before my strength ebbed. My hasty escape, ill-planned as it was, now indeed appeared to be the efforts of a fool.

An hour or more later the silence of the dark sea was pierced by a strange whistling sound. I became instantly alert as it grew more shrill, and instinct saw me grab the shaft of an oar as something struck the side of the boat with a punctuative thud. But before I could identify the source of the intrusion, a brine-soaked missile sped by only inches before my face. A second, then a third passed over the deck before the

28

realization struck me: the *Winged Messenger* had drifted into the path of an active, perhaps agitated, school of flying fish.

Seconds later the air was filled with the leaping creatures, the combined shrillness of the eerie sounds they made nearly deafening. A few struck me with full force, though these were not as dangerous as the ones that glanced off me in their headlong flight, their rigid pectorals slicing into my flesh like a well-honed razor. At first I tried to bat them away with the oar, but the futility of this was evident, and accordingly I sought shelter under the canvas, which I hastily unwrapped. Thus did I remain as the school, propelled by a force that only they could comprehend, continued to assail the *Winged Messenger*.

The barrage ended, and once again the sea was still. I rose from beneath the canvas, nearly slipping on one of at least a dozen fish that frantically flapped on the deck. While momentarily preoccupied with stepping gingerly amidst their still menacing fins, I did not overlook the significance of their presence on board. Here was food, more than I could have hoped for! And in addition to this, a like number of the scaled denizens floated within a few yards of the vessel, these doubtlessly stunned from ramming the hull. I plucked them from the water rapidly and, after tossing them to the deck, I ascended the bow. There I tended to the cuts I had received, and I watched as, one by one, the doomed creatures ceased their gyrations.

There was a sharp, albeit rusty knife in the tackle box, and I used this to remove the head, tail, and fins from one of the fish. My limited skills were apparent as I then carved out a substantial fillet, one in which more than a few bones were left, Once over my initial revulsion I bit off a piece of the surprisingly soft flesh, and I chewed it carefully. It was tasteless, and its slimy texture caused me to shudder; but it was nourishment, all that I had, and I was determined to make the best of this food supply that had been provided by an otherwise hostile world. I devoured more than half of the fish, and the rumbling soon abated.

For at least an hour, probably longer, I cleaned the pile of fish, most of which weighed between two and three pounds. I stacked the fillets in one of the compartments under the rear seat, and I filled this cubicle with seawater in the hope that the brine would preserve them longer. Other fish passed within earshot while I worked, though none appeared in the drifting path of the *Winged Messenger*. When finally done I again sought slumber, this time atop the folded canvas, and my rest was only occasionally broken by the night visions that so often troubled me.

Dawn came rapidly, but this time I did not have to prepare for the onslaught of Ama, for the lingering clouds now blotted out all of the sky. The currents that bore the *Winged Messenger* throughout the long day` were stronger than before; and without the concern of being scorched, I was able to continually scan the waves for some hint of land. But none appeared; and the only thing that penetrated the monotony of the still sea during the many hours was the appearance of a huge, dark shape two hundred feet distant—this breaking the surface for only an instant before submerging under a froth of bubbles. By the end of the afternoon I felt myself victimized by a heightened sense of frustration, though in spite of my self-recrimination I was unable to help it.

The sun remained hidden the next day, while I continued to scan the surrounding ocean with renewed hope. Then, near what I approximated to be midday, I noticed a speck far off the port side. I stared at it for a minute, until I believed that I was being toyed with by an illusion, for the distant object appeared to be growing larger. But I soon realized that this was no caprice of the mind, for the thing— unquestionably a living creature—became more visible with each second that passed. Soon it was less than a hundred yards away, and I found myself shuddering involuntarily, not only from the sight of this awesome nightmare but from the realization that the airborne horror was flying directly toward me!

The creature, whose wingspread measured at least thirty feet from tip to tip, possessed more reptilian characteristics than avian. Bloated, reddish veins protruded in quantity from beneath its taut, olive-drab hide—this both on its spastically jerking wings and its barrellike torso. Atop a long, scrawny neck was a disproportionately small head: the pointed, clattering beak and wicked, lidless eyes seeming more grotesque beneath the misshapen crown of tumors and scales. Two gleaming talons, these drawn tightly to the underbelly far back near the juncture of the rigid tail, completed the not-too-pleasing picture of the unexpected monstrosity.

Two, three times the curious thing circled the

Winged Messenger at a distance of twenty yards, while I watched its every move warily, my fingers whitening around the oar shaft. Then, with a piercing screech that doubtless resounded over a radius of miles, it sped toward me; and I was forced to the deck by its now extended talons, which raked the air about a yard above me. It dove a second time, then a third, the steellike nails stretching closer as it overcame its fear of the unfamiliar vessel. I thrust the oar at the creature in a desperate attempt to ward it off; but this only served to further enrage it, and with a few savage swipes it mutilated the hardwood blade.

Momentarily puzzled by the unexpected resistance the horror retreated to a respectable distance and resumed its circling of the boat, an exercise that I knew would be of short duration. As I glanced at the splintered end of the shaft, I was struck with an idea. I knelt down on the deck, my eyes never moving from the reptile, and I fumbled with the latch of the tackle box, until it was open. From it I removed the knife, and with a few hasty strokes I fabricated a questionable point. Thus armed, I awaited the inevitable onslaught of my winged tormentor.

Once again the chilling screech dissected the stillness, and the creature, whose speed belied its awkward appearance, bore down upon me. I crouched over, the makeshift javelin poised, and I awaited its descent. Closer, closer, until the force of the wildly flapping wings nearly drove me backward. But still I restrained myself, and not until one of the reaching claws had found my shoulder did I act. Uncoiling like a taut spring I leaped up, and I utilized all my strength as I drove the shaft deep into a potentially vulnerable area of the underbelly—this eliciting grotesque screams of agony from the now severely wounded thing. Its membranous wings carried it upward and away from the *Winged Messenger*, though not before I was spattered with its vile lifeblood, a purplish ooze that poured forth from the gaping lesion.

I had assumed the wound to be mortal, and perhaps it eventually would prove to be so; but for now the shrieking reptile, leaving a trail of blood in its wake, set off in the direction from which it had come. Many minutes later, when the final echoes of its cries faded beyond the rippling horizon, it fell to a seabound grave.

After examining the gash on my shoulder, which was not as serious as I had initially feared, I lowered myself into the water to rinse off the putrid gore, already caking on my clothes and skin. I gnashed my teeth as the brine penetrated the wound, as well as the cuts previously inflicted by the sharp fins of the leaping fish. But this soon relented, and for a few minutes I luxuriated in the warm sea, until I was urged back on board by the appearance of a large, angular shape that glided slowly through its element some yards below. From the hoped-for safety of the *Winged Messenger* I watched as the indistinguishable form, likely drawn by the blood of my erstwhile attacker, passed below the hull at least half a dozen times. Then it was gone, and I breathed a sigh of relief as I realized that, for the time being at least, I would not have to face another of this hostile world's terrors in so short a span of time.

The overcast day passed uneventfully, as did the

chilled night. Daybreak saw the killer sun remain hidden, and I was again able to scan the waves with impunity, though my hopeful vigil continued to go unrewarded. The only variance during the endless hours of morning and early afternoon was the slight breeze that began to stir, marginally agitating the surface of the glassy sea and causing the cumulus layers to swirl. But nothing else penetrated the monotony of the bobbing journey; at least, not until later in the day.

From the same direction as the previous afternoon, which I approximated to be due north, sped four—no—*five* winged devils, all identical to the one that had first attacked me. They flew in a ragged formation a few hundred yards away, the conjoint thunder of their flailing wings only now piercing my senses. I could not say if the motivation for their approach was spurred by vengeance, curiosity, or a more carnivorous interest—though I did surmise that their wounded brother had perhaps not died but had somehow limped back to the foul nest in which these horrors were spawned, and that before perishing it had aroused them to flight. But whatever the case the end result of this visitation could hardly be doubted and, despite the seeming futility of my efforts, I made ready to defend myself against the onslaught.

It was a hundred yards, then fifty, before the savage quintet—like their kin wary of the strange thing atop the waves—began to circle. With the knife in one hand, the sole remaining oar in the other, I stood near the stern and glared at the clattering horrors. I was loath to expend the valuable oar for this purpose, but my options were limited, for the water skis, which I might otherwise have utilized, had been lost during the passage, and there was nothing else at hand. Moreover, it occurred to me that the preservation of the implement would avail me little if I were dead.

One of the creatures, more bold than its fellows, broke from the line and angled toward me, the others exhorting it on with their shrieks. Its fear of the vessel appeared nil as its extended claws raked the air, and the meager blow that I proffered with the blade of the oar only served to further infuriate it. For what seemed an eternity it hovered atop the *Winged Messenger*, while I lay supine on the deck; and not until its talons had wrought havoc with the weathered bow did it ascend. Straight overhead it rose, and it screeched triumphantly in acknowledgement of its boldness—as did the others, which one by one began to narrow the distance that separated us.

I scrambled to my feet as the reptiles neared, though in so doing I was nearly hurled headlong toward the idled motors by something that I could not have anticipated. The heretofore gentle breeze had intensified in recent minutes, and the force of the wind that now rocked the vessel was considerable. Indeed, even the winged horrors overhead were experiencing some minor difficulty in maintaining their positions, though the power of their own formidable appendages proved more than enough to nullify the gusts. Soon the irritant was ignored by all, and the brunt of their assault commenced.

Their grotesque shrieks pierced the air as the leathery creatures, either singly or in pairs, swooped down toward me. Only their immense size prevented any more from attacking at one time, or I would not have endured for as long as I did. The difficulty of my efforts was heightened by the elements, which saw me driven to the deck almost as many times as the talons of my aggressors. In their frenzy they gouged large chunks from the *Winged Messenger*, and I feared that the vessel would be reduced to kindling around me. Once, when the five hovering monsters chose to relent for a few seconds, I chanced a look into the depths of the choppy sea; and I shuddered involuntarily as I noted the two dark, silent forms that glided back and forth, these drawn to the scene of the pending carnage by some primitive instinct. Whether from above or below, it now appeared that my destruction was assured.

As I readied the now mangled oar shaft for what I believed might be the final stand, I suddenly realized that I was perspiring freely. Initially I assumed this to be a logical result of the current circumstances, but a glance beyond the broad wings of the reptiles revealed otherwise. Borne by the powerful gusts, the dense clouds that for days had hung overhead now floated away rapidly, their dissipation a brief precursor to the appearance of the fiery sun. Ama, on its downward arc toward the western rim, bathed the seas with its deadly rays, and in only seconds my exposed skin felt as if it was on fire. Still, it hardly seemed to matter in light of the tenuous situation— or so I presumed.

The exultant shrieks of the reptiles altered to cries of apparent terror as I returned my momentarily diverted attention to them, and initially I could not comprehend the reason for the sudden turnabout. They descended no more, but instead sought to flee the scene of their unfinished assault. In their blind frenzy they interfered with one another, and for a few moments the air was filled with the sounds of savage combat between an especially incensed pair. Then, as the two separated and set off in the twisting wake of their brethren, it became more than clear to me: the sun! The deviation in their behavior coincided with the emergence of Ama, no less an enemy to the creatures of this world than it was to man. Doubtless emboldened by its prolonged absence, the winged horrors had left the safety of their sheltered aeries to seek out the destroyer of their kin; and in so doing they had challenged the fate that, without question, they would now meet.

Despite their frantic beating of wings, the creatures could muster no speed; and they were still within twenty yards of the boat when their smooth, drably hued flesh began to blister. The rapidly enlarging pustules reached the size of baseballs before they burst, many of the first ones simultaneously, and the sea was pelted with a rain of thick, grayish ooze. It was a repulsive sight to be sure, and yet I found that I could not tear my eyes away, for I was fascinated by the obvious vulnerability of the doomed monsters, those that I had thought to be invincible.

The erstwhile leader, with much of its flesh seemingly dissolved, soon began spiraling toward the waves; and its anguished shrieks continued to pour forth as it floated ponderously atop the surface of the unfamiliar element. Then, moments later, its cries were silenced under a brief froth and a darkening stain as one of the waiting denizens bore the immense prey to its haunts far below.

A second reptile met with a similar end, this time disturbingly close to the shattered bow of the *Winged Messenger*. But the remaining three, their miniscule brains refusing to acknowledge the certainty of their deaths, propelled themselves northward with appendages that were all but decomposed; and not until they were more than a hundred yards distant did another plummet downward. I chose not to witness the inevitable as I realized that my own skin was now beginning to redden from the lengthy exposure, a revelation that urged me to the deck beneath the hastily unfurled canvas. Thus did I remain, my singular fear now being the possibility of an assault from the as yet unrevealed horrors below.

The unnerving shrieks of the doomed reptiles grew fainter, and then were gone; Ama fell below the horizon, while Zil and Dal rose in the cloudless night sky. I was pleased to inhale the now cool air as I emerged wearily from the makeshift refuge, for despite my still tenuous situation I had survived the ordeal. The cuts and bruises I had sustained were too numerous to tally, while the condition of the battered vessel was at best questionable; but I still lived, and, as I had learned so often the first time, when a spark of life remains ignited there can be no loss of hope.

Careful scrutiny revealed that the *Winged Messenger*, while splintered in countless places, would remain afloat, at least for the time being. There was half an-inch of water on the deck, but this had been deposited aboard by an occasional upthrusting wave from the angry sea, rather than a hole in the planking. I baled out as much of the still gathering water as possible with my cupped hands, and I repeated this procedure less than two hours later, when the snaking whitecaps were leveled in the wake of the dying gusts. Then, after dining on the tasteless fillets and the dwindling water, I stretched out on the utilitarian canvas, and my overwhelming fatigue bore me rapidly into a dark, dreamless sleep.

The next morning I was cheered by the sight of an immobile speck on the horizon to the northeast, without question a body of land. Its characteristics became more defined as the hours passed and, by the time the sun hovered at its zenith, I could discern a rugged, rockbound coastline. But not until a short time later, when the sheer cliffs that ringed the southern edge of the mass were only a few miles distant, did I find myself trembling with both anticipation and anxiety. The *Winged Messenger* angled past the jagged, treacherous outcroppings that guarded the small, gentle strand called the Sands of Mogar—all of these familiar landmarks dispelling the slightest doubt of where the fortuitous currents had chosen to bear me.

I had returned to Boranga.

CHAPTER TWO

A CITY OF ASHES

Even had it been my desire, which it was not, I would have been unable to duplicate the original landing that Denny and I had been forced to make, for this time I was still a considerable distance from the beach, and the rapid current in which I rode offered no hint that it would immediately release me. The *Winged Messenger* now seemed an appropriate designation for the battered vessel that sped toward the southeastern tip of Boranga, the rocky shore upon which—as more and more I was coming to realize—I would doubtless be crushed.

I knew that I had to do something quickly, but what? My exertions were limited by the unrelenting Ama, from which I shielded myself by utilizing the canvas as a burnous. Even if I could fabricate a pair of oars from the splintered wood of the ski boat, I would be sorely pressed to extricate myself from the powerful forces that controlled the sea. My only choice, though loath to admit it, was to conserve my strength and wait until the exact nature of my plight was more clearly revealed to me.

The distance that separated the *Winged Messenger* from the unending stretch of perpendicular cliffs shriveled to less than three hundred yards, and the sea grew increasingly hostile as numerous eddies spun the prow in all directions like a helpless top. Then, quite unexpectedly, the narrow southern tip of Boranga was gone, and the still rockbound coast curved sharply northward. The turbulence eased beneath the vessel, and a now barely noticeable current altered its course slightly to the north-northeast. I expended a sigh of relief for this temporary reprieve, though I knew that my problems were hardly ended, for nowhere along the eastern coast, now visible for miles in the clear afternoon air, was there an open strand upon which I might beach the deteriorating craft.

More hours passed, and the descending Ama fell beyond the towering rock walls, the nearest of which was almost a quarter mile from the bobbing vessel. As the cooling twilight began to descend, I gathered up the anchor and made ready to cast it over the side, for I felt certain that by morning, I would otherwise drift far from the island—something that I could not let happen. I had to stop: first to regroup my thoughts, second to perhaps fabricate a pair of oars from—

I nearly dropped the anchor on deck as the gentle bay, which remained hidden until the last minute by the subtle curvature of the rugged coastline, was revealed. The granite sentinels were broken, at least for a mile or so, by a shimmering white beach, upon which lapped an unending barrage of less than formidable waves. Further inland, about fifty yards or so, the strand was rimmed by a verdant wall—the palms, brightly colored fronds, and other lush species indicating the existence of a tropical jungle. Without a doubt this was Boranga's eastern forest: the home of the Mogars, the steamy wood in which the satong stalks during the dark hours. Here was a fortuitous point of embarkation—surely no worse than any other upon this wretched island—for the hazardous journey to the Other Side, the godless place where the monster called Ras-ek Varano had taken my beloved Adara an eternity past.

My alternatives all but exhausted, my desire to reach land heightened, I decided to swim for the beach, despite the ever-present danger of the horrors that lurked below. But before I chanced this risky venture I noticed something in the water, and it was not any of the fierce denizens. The rock-strewn ocean floor had risen from the fathomless depths and now, by my estimation, it was no more than twenty feet below the hull of the *Winged Messenger*. As I gazed downward I began to see it more clearly, for the vessel was drifting in the path of the unexpected incline. Soon it was only a few feet below, and I was sure that the bottom of the boat would scrape against the foremost of the protruding rocks, when it leveled.

After tying one end of the towrope to a cleat on the bow and the other around my waist, I plunged into the shallow water and trudged slowly toward shore. Footing was far from ideal on the stony bottom, but I managed to negotiate the nearly quarter mile without difficulty. As darkness began to enshroud the island I climbed wearily onto the beach, and with the remnants of my dwindling strength I towed the *Winged Messenger* as far back from the waterline as I could. I then crumpled to the sand, where I struggled to regain my wind; and even the portent of the land upon which I now tread for the first time in endless months did not initially pierce the barriers of my fatigued brain.

Soon the darkness was total, and the smaller Dal began to climb in the ebon sky. I was hardly aware of the moon's appearance as I continued to lie supine on the sand, my breathing heavy; nor did I notice the sounds that emanated from deep within the forest, not until their heightened intensity aided in the dispelling of my own torpor. I rose quickly to my knees, and with my senses again functioning I absorbed the shrieks, the throaty roars, and the other less recognizable calls—the sources of which sounded only yards away. The night hunters of Boranga's jungle were afoot, and I did not doubt for a moment that the scent of easy prey would summon them to the strand that bordered their haunts.

I urged my shaky legs toward the *Winged Messenger*, and for the last time I utilized the battered vessel to achieve an end. No care was necessary in tearing free large splinters from the hull, the noise of my labors briefly silencing the nearest of the stalkers. I piled the wood high, and I doused the cairn with some of the remaining gasoline, which flamed high as I ignited it with a match from a waterproof packet in the tackle box. By the time the fuel burned away the wood was ablaze, and I felt reasonably sure that the substantial fire would suffice to frighten away even the most fearless of my potential attackers.

During the first few hours of night I continued to heap additional wood upon the well-fueled blaze, and I gratefully partook of its warmth as I scanned the nearby foliage. Four times I perceived sinewy shapes emerging from the verdant wall, though the curiosity of each indistinguishable creature was quickly overcome by the sight of the hated fire, which drove them back into the dark forest. Soon they came no more, and despite the continuance of their menacing cries I was afforded two or three hours of broken sleep.

Ama's first traces jarred me from a troubled slumber. I quickly shook free of my stupor, for I knew that within half an hour, perhaps less, it would be impossible to stand upon the beach. From the *Winged Messenger* I took the fishing knife, the supple towrope, and the container of murky water, which I fastened to my belt. Then, after a last wistful look at the splintered vessel that had borne me so far, I strode toward the waiting foliage, and once again I penetrated Boranga's grim interior.

The jungle still abounded with noises, though it was the timid creatures that ruled during the daylight hours; only an occasional roar was audible above the shrill cries of countless birds and the chatter of monkeys, none of which were visible in the dense wood. I was soon oblivious to their presence as I forged a path through the brush, my direction, as best I could guess, due north, toward the Other Side. But long before this, perhaps within a day, I would reach

Mogara, the primitive city where Denny McVey, the Omogar, had once shared in an unspeakable reign of terror. I cannot say for certain why I wished to go near the city, for regardless of whoever now ruled, my freedom—if not my life—would surely be imperiled. However, the proximity of the place where I had last seen my friend alive would not allow me to ignore it, and I knew that—if from nothing else than a safe distance—I must again gaze upon the collection of crude hovels that was Mogara.

My path was easily defined, for I paralleled the foothills of the coastal mountains as they again stretched northward without pause. A narrow veldt, its width varying from twenty to fifty yards, separated the formations from the jungle; and had it not been for Ama's searing rays, I would surely have taken advantage of its comparatively smooth surface. But instead I utilized the protection of the overhanging foliage along the forest's edge, at least until later in the afternoon when the arcing sun was no longer a menace.

Mogara loomed nearby; I cannot say how I knew, for I was not the product of a habitat such as this, where nature elevates all the senses. Perhaps it was the diminished din of the surrounding creatures that caused me to halt in my tracks; but whatever the case, I was more than certain of the hostile city's presence, and I knew that stealth, as well as other precautions, would be necessary for me to approach Mogara with impunity.

The forest had inched nearer to the base of the hills during recent hours, until the grass-dotted plain that divided them was no more than ten yards across. I carefully negotiated a particularly lush sward, and only when I stood firmly upon a rocky incline did I breathe easier. Then, after rummaging amidst the loose stones that over the years had been deposited along the base from the higher elevations, I chose one that was more round than the others. It weighed between forty and fifty pounds, and its handling was a tedious matter; but I did not care, for it was exactly what I wanted.

Doubtless I would have been thought mad by anyone who might have chanced to witness my subsequent actions. I carried the stone a few yards from the hills, and I lowered it atop the emerald blades. Then, with a loud grunt, I rolled it ahead of me as far as I could, about seven or eight feet. I followed in its path and repeated the effort, all the while casting glances about me for hints of possible intruders. My progress was slow, preoccupied as I was, and the first hundred yards that I traversed seemed to consume an eternity. But my labors were not in vain, for the next roll saw the stone vanish beneath what appeared to be solid earth. I heard it crash below, and I sidled slowly to the edge of the gaping hole—where, now panting heavily, I gazed downward knowingly. I had avoided this particular satong pit, the traps that the Mogars dug with much cunning to protect their city from the terrible man-beasts, though I knew that it would not be the last.

I found a stone of similar bulk nearby, and my trek continued for another few hundred yards, where a second pit was revealed. Six more dotted the way along the mile that ensued, half of these carpeted with sharpened wood stakes. There was one other that I passed, but I could hardly count this, for it was already opened wide, and the horrid stench that wafted from its depths assured me that it had long since succeeded in its grisly work. Needless to say, I chose not to look over the edge.

Soon the jungle melded with the foothills, and the heavy underbrush negated the use of the stones. I snapped a thick branch off a nearby tree, and after trimming its leaves I utilized it to probe the ground before me. This method was slower, but still necessary, as witnessed by the two traps that I managed to avoid.

The normally ceaseless sounds of the forest, which had continued to diminish in intensity, were now virtually nonexistent. A deathly pallor seemed to enshroud the wood, and I shuddered slightly in the midst of what had been a torrid clime. At first I found this difficult to comprehend; then, as I peered out from the foliage across a broad clearing, I quickly grasped the answer to the enigma.

Mogara was dead; the once verdant ground upon which it stood had been blackened by fire, and much time would pass before anything grew there again. The bamboo shanties had been razed in a like manner, most incinerated completely—though remnants of a few remained. Charred skeletons dotted the landscape, a particular stack of five or six befouling the narrow stream that paralleled the city—the tributary that Ter-ek and I had followed many months past. Only the crimson obelisk, the stone erected decades past in obeisance to the devil whom those of Boranga worshiped as their Master, remained standing, doubtless as a perverse monument

47

to what I could only assume was his inconceivable handiwork.

Casting aside precaution, I wandered the dead city in disbelief. Countless questions raced through my head as I stepped numbly amidst the blackened bones: had this happened before the Homaru takeover, or after? In either case, what was the fate of Denny? Had Ter-ek survived, so that he might seek out his beloved Aleen on the Other Side? And what of Lar-ek, the Homaru king; Heran, elder of the Mogar Council; Dovan, his son. Yes, my curiosity even extended to the unspeakable Ophira and to the Princess Oleesha, her equally vile spawn. But I feared that the answers had perished along with the unfortunates whose remains littered this graveyard, and the frustration that I now experienced could hardly be measured.

I staggered toward the still defined area where the larger dwellings of the ruling triumvirate had stood, and I scoured the ashes for some small clue, but in vain. Then, after bypassing the charred rubble through the heart of Mogara, I approached the large door at the base of the obelisk, the portal to the underground chamber in which the Mogars gathered to revere the Master. I utilized one of the now tarnished gold rings to cast it open, and I was immediately felled by the odor that wafted from below, the stench of Death itself being released from interminable imprisonment in the dankest, most loathsome of pits. Not until I ceased retching, not until I controlled the trembling that had assailed my body did I crawl to the edge, and I cried out in disbelief as I absorbed the scene below.

It was a charnel house, an impossible cairn of death that rose from the floor of the chamber almost to the opening. Hundreds of human beings, among them children, had been incinerated as a single entity in what they had believed to be their sanctuary. What manner of monster could have perpetrated such an act? But of course I knew, and my revulsion quickly altered to rage as the image of his malformed, mocking face took shape in my mind. With a bestial growl I slammed shut the door of the mass tomb, and I scrambled away on my hands and knees, for as yet I was unable to walk.

I soon regained the strength of my feet, and I strode mechanically toward the northern perimeter of the clearing. Darkness was falling rapidly, but I was hardly aware of this as I sought to free my overtaxed brain of the horrible images that manifested themselves within. I then pierced the foliage without pause, not once glancing behind at the ebon city of death that had been Mogara.

CHAPTER THREE

CHALLENGES OF THE FOREST

The cool night air of the forest eventually drove away the foul odors, if not from my memory then at least from my nostrils. I continued to probe for satong traps as I tramped through the brush, until my weariness—heightened by the recent episode in Mogara—forced me to a halt. The cries of nocturnal predators echoed in the distance, though, like the creatures of the day, it appeared that they too shunned the dead city, for none were nearby. But this did not hinder me from igniting a substantial fire in the center of a small clearing, for besides its warmth the blaze lent security against the possibility of attack by a less timid hunter.

I had gathered a few large fruits earlier in the day, but now found myself with no stomach for downing them. Instead, I sipped the last of the clouded water from the *Winged Messenger*—this despite the fact

50

that the more inviting stream passed within fifty yards of my encampment. But I had little desire to move, and once I had made myself reasonably comfortable atop a bed of fronds I fell into a fitful sleep. As I expected, as I feared, the visions of Mogara's fate were by far the worst nightmares that I endured since reentering this strange world.

Dawn found me little rested, though this did not prevent me from resuming the trek. First I refilled the water bottle from the stream, which I found snaking through the foliage only a few yards past the western rim of the clearing, and I rinsed off the caked dirt of the previous day. I then stepped into the barely ankle-deep water, and I utilized the tributary to avoid the deadly pits that abounded in this part of the forest. Not until nearly two hours later, when reasonably certain that I was beyond Mogara's sphere, did I quit the slippery stones for the more substantial floor of the jungle.

I was now faced with a decision: should I continue due north through the steamy forest, or should I follow the stream, which angled toward the north-east to join the Otongo, the large river whose headwaters were in the northern coastal mountains? The latter choice seemed more logical, for it was the quicker, better defined path to the Other Side; but I ultimately disdained this way, for I feared my vulnerability along the open river, where once before *he* had found Adara and me in the midst of our flight. I opted instead for the shelter, however potentially dangerous, of the jungle, and accordingly I returned to the base of the ever-present foothills, a distance of about half a mile.

Once again the forest teemed with sounds as I strode along its edge, always beneath the protection offered by the overhanging fronds from the fierce rays of Ama. Eventually the strip between the hills and trees widened, and by the latter part of the afternoon, when the sun was of no consequence, I was able to make considerable progress. Then, quite unexpectedly, the sky darkened, and within minutes I was being pelted by windblown sheets of rain—this driving me back into the foliage. I crouched under an especially broad leaf while waiting out the storm, which during its hours of unrelenting fury soaked the already softened loam and turned it into a quagmire. When the downpour ceased I tried to continue, but with each step the mud grasped at my ankles, and it was this, coupled with the lateness of the day, that provided more than enough incentive to terminate my trek until morning.

I camped near the base of an unusual tree, a broad-boled titan whose roots snaked along the surface of the loam before disappearing underground. The saturation of all that surrounded me precluded the lighting of a fire, which would have been doubly welcome; and so, chilled and damp, I sought slumber without such a luxury. I hoped that the stalkers of the dark hours, none of which I had yet heard, would be deterred from this particular hunt by the foul weather.

The thick roots undulated slowly as they reached upward, their dirt-caked tips meeting to form a conical cell around me. I gazed at them with curious eyes, and I proffered a dull smile as they danced about me, one or two occasionally brushing against my arm. A particular root, thinner than the rest and covered with tiny yellow flowers, swayed only inches before my face, and I found myself taken with the pungent aroma that wafted from the tri-petaled buds. When the appendage began to withdraw I mumbled a protest, and I went to reach for it, but for the moment I was unable to move. Still, the fragrance lingered after it was gone, and I verged on euphoria as I continued to absorb it.

One by one the tactile ends of the roots fell away from the others, and they snaked across my arms, my legs—all of my body—while I continued to stare at them dumbly. Then, after encircling my flesh, they began to constrict, and when a firm grasp was assured they withdrew in the various directions from which they had emerged. Only now, with the dulling effects of the narcotic flowers minimally abated, did I realize what was happening: *I was being torn apart!*

Searing bolts of pain assailed me—these, if anything, freeing me from the remaining shreds of the torpid web. I cried out in agony, the piercing sound shattering the silence of the black forest. The tentacles, upon sensing the vibrations of my scream, eased their hold; and I was spared the torment for a few brief moments, after which they again began to pull. But the fleeting respite had imbued me with a new strength—this born of desperation—and I channeled nearly all of it into an attempt to loose my right arm from a particularly stubborn captor. My teeth gnashed together loudly and my body quivered as I struggled against the creeper, until the now over-matched thing grudgingly relinquished its hold.

Quickly overcoming the numbness in my wrist, I drew the knife from my belt and began slashing at the appendages. I was soon drenched in a sticky, rust-colored sap—the lifeblood of these silent horrors, which began to fall away slowly. Then, from amidst the writhing mass, the flowered root emerged, and I was nearly overwhelmed by the narcotic fragrance. But I shook free of the spell, and I held my breath tightly as I severed the digitlike tip—this causing the seeping thing to recoil.

I finally tore free from the last of the tentacles, and I emerged from the squirming core upon legs that were less than steady. For ten, perhaps fifteen minutes, I staggered blindly through the mire, not knowing what I was seeking, but aware of the need to place much distance between myself and the wooden giant that had nearly destroyed me. Then I stumbled, and the coolness of the saturated loam as it clutched at my face was the last thing of which I was aware.

The rays of the fierce sun filtered dimly to the forest floor between the dense, overhanging foliage. I was vaguely aware of the encompassing warmth as I shook my head from side to side in an attempt to penetrate the haze before my eyes, an effort that only heightened the pain of my abused body. Again near blackness—I remained still for long minutes—and not until I could discern the closest of the trees did I raise myself off the ground, this time slowly.

My body was covered with bruises; there were no

cuts or lacerations, just dark, ugly welts, at least a dozen of them. I shuddered as I recalled the touch of the things that had caused this, though I was thankful that the damage had been no worse. Doubtless I would be sore for days, a reality that I would have to live with, for I had every intention of resuming my trek immediately.

I walked slowly to the foothills and regained the broad path, which had been dried considerably by the intensity of Ama. The fact that I could utilize it attested to the lateness of the day; for the sun, already in the initial stages of its downward arc, was far to the west, beyond the towering trees. I had been imprisoned in darkness for a long time, and I chafed at the delay it had caused—though I suppose I should not have complained, for, defenseless as I had been during the many hours, I was fortunate just to have survived.

Little more than a handful of miles were traversed before dusk, which fell rapidly. I was angered on the one hand, but relieved on the other, for I doubted whether I could have continued much longer under the present circumstances. This time I did not return to the forest, but instead remained by the base of the hills, where I located a marginally comfortable niche. With stone surrounding me on three sides and an adequate fire in front, I slept securely, if not peacefully.

Feeling somewhat refreshed I resumed the trek at dawn, and a substantial number of miles fell behind me during the first few hours. Then, late in the morning, I chanced to notice something atop the surface of the plain, something that seemed out of place here. My curiosity forced me from the shelter of the trees, and I risked exposure to the sun, now directly overhead, as I hastened to the edge of what was clearly a filled-in grave. There was a headstone, a hastily contrived marker, upon which words had been chiseled. They read,

> Oleesha, princess of the Mogars
> killed by a satong
> she deserved no better

The death of the cruel woman, whose past deeds reeked of perverse notoriety, was hardly the cause of the emotional wave that coursed through me as I stared in disbelief at the stone. I dropped to my knees, and I tried to grasp the portent of the epitaph, which had been carved out *in English!*

I had momentarily forgotten Ama, an oversight that my prickling skin soon rectified. But still I could not tear my eyes from the marker, and I stumbled more than a few times as I backed toward the safety of the forest. This revelation could only mean one thing: Denny McVey was alive! No one else here could write in English. And moreover, he had somehow regained the memory that had been wrested from him as a result of the accident that first cast us upon the shore of this island. Even now he might be somewhere in the nearby wood or, more likely, wandering about some other sector of Boranga in search of me! Perhaps he . . .

There was, of course, another alternative, one that

I found difficult to consider. Many months had passed since this incident, a fact of which I felt reasonably certain; and Denny, despite the strong will that I knew he possessed, would have been sorely tested to survive the rigors of this harsh land. Granted, I had managed to endure the first time, but then I had been tutored in the ways of Boranga by Ter-ek, and there were few more capable than the Homaru warrior. In any case, one thing was clear: Denny had survived the Mogara holocaust and, until I learned otherwise, the hope that he still walked the land could not be allowed to die. After I found my Adara, after I rid this island of its disease, I *would* again find him.

With a last wistful look at the marker I resumed my trek. I was immediately aware of the longer, more purposeful strides that propelled me through the brush—this effort doubtless resulting from the now fortified realization of my objective on Boranga, the impossible tasks that the fates had capriciously delegated to me. Not before half the afternoon had passed did I stop to rest, and then only for a few minutes. I had been away from Boranga for too long and now, believing every hour to be invaluable, I was determined not to waste the time afforded me. Only common sense would deter me from carrying my quest into the dark hours, a thought that I had toyed with at length before discarding.

A few hours before dusk, the previously unending din of the forest was suddenly stilled. It did not abate gradually, as it had near Mogara, but instantaneously, as though a switch had been flicked off. My fingers tightened around the knife handle, and I glanced suspiciously at the foliage surrounding the small glade in which I stood. At first I noticed nothing, for not even a soft breeze rustled the leaves; then they began to shake, and many were trampled by those who now forged into the clearing and encircled me.

My assailants appeared to be human, or at least humanoid. They were short, squat, and all were covered with long, frizzled white hair—which grew from every available inch of flesh on their bodies, save for their palms and the bottoms of their feet. Round, bloodshot eyes, the only organs visible through the mass of whiskers, glared at me hatefully as the fifteen or more creatures, each armed with a stone hatchet and spear, began to tighten the ring.

I brandished my knife as I tried to follow the movements of all, an impossible feat. They continued to close, finally halting less than five yards away. One of them stepped forward from amidst his brethren, and he wagged a hirsute finger at me as, much to my astonishment, he spoke.

"Put weapon down, or we kill!"

The words were rudimentary; the tone harsh, guttural. These beings were, quite obviously, far down along the evolutionary scale. But the message of their apparent leader was clear, and I had no choice but to comply. I might have dispatched more than my share of them had I attempted to fight my way free, though without question I would have eventually succumbed to the overwhelming odds. Besides, the hairy one's terse instructions indicated that they did not wish to kill me, at least not at the moment.

I dropped the knife to the loam at my feet, and I extended both palms in a gesture of peace. "Why do you stop me?" I asked. "I am not your enemy. Let me pass, and I swear that I will not come this way again."

All eyes turned to the leader, who scratched his chest absently as he pondered my words. Then, after deciding on his next course of action, he stamped a clublike foot three times and he waved both arms animatedly.

"You are prisoner of Ghel, king of all Haghrs!" he bellowed. "Now you come!"

He pointed eastward as he leaned over to gather up my knife, and I was compelled to obey, for at least half a dozen of the menacing spears probed my body. One of the crude weapons—this wielded by an over-zealous Haghr—drew blood from my left shoulder, and I bit my lip in defense of the pain, but I did not cry out. Instead, I quickened my steps to comply with the surprisingly rapid pace they maintained; and this seemed to satisfy them, though all during the brief trek the tips of their weapons were never more than a few inches from my flesh.

They led me to the hills, which for the last two miles had again rejoined the forest. The foremost of the surly bunch then disappeared amidst the formations, as did those in his immediate wake, and not until I had neared to within a few feet did I notice the almost imperceptible fissure into which they sidled. I was urged through the narrow passage, and for a few moments I felt overwhelmed by the choking confinement—this terrible phobia that I had not known before my first sojourn on Boranga. But it quickly passed as the rift widened, and once again my hirsute captors swaggered ludicrously on either side of me.

The defile, after twisting and turning for about fifty yards, ended in a box canyon, the sheer granite walls encompassing the village of the primitive Haghrs. There were three, possibly four, dozen randomly spaced hovels, few of these mud and straw contrivances of uniform shape or size. The floor of the canyon was dotted with bones, refuse, and excrement, this accounting for the stench that over-whelmed me as I neared. At the communal cooking fire the Haghr women, large-breasted creatures only slightly less hairy than the males, paused from their labors to witness the procession. They shuffled toward me—as did a score of pasty-skinned, obnox-ious children—the shrill voices of all melding obscenely into a vitriolic tongue-lashing of their unexpected prisoner. A few tried to reach me, and I suppose that given the chance they would have torn me apart; but Ghel would have none of this, and with a guttural bark he drove his stone ax-head into the face of one clutching female. The latter, spitting out blood and teeth, was helped away by her mate—while the rest, now subdued, backed away to let us pass.

I was led to one of a pair of tall wooden stakes at the far end of the village, where my arms and legs were bound securely with leather thongs. Then, after assuring themselves of their handiwork, Ghel and his party walked away. Following their lead, the rest of the Haghrs dispersed to the various occupations that had heretofore warranted their interest, and I was left alone where I had been tied, almost as if I did not exist. This turnabout stunned me, though without question it was far better than standing defenseless against any further cruelties on the part of my captors. If nothing else, the isolation would afford me time to mull over possible means of escape from this pestilent canyon.

The first thing I tested was the trimmed stake, which clearly had not sprouted from the spot, but had instead been driven into the hard earth by the efforts of many. I pulled easily against it initially, then more vigorously, until my face reddened; but the Haghrs had done their work well, for it would not move even an inch. I thought of shinnying the pole after dark, but my awkward position, coupled with the fact that it had been hewn from a smooth hardwood, made this impossible. My only hope was to work on the bonds, a task which I began warily, for I could not rely on their seeming lack of interest to prevent an occasional Haghr from glancing in my direction.

An hour or so later I had accomplished little more than scraping a few square inches of skin from my wrists, and accordingly I abandoned my futile efforts, at least for the time being. My attention was now diverted to a commotion near the hub of the village, from where loud shouts and screams emanated. Scores of Haghrs had already gathered, and I was unable to see the participants through the crush of bodies—though I did recognize one of the voices, the authoritative guttural of Ghel.

"What means this?" the Haghr chieftain barked. "Why you bring Mruf before me?"

An agitated voice replied, "I come home, find Mruf on woman!"

The crowd gasped conjointly as Ghel asked: "What you say to this, Mruf?"

"I not to blame!" the accused whined. "Ivuura call me inside, beckon me to mat. She————!"

"Mruf lie! Mruf lie!" a shrill voice cried. "For long time he want me. Now he find me alone, and he force me to—*aaiyee!*"

The female shrieked uncontrollably, and the uproar began anew, with the assembled Haghrs calling for the justice of Ghel. There was a struggle, after which the crowd parted, and I saw four burly tribesmen dragging their thrashing fellow along the rock-strewn earth. Ghel, swaggering a few yards behind, indicated the stake to my left, and the taunting crowd followed as the assigned guards bore their captive across the thirty or so yards. Mruf was then bound to the pole, his wrists lashed together far more tightly than mine, and despite his incessant whining protestations, all eyes turned for the moment to Ghel.

"Mruf wrong woman, so he will know justice of woman, and not Ghel," the Haghr king announced.

The people stepped back, all save the female called Ivuura, who grinned wickedly as she approached the quaking prisoner, her long fingernails extended in a catlike manner. She summoned her sisters in a shrewish voice as she neared Mruf, and within seconds she was joined by at least twenty of them. Together they loosed a chilling cry, and they fell upon their victim in a frenzy, while the throng slavered obscenely in anticipation of the carnage.

It was my misfortune to have a ringside seat to the horrid scenario that ensued, and I found that, despite my revulsion, I could not help but stare. The savage females pulled out wads of hair from the screaming Mruf, until nearly all of his ghostly white flesh was evident. Then they raked his body with their nails, the spurting crimson gore soaking their own unkempt fur. Once I heard Mruf's shrieks rise even louder, if such was possible, as one eye, gouged from its socket, fell to the dirt, where it was kicked from sight by the flailing feet of the Haghr females. Only then did I tear my eyes away, for it had become more than I could stand.

Soon the cries of Mruf had altered to low, pathetic moans, and he seemed oblivious to the frothing women as they slashed at his arms and legs, his face, even his bulging genitals. It appeared as though he survived in much the same way as an animal, his brain too miniscule to accept the reality of his demise. Then he slumped over, but still the women did not relent, until Ghel stepped forward and began swatting them from side to side. At first I thought that, in their madness, they would turn on their king; but they thought better of it, and one by one they slunk away, like beaten curs.

The creature named Ivuura suddenly rose, and, still frothing, she waved a finger in my direction. "That one! That one!" she shrieked. "He would have me too! I kill him!"

I struggled vainly as the repulsive Haghr female, after scurrying toward me on all fours, began clawing at my legs. But before she could effect much damage, her mate pounced on her; and he cuffed her soundly on the side of the head at least half a dozen times, until she was marginally conscious.

"No more!" he bellowed. "This one is for Ama. Go now, or you will anger Ghel."

Ivuura crawled away, and the remainder of the Haghrs, for the time being emotionally spent, began to disperse. I glanced at Ghel, who, having cut loose the unfortunate Mruf, now toed the supine, blood-caked body.

"Get up, spawn of satong!" he roared at the motionless hulk. "You have work not yet done. Get up, or I cut out heart!"

I thought for sure that the Haghr king was wasting his breath, that Mruf was long since dead. But to my astonishment, the abused body began to quiver in response to the merciless kicking. Ghel backed away as his underling, streamlets of sticky gore oozing from his eyeless socket, rose upon thick stumps that were far from steady. Without a word he followed in the wake of his brethren, who—now that justice had been meted—barely noticed him. For the primitive Haghrs, the matter was closed.

Darkness fell; the hirsute tribe, after gorging themselves with charred meat from the large fire, disappeared inside their hovels, where the grotesque sounds of their lovemaking fouled the air during the first few hours. I was given no food and only a few sips of water by a surly guard—who squatted nearby and noisily partook of his own repast. My ankles were untied shortly thereafter, and I fell to my knees, a position that while far from comfortable was a considerable improvement.

Sleep did not come, despite the weariness, despite

the gnawing hunger. My discomfort at times was unbearable, and I worked in vain to loose the tension that knotted my body. In such a manner was I left to contemplate my fate during this, my first night as a prisoner of the Haghrs.

CHAPTER FOUR

THE REDBEARD

At daybreak the fourth of the guards who had maintained a vigil throughout the dark hours rose wearily and swaggered toward the hovels, leaving me alone. With bloodshot eyes I gazed at the morning activities of the village, which only minutes earlier had begun to stir. Haghr men, women, and children performed their ablutions wherever they chose, like mindless animals—a few even kicking dirt over their foul leavings. The females then gathered at the communal fire, which had all but died during the night. They added dried straw and leaves as they stirred the embers, until once again they had a substantial blaze. From a nearby cave the grunting males emerged with the carcasses of various rumi-nants, bush pigs, even a huge ghoma, and they heaved these atop the fiery cairn—the added fuel causing the fire to sputter. Within moments my senses were reeling from the odor of singed fur and roasting flesh, though eventually I hardly noticed it at all.

As the morning wore on I sensed something different about the village. Unlike the previous day, when all seemed muted and surly, there was now an almost festive air about the Haghrs as they jabbered incessantly in the midst of their labors. There were even sounds that I presumed to be laughter, though this staccato rumbling was, to me, anything but mirthful. I was curious about their seemingly uncharacteristic glee, though the many glances they cast in my direction hinted at my possible role in whatever titillated their thoughts, and I feared that the eventual knowledge would not be to my liking.

Ghel soon emerged from the largest of the hovels, and he strode toward me. At least half a score of Haghrs were at his heels, these underlings grunting loudly as they dragged two stones of considerable weight along the ground. They halted within a few yards of me, where Ghel, after glaring at me with his bloodshot orbs, hurled a barrage of orders at his panting charges.

"Faster, faster!" he roared, as they scurried to do his bidding. "It is nearly time."

They grabbed my ankles and spread-eagled me atop the gravel, my bound hands still wrapped around the pole. Every shred of clothing was torn from my body, and I winced as the tiny stones cut into my back. They secured the hemp that they had used to haul the stones about my ankles, and they rolled the small boulders back a few inches, until there was no slack. My muscles were now stretched to their limits, and the slightest move caused me much pain.

Ghel, once assured that his men had carried out their tasks well, ordered them back to the core of the village. All of the Haghrs, even those tending to the still roasting feast, then shuffled to their respective huts. They paused outside the frond portals, their eyes on the king, who raised both hirsute arms in supplication as he uttered a string of unintelligible words in a dull monotone. Then he vanished within his own hovel, and the rest followed his lead, until only the crackling of the fire pierced the silence of the deathlike canyon in which I lay.

Ten, fifteen minutes passed while I struggled against my bonds, a futile exercise that I eventually abandoned. I gazed upward resignedly at the limited expanse of blue sky that was visible between the lofty peaks, and in my mind I conjured a thousand fiendish tortures that the Haghrs might inflict upon me when they emerged. But the village remained still, and I continued to be puzzled, until the topmost portion of the sun appeared over the rim of the highest crag, this immediately warming the canyon. Suddenly I understood, for the words of Ivuura's mate, which had meant nothing the previous day, now echoed clearly in my brain: *this one is for Ama*. These primitives had chosen me as a sacrifice to Boranga's fiery orb, which during its brief appearance above the hidden canyon would doubtless sear the flesh from my bones.

I resumed my frenzied exertions, while Ama continued to arc higher. Soon the canyon was an inferno, the unimaginable heat immersing me in a languid pool. Through a multihued haze I imagined that I saw a figure on the far side of the Haghr village, a wavering, spectral shape that floated alongside one of the rock walls. It bypassed the uneven rows of hovels as it neared, but not until it was within yards could I discern its features more clearly.

It was a man; not one of gigantic proportions, as my clouded vision had earlier imagined, but one who, while well muscled, was of average height. The man was garbed in nothing more than a loincloth and a pair of sandals. His abundant shock of red hair was unkempt, as was his full beard. He hefted a sleek javelin in one hand and a long knife in the other— both these weapons far superior to the stone contrivances of the primitive Haghrs. At first I mistook him for my executioner, and in a perverse way I felt gratified, for a quick death was by far preferable to the fiery alternative. But then, as I continued to stare into his curious, widened eyes, a flickering hint of recognition registered, and my jaw sagged in disbelief.

"Denny!" I gasped. *"Denny, it's me, Rollie!"*

For long moments Denny McVey stood there, motionless. Then he knelt at my side and he grasped my hand tightly, his body trembling. When he finally spoke it was in a muted tone, and the detached, monotonic voice that I heard was a far cry from the ebullient one that I had known for so long.

"The fool Haghrs will not come out while Ama crosses over their village, unless there is a good reason. Will you be able to walk?"

"I think so."

He began cutting me loose. "Silence is imperative, even though they are deep in what they consider prayer. We'll go through the village to save time, for you've already been exposed too long. Come, let's get out of here."

The last strands were severed; I rubbed my wrists and ankles, and I gritted my teeth against the pain of my reddening flesh. Denny helped me to my feet, and after regaining my balance we strode stealthily toward the core of the village. We dissected the first row of huts, and then we passed by the large fire, where the feast in honor of the sacrifice to Ama was nearly done. Our eyes darted back and forth across the covered portals of the crude dwellings, but initially no Haghr chose to break the tradition of his people.

Nature suddenly chose an inopportune time to toy with us, for high in one of the nearby mountains a chunk of stone broke loose, and a resounding rumble filled the canyon as it plummeted downward. It struck the ground a hundred yards distant, where it shattered into small bits of rubble. But even then the echoes refused to die, and for at least ten seconds they bounced off the facings.

Denny gathered up a discarded spear and handed it to me as our pace quickened. But we were too late, for the noise had alerted the meditating Haghrs, and a few of them now poked their heads through the portals.

"Redbeard!" one of them bellowed. "Redbeard takes prisoner!"

They poured forth from all sides of us, and their anger at this affront was apparent as they brandished their crude arsenal with only one thought in mind. Denny smiled grimly as he prepared to meet the onslaught, and he glanced at me for an instant.

"Back to back, my friend," he stated. "We'll give these devils something to remember!"

We met the intitial attack like two cornered beasts, the training that I had received from the skillful Ter-ek long ago now serving me well. Six, seven Haghrs were victimized by our thrusting weapons before they backed away. Then, in response to the vitriolic urging of Ghel, they re-formed for another attack, this time as a singular entity. But Denny and I did not allow them the offensive; instead, we gathered up two of the long-handled stone clubs from amidst the writhing bodies, and we waded into the hirsute tide, where we caved in the skulls of more than we could count. Crimson gore, some of it doubtlessly belonging to us, spattered our bodies, though far more of it stained the white fur of the Haghrs—who, if not skilled, were anything but cowards.

Ghel suddenly ordered his people back, and they complied, while we sought to catch our breath. During the conflict I had ignored the heat, as had Denny; but our exertions only served to heighten the effects of Ama's deadly rays. This revelation nearly felled me, and only Denny's strong grip on my arm prevented me from succumbing. With a curt nod I indicated that I was all right, and we again turned our attention to the Haghrs, who were preoccupied with their own fears.

"See! Ama is angry!" Ghel roared, indicating the now fully revealed sun high overhead. "We must beg Ama to forgive, so he not destroy us all. Go!"

The Haghrs scattered for their hovels, and in

moments the hub of the village was devoid of life, save for ourselves and those who had fallen before us. We wasted little time in negotiating the remainder of the scorching canyon, where the narrow fissure shielded us from Ama's wrath. We then pierced the forest, which despite its steaminess seemed cooler than the rockbound inferno. I followed in Denny's wake for about a quarter of a mile, until the fatigue that I had denied for so long overwhelmed me, and I crumpled to the ground.

Denny, who seemed little the worse for wear, propped me gently against the bole of a tree. His concern was evident as he knelt at my side, but I quickly allayed his fears as soon as I regained my breath. For long moments we stared at one another, almost as though we were strangers; then the months of uncertainty were stripped away, and a strong handshake was turned into a backslapping embrace as we roared our approval of the joyous reunion. Not until the pain caused by my exposure to the sun registered in my brain did we separate, and Denny chided himself for his self-assigned lack of diligence as he assisted me to the loam.

"You have no cause to fault yourself, pal," I told him through gritted teeth. "I owe you my life. Besides, seeing you again is a more than adequate balm."

Denny shook his head. "For getting me to shore when I was knocked out, and especially for what I almost did to you in Mogara, my own debt to you has hardly been repaid."

Shrugging this off, I asked, "Then you remember everything?"

"The first I could only surmise; but what happened later is as clear to me as if it occurred yesterday. To think that I would order the death of my . . ."

His voice trailed off, and he trembled slightly, while I placed a reassuring hand on his arm. "I know that you weren't to blame; but we'll talk about that later. For now, I'm curious to know how you survived the fall of Mogara. When I saw what had happened————"

"You—you were there?" he exclaimed. "You saw?"

I nodded. "Having previously witnessed the atrocities of Ras-ek Varano, I suppose that this should not have affected me so. But the way they perished!"

Denny turned his back toward me, and I heard him mumble, "The Master was not responsible for Mogara."

"He wasn't? Then who destroyed all those people?"

"I did."

His words, though barely audible, fell upon my ears like a thunderclap. My senses reeled, and a wave of nausea coursed through me as I stared at his now sagging back.

"Are you crazy?" I snapped. "How can you say such a thing?"

He whirled to face me, his mask of terror lending credence to the fact that his words had not been spoken in jest. His body shook as he backed away, and he spoke with difficulty.

"For endless months I have lived with the torment, and there has been no one to share it with, even had I

73

chose to do so. I'll tell you everything, Rollie—but not now. First I must tend to these burns, for I know from experience that the pain will only grow worse. I have an ointment that will help, but I'll have to leave you for awhile to go and get it. You'll be safe here."

"But what about the Haghrs?"

"Those fools? They'll spend the rest of the day gorging themselves on that pile of food, and with their bellies full they'll sleep all afternoon and night. But for your own peace of mind we'll hide you in the heavy brush over there. I'll leave you this spear to ward off any predators, though I know that few will hunt before nightfall. Here, give me that Haghr atrocity."

We exchanged weapons, and Denny helped me to the brush, while I nearly bit off my lower lip from the increasing pain. Once I was nestled amidst the moist foliage, he left me; and an uneventful hour passed before he returned. He brought with him a large skin of water, two poncholike garments fabricated from animal hide, a pair of sturdy leather sandals, and most importantly a small pouch containing a black, foul-smelling salve. This he rubbed gently over every inch of crimson flesh, and after a brief stinging sensation I was amazed to feel the burning lessen. In only minutes I could sit up without pain, and I quickly became immune to the stench of the balm in light of its remarkable healing properties.

Once assured that his ministrations were a success, Denny again left me, though this time only for a few minutes. He returned with an ample supply of purple berries and a couple of large, oddly shaped tubers, all of which he proffered to me. The berries were tart, the raw tubers bland, but I downed them hungrily as I listened to my friend's story.

"I suppose you know what happened immediately after the Mogars found me on the beach that night," he began. "How could I have denied being who they thought I was, since I didn't know myself? In any case, by the time Oleesha had finished with me I *was* the Omogar, and there was nothing that could have been done to convince me otherwise. I was imbued with the depravity, the cruelty of Oleesha and her vile mother, and for that time I was no better than either of them. You witnessed an inkling of what I had become, and you could not have known that I rejoiced at the thought of your supposed death, for we all believed that the Master had seen to the disposal of you and the Homaru during his appearance in Mogara.

"Thereafter I became embroiled in the intrigues of the struggle to rule Mogara, and as my confidence grew so did my powers. I devised 'accidents' for members of the Council, despite the long-standing internal truce, and three of them were never seen again. Needless to say, my tutors were ecstatic over my rapid progress.

"A month or more later, two hunters chanced across a vast Homaru encampment near the western rim of the forest. By stealth they penetrated the core of the tents, where they learned of the plot to overthrow the triumvirate and place the Council in power. These warriors, both loyal to Ophira, utilized all their skills in negotiating the deadly forest during the dark hours, and they reached Mogara not long before dawn. We were advised of what they had heard, our subsequent actions resembling those of rabid dogs as we absorbed the impact of the revelation.

"Ophira was the first to regain some semblance of control, and, now realizing that the Mogar way of life as she knew it was doomed by the pending coup, she conceived of a fiendish way to thwart the designs of the Homarus and their Council allies. She slapped Oleesha and me into marginal coherency, and she ordered us to gather up all the casks of zinn oil—a highly flammable substance that, in limited quantities, was used to light the interior of all Mogar dwellings. With the village still asleep we raced through the streets and I doubt whether we missed dousing a single hut, despite the frenzied nature of our activities. One entire cask was hurled into the underground chamber by Ophira—though at the moment I could not imagine why she chose to do this, for the unoccupied burrow was seldom used.

"Finally our labors were done, and we hurried to the foothills, though not without deliberately spilling a trail of zinn oil in our wake. We paused at a safe elevation of about fifty feet—where Ophira, exercising her right of power, set a torch to the oil. The thin flame raced toward the city, and within seconds we were forced to shield our eyes from the inferno that flared before us. A few Mogars were incinerated as they slept, though most were roused by the intense heat or the crackling of the fire. Men, women, and children—some ablaze, others just terrified—scurried about like helpless rats, unable to comprehend what was happening. They perished singly, in pairs, in heaps of considerable numbers, while we laughed uproariously from the safety of our perch.

"Suddenly a cry arose from the throat of one frenzied Mogar, and soon it was echoed by all who still lived: the Master! Like you, Rollie, they all believed this to be the work of Ras-ek Varano, possibly retribution for some past deed that had angered him. They raced toward the obelisk, hundreds of them, and they poured into the chamber, until the only movement above ground was the writhing of the charred bodies that had as yet refused to die.

"The frothing Ophira shrieked in triumph as the door was pulled shut over the surviving Mogars, who were doubtlessly cringing below. She told her daughter and me to remain where we were, and with torch in hand she began the easy descent to the village. Only then did the two of us comprehend the reason for what she had earlier done, a revelation that sent Oleesha into moaning fits of ecstasy. Normally I would have reacted no differently; but for the first time some minute speck of humanity was ignited deep within me, and I felt disgust, if not total abhorrence, for what was about to happen.

"Making use of the stream for as long as she could, Ophira forged a path through the still burning city to the obelisk, this small area not having been touched by the flames. Though slight of stature, the strength of madness enabled her to open the heavy door about a foot, and with a wicked smile etched on her face she hurled her torch into the chamber. A loud roar ensued within moments, this intermingled with screams of horror and agony that even today continue to haunt me. The terrible cries drove Oleesha to her knees—where she writhed sensually, her piercing eyes now glassy. But my own feelings were those of remorse, of revulsion; and while I possessed no clues to the contrary, I began to doubt my identity as the son of Amogar.

"The cruelty of Ophira, which transcended evil itself, soon proved to be her undoing. Instead of hurrying from the scene of her atrocity, she could not help but peer into the chamber in hope of witnessing the torment of her erstwhile subjects. A jet of flame shot through the crack, and she was driven to the ground as it struck her squarely in the face. She shrieked insanely as first her hair, then her garments, and finally her flesh were charred, until minutes later she had become just one more unrecognizable lump amongst the many that dotted the floor of Mogara.

"The death of her vile parent, heaped upon the madness of the terrible night, was more than Oleesha could stand, and with a shriek of finality she fell unconscious at my feet. I was now numb from all that I had observed, and for a few minutes I was unable to move. But the worsening stench of the dying Mogara soon became unbearable, and I knew that I had to get as far away as possible. I slung the princess over my shoulder, and I traversed the lower hills for about two hundred yards, until I was well beyond the perimeter of the smoldering city. With the first traces of dawn in evidence I entered the forest, and not since that day have I chanced within two miles of Mogara.

"Later that morning I was able to revive Oleesha, and I quickly learned that she was little changed from the recent events. On the contrary, her mother's death caused her no grief, her sole regret being the loss of the kingdom that would one day have been

78

hers alone. Now her rule extended no further than the individual whose misfortune it was to be near her; and for seven days, one hellish week, she loosed her venom at me, while I served her like the most menial slave. I would have deserted her in an instant, but I was unable to do so, for the terrible powers that she manifested through her wicked eyes had not diminished in the least. And so I hunted for her, prepared meals for her, saw to her safety and comfort—while all the time I wrestled with the mystery of my own identity, fleeting hints of which taunted me endlessly.

"One morning, not long after delivering a vicious tongue-lashing at me for some trivial matter, the still incensed witch came at me from behind and struck me on the side of the head with a jagged stone. I was senseless for quite awhile, and I came to just in time to witness her shrieking demise at the hands of a satong, which roared triumphantly as it tore her incomparably beautiful body to pieces. Preoccupied as it was, it did not notice my approach from the rear, and it perished in seconds as I drove my spear through the base of its brain.

"The death of my tormentor, coupled with the destruction of one of Boranga's most feared creatures, should have proved satisfying; but these paled by the realization that, most likely because of the blow inflicted by Oleesha, my long dormant memory had returned. I knew who I was and, worse, I remembered what I had been. I was stricken with inconsolable grief over your supposed death; I was overwhelmed by the horror of the atrocities that I had been a party to in Mogara, in particular the final devastating act.

My guilt was more than I could bear, and I ranted like a madman as I sought a rapid way to end my worthless life. But before I could accomplish this my body began to tremble uncontrollably, and I was thrust into blackness by the wave of emotions that swept over me.

"At least an hour, possibly more, went by before I regained consciousness. I first felt regret that I had not fallen to a roving satong, or any other predator, while helpless on the ground; but then I altered my thinking as I realized that such a death would have been the easy way out. For me, living would be the greatest punishment of all, for the thoughts, the nightmares of what I had been party to would be worse than death itself. You can be certain that I was not wrong in this assumption.

"And so I became a part of this stinking forest. Redbeard, they called me—the Haghrs, the Zriurs, and the other handful of tribes so primitive that even the Master has long shunned them. Can you imagine Ras-ek's interest in a Haghr female? I became their enemy, for their limited intelligence enabled me to torment them with impunity. Often I would steal their food from under their noses, the very task that brought me to the village of the Haghrs during their sacrifice to Ama. I believed that, sooner or later, I would be destroyed by one or another of them, but I didn't really care.

"Such has been my existence for these long months, Rollie, days haunted by terrible memories, nights tortured by visions in which each perversion, every unspeakable atrocity is enacted again and again. Often I've thought of you, and once in awhile

I felt a spark of optimism that somehow, somewhere, you still lived. I even considered searching the length and breadth of Boranga, but I always abandoned the idea, for this jungle was, and is, the place of my exile, and I've never left it."

His bitter narrative finished, Denny hung his head and turned away from me. For long moments I sat there, at first unable to speak as I tried to assimilate what he had related, to comprehend his anguish. I then placed a hand on his shoulder, and he looked up at me—the once youthful face that so often sported the impish grin now gone, replaced by a troubled, aged face, not unlike my own. His eyes found it difficult to meet mine, despite the smile that I proffered.

"Listen to me, you hardhead," I chided, "and know that what I say is the truth. What happened to you could easily have befallen me, or anybody, who might have had the misfortune to come under the influence of that Mogar witch. You had nothing to do with the actions, however unspeakable, of the creature called Omogar—*nothing*. My own death sentence, which you decreed, elicited shock, sorrow, but not hatred, for I knew that it was not Denny McVey who spoke, but Oleesha. Your mind, your soul, the essence of your being was hers to command, to toy with as she saw fit. What you were before the shipwreck, what you are now, what you still can be, that is all that matters. Please, Denny, believe me!"

He shook his head. "The images, Rollie; how can I escape the images? They will never stop haunting me!"

"I don't deny that, for I have my own nightmares, and they have tormented me without pause since my last sojourn on Boranga. It is for this reason that I have returned, and now—more than ever—I need your help. Hear my story, please, and then make your choice."

Denny nodded, and for the first time since assigning them to paper in my hospital room, I related the strange events that transpired following my escape with Ter-ek from Mogara. The man the primitives called Redbeard listened intently, his brows furrowed, and not once did he interrupt as I described my experiences in detail. When I was finished he rose to his feet, and for more than a minute he paced the limited confines of our sanctuary, apparently deep in thought. Finally he knelt before me, and he looked me squarely in the eye.

"I'll help you find your Adara," he stated strongly, "and together we'll put an end to Ras-ek Varano's reign of torture and enslavement."

CHAPTER FIVE

PETER'S CAVE

We awakened before dawn, far earlier than the Haghrs, and with Denny in the lead we forged a steady trail northward. The salve he had applied to my burns had worked miraculously in the short time, and I felt only slight discomfort as I matched his every stride. We wanted for nothing, since fruit and nut trees abounded, and there were packets of dried meat, as well as various weapons, in the skillfully concealed caches that Denny had scattered about his kingdom. A few beasts crossed our path, but save for a fierce spotted cat, a half-starved creature that we were forced to destroy, we were not challenged. We did encounter a small band of Zriurs, grotesque-looking beings only a fraction higher on the evolutionary scale than the Haghrs; but Denny, who would otherwise have toyed with them, now chose to give them a wide berth in light of his newly found purpose.

Late in the afternoon we paused, and Denny motioned me to silence as we listened to the terrible sounds in the distance, familiar screams that rose above the commonplace din of the jungle. These were the cries of the satongs, Boranga's hideous man-beasts, whose domain we now approached. The descending night was already rousing them from their daytime lethargy, and soon they would be emerging from the hills to walk the forest in search of a kill, a fact that prompted Denny's concern.

"We'd best angle deeper into the jungle," he stated, indicating the dense foliage. "The further away from the hills, the better. We won't be outside their sphere by any means, but it will at least heighten our chances of survival."

Shaking my head, I told him: "I was not paralleling the foothills by accident. Not until after I had decided on this path did I come to realize the reason for choosing it. I wish to continue into the heart of the satong's land."

"Rollie, are you crazy?" he exclaimed. "Why would you want to risk your life by journeying to such a hellish place?"

"Do you recall my telling you about Peter Collins' cave, where it all ended the first time?"

"Yes, but—"

"I must go there again."

"Why, Rollie, why? What happened there belongs to the past. What could you hope to find, assuming that we even reach the entrance without being torn apart?"

"I don't know; but somehow I sense this cave to be the focal point. I can't explain it, Denny, but I must return there. If you don't want to go, I'll understand—"

"Don't be ridiculous!" he snapped, shrugging his shoulders. "You're just as stubborn as you've always been. Anyway, we'd best stop here, or we'll find ourselves at their doorstep after dark. Tomorrow will be soon enough to hunt for your cave."

I clapped him on the shoulder, and I began looking for a sparsely foliated patch of ground to build a fire. But Denny nixed my efforts as he indicated the surrounding jungle.

"From experience, I can assure you that there are better places to make camp in so dangerous a part of the forest. My first choice would be a crevice in the hills; but I've noticed none that would suit our purpose, and dusk is falling too rapidly to waste time looking for one. That leaves the trees."

Eyeing him strangely, I asked, "What do you mean?"

"I mean that we spend the night above the ground."

"You're not serious!"

He smiled. "Satongs are notoriously skilled stalkers, but even the best of them cannot shinny up a tree without making his presence known. Now, help me find one that will suit our purpose."

Acceding to his know-how, I chose not to debate the matter any further. Instead, I turned my attention to the surrounding wood titans, of which there were countless varieties. One in particular—its broad trunk disappearing into a dense, verdant umbrella—immediately caught my eye, and I pointed it out to Denny, who shook his head.

"I once made the same choice," he said, "and I nearly paid for it." He gathered up a long, narrow branch that lay in the grass nearby. "Here, boost me up and I'll show you what I mean."

Utilizing the bole for leverage I hoisted him upon my shoulders. He thrust the end of the stick into the lower boughs, and he poked about for a few seconds, until it was nearly torn from his grasp. He pulled hard against the force, the effort sending both of us to the soft loam. The branch, now held tightly in the fangs of an oddly colored snake, fell less than a yard away. This topaz-hued creature, about two feet in length and the thickness of a man's arm, dripped a milky venom as it thrashed wildly on the ground. Nor did it relinquish its life easily after Denny, who had regained his feet rapidly, severed it with the razorlike edge of his ax. I also scrambled to my feet, and I watched in silent horror as the two spurting pieces writhed in opposite directions—the evil looking head, still bearing the branch, the first to vanish amidst the dense underbrush.

"The *agyf* is partial to this kind of tree," he explained. "I'm certain there are more of the same just above us. Their bite, as you can guess, is lethal."

Brushing myself off, I glared at him and yelled, "A demonstration wasn't really necessary! You could have just—!"

He began to laugh, and once again there appeared the long missing twinkle that denoted his previously

86

incomparable sense of humor. I was unable to remain angry with him, and a broad grin creased my face as I thrust him playfully to the ground. Uproarious laughter soon echoed from the nearby hills as the endless months of horror and anguish endured by both of us were briefly forgotten, and not until the piercing scream of a satong rose above our merriment did we reluctantly separate ourselves from this emotional catharsis. I helped Denny to his feet, and I beamed inwardly as I realized that, even more so than the previous day, I now had my friend back.

The surrounding trees soon yielded one to Denny's liking: a narrow, sparsely foliated plant that I would surely have shunned. But after a few minutes I understood the reason for his choice, and I marveled at the skills he had acquired in order to survive amidst this hostile environment. Only a few boughs of its broader neighbors stretched to within inches of the relatively isolated tree, these deftly severed by the Mogar hatchet to eliminate the possibility of any arboreal reptiles using them to bridge the gap. Denny also trimmed some of the anemic upper branches as an added precaution, despite the seeming dearth of life there. Then, from atop one of the thick lower boughs, he instructed me to hand him up a quantity of large fronds—with which he fabricated a pair of verdant cots on the tenuous perches, about eighteen or twenty feet above the forest floor.

Once done, Denny climbed down the trunk and gazed admiringly at his handiwork. I too stared at the lofty mattresses as I exclaimed, "Do you really think that I'm going to spend the night up there?"

A chilling shriek from nearby in the forest ripped the air. "I do," he smiled.

We shared a hasty dinner, and then, with darkness nearly total, we scaled the tree and stretched out upon the frond beds, which proved surprisingly comfortable. Still, I felt uneasy knowing that nothing more than a pair of parallel branches separated me from the earth below and that any altering of my position might result in an excess of shattered bones. But Denny's reassurances, coupled with the gentle swaying of the limbs, soon lulled me into a slumber that I would have thought impossible.

I cannot begin to guess at the number of stalking satongs that passed within yards of our sanctuary during the night, for after the fourth or fifth series of footfalls and muffled grunts I grew accustomed to their proximity, and they no longer roused me past the first hour. Not until well into the night did a particularly keen-eyed creature discern our outlines against the blackness of the forest, though as Denny had predicted we were amply forewarned of its presence. Its massive bulk caused the tree to shake before it could climb even a few feet, and we were jarred from our sleep in an instant, our weapons poised.

The satong, its bulging eye absorbing our alertness, now abandoned all pretenses of stealth as it roared menacingly, and its accelerated ascent would have seen it reach us within seconds had Denny not launched one of the hefty axes downward. His arm was doubtless affected by the swaying tree, for the weapon—rather than burying itself in the huge, fleshy skull—merely struck a glancing blow before caroming away. But this was enough to stun the monster, and it fell to the ground, where it staggered about blindly for a few moments.

"Hold tight, Rollie!" warned Denny. "This devil's not nearly through with us."

Indeed, the enraged creature, after shaking off the pain, wrapped its hirsute arms around the trunk and began shaking it violently. I thought that in its frenzy it might uproot the tree, or at least snap it; but the supple stem held—this further incensing the horror, whose deafening shrieks now echoed from the hills.

Its diminutive brain seeking some answer to the problem of snaring its elusive prey, the satong momentarily ceased its efforts and backed away from the bole. With Denny hanging precariously by one of the limbs, it was up to me to seize the opportunity and turn it to our advantage. Having mastered the Borangan spear during my training in Var-Dor, I chose this weapon to hurl at the bellowing creature on the ground. Despite my awkward position, my aim was true. The barbed point lodged deep in the satong's twisted face, and its screams were silenced as it toppled to the ground, dark gore spurting from the jagged wound.

While assisting Denny to the safety of the sturdy limb from which he hung I chanced to gaze down at the dying creature, which somehow, miraculously, had urged itself to its knees. A bone-numbing sound now rose from its foul throat, a mournful lowing punctuated by wracking spasms of coughing. The forest became silent as it filled the air, and it dominated without pause for at least a minute. I gazed questioningly at Denny, whose eyes were now widened in horror as he absorbed the unholy noise.

"The satong's death cry!" he exclaimed. "Rollie, let's get the hell out of here, *now!*"

"What does this mean?" I asked.

"Knowing that its death is near, the satong instinctively summons its brethren to feast on its carcass. Listen!"

As if on cue, the cries of innumerable satongs arose simultaneously to drown the now pathetic wailing of the monster below. "Every one of them will be here within minutes!" shouted Denny, already scrambling down the trunk. "We'd be doomed under any circumstances, but with their already heightened lust for blood! . . ."

He did not have to say more. I scraped my hands on the bark as I shinnied down, and in seconds I was close on his heels. Neither of us proffered even a glance at the dying beast, who had cost us one of our valuable weapons. Denny scooped up his ax without so much as breaking his stride, and we raced headlong toward the foothills, which we reached only an instant before the first of the hulking man-beasts emerged from the forest.

They came from all directions, singly and in pairs, and the last moans of their brother were stilled as those whose nocturnal hunt had heretofore proven fruitless fell upon him ravenously. The scent of blood, the slavering, sucking sounds—all of these summoned more and more to the cannibalistic orgy. A few passed within yards of our questionable place of concealment amidst the rocks, but their single-mindedness disallowed them the discovery of the additional kill, which they would have relished.

For the greater part of an hour we inched our way along the base of the hills, and despite the fact that we had not observed a satong for more than half that time we did not relax our vigil. As we were both aware, our direction was taking us further into the heart of their dominion—though on this particular night, considering the still audible sounds that emanated from behind us, it seemed the safer place to be. Then, much to our relief, we discovered a crevice in the granite barely wide enough to allow us ingress, and there, huddled uncomfortably, we spent the remainder of the night. Needless to say, neither of us were afforded even a minute of additional slumber, though the fatigue we shared would have driven most into the deepest well of blackness.

At dawn, the grotesque sounds of the night feeding had been replaced by the shrill cacophony of birds from the depths of the forest. The satongs had returned to the hills to sink into the day's lethargy that denoted the mindless, bestial killer. Denny and I emerged from our niche to stretch the soreness from our cramped muscles, and in the light of day I noticed the weariness in my friend's face, more than likely a mirror of my own.

"Does any of this look familiar?" asked Denny, indicating our surroundings.

I shook my head as I glanced about. "It hasn't looked any different for miles now. Besides, on that particular night I wouldn't have noticed a thing, not with Ras-ek Varano at our heels."

"Then where do we start?"

"The entrance to the cave was higher up in the hills. I do recall that our ascent was not too difficult. Let's continue along the base, for it's pretty steep around here. We'll know when to climb."

For the next few hours we cautiously paralleled the foothills, which at times pulled away from the edge of the forest, only to rejoin it further along. The fierce sun overhead now proved to be of little consequence, for the dense cloud cover that dominated much of Boranga shielded us more than adequately. In fact, the air was chilled by comparison to the sweltering jungle, and I was pleased by Denny's foresight in providing the heavy ponchos, which heretofore had seemed an unnecessary burden. Despite our wariness we encountered none of the man-beasts, and only a single cry in the distance near midmorning hinted at the fact that we now walked their domain.

Eventually the steep, jagged hills fell behind us, and a smoother, more gentle, incline angled toward an as yet unseen plateau. We were now visible to anything that might have been wandering above, and this raised our level of anxiety. But our luck continued to hold, and for the first quarter of a mile we observed nothing on the slope.

The jungle had again melded with the granite formations when I suddenly motioned for Denny to stop, my unexpected action causing him to draw his long knife as he glanced about for some sign of danger. Then, noting the puzzled look on my face, he sheathed the blade and turned toward me.

"You scared the devil out of me," he stated. "What's wrong?"

"We'll climb here," I replied.

"Do you recognize something?"

"No. Like I told you before, there was no time to observe landmarks. It's just some strange sensation, a feeling as if—as if a cold and evil manifestation had hewn a trail across this ground not long ago. We have to start somewhere, so it might as well be here."

We ascended slowly, cautiously, the path seemingly well defined to me, for the eerie chill that numbed my bones did not lessen. The forest din soon faded, and for long minutes the only sound was that of our sandals scraping atop the stone. Then we heard noises from above, grotesque sputtering sounds that grew louder with each tentative step. Our climb was slowed to a crawl, and when we finally neared the ridge we paused, for the obscene cacophony was almost deafening. But time was a luxury that we could not afford to waste, and with this in mind we peered hesitantly over the rim at the incomprehensible scene on the narrow plateau.

There were satongs, dozens of them, sprawled about the ledge amidst heaps of their own excrement, as well as the bloody, shredded remains of their previous night's kill. A few pairs were entwined obscenely in the wake of their bestial mating—the females, save for the bulges on their hairy chests, barely distinguishable from the males. All appeared to be deep in slumber, though the terrible noises they made could hardly be thought of as snoring. We were repulsed by this scene, and yet our disgust was marginal in light of a far more significant discovery. About twenty-five yards further north was the narrow opening of a cave, dotting a sheer granite facing. Denny was the first to notice it, and after pointing it out he gazed intently at me while I studied it. I then nodded at him knowingly, for there was little doubt in my mind that I was again near the threshold of Peter Collins' cave.

We backed away from the ridge, and we sidled along the slope as quietly as possible, until we were directly opposite the opening. Less than ten yards of the narrow plateau now separated us from our objective, though this was anything but a gratifying revelation—for the minimal distance was carpeted with heaving satongs, one interlaced pair lying right in front of the adit.

"What do we do now?" I whispered.

"Simple: follow me."

Denny stepped boldly onto the plateau, and I was far too dumbfounded to stop him. By the time I recovered from the initial shock of his action he was within a couple of feet of the nearest creature. He motioned for me to follow, and I complied, though not before warily scanning the undulating wave of monstrosities that lay in our path.

Neither of us dared to breathe as we waded through the layer of slumbering man-beasts, an unnerving task that saw us meld haste with extreme caution. The slight, unavoidable scraping of our soles on the stone surface was hardly enough to rouse the creatures from their torpor, especially in light of the din that engulfed us. Only one, the female that slept with her mate at the opening, chanced to stir as we neared; but the bulging eye near the top of the hairless skull remained shut as we stepped over the pair, and we passed safely into the blackness of the tunnel.

"What kind of fool stunt was that?" I roared at Denny, after we had placed a comfortable distance between ourselves and the mouth of the cave.

He smiled. "We made it, didn't we? Was there any other way?"

"You might have at least warned me!"

I squeezed in front of him, and for the next couple of hours we traversed the low, narrow passage in silence. My thoughts often drifted to the last time I had come this way, and now, more than ever, I felt that there was a definite purpose in my returning here. The chill that had earlier permeated my body was no longer prevalent, though my level of anxiety was almost beyond the limits of reason.

Finally we reached the seaward opening, and once again I stood in the broad cavern where Peter Collins' boat had been painstakingly constructed over a decade. The tide had receded not long ago, and on the slippery stone floor I could discern a few dark stains, these the remnants of the battering my body had absorbed at the hands of Ras-ek Varano. But the bitter memories of that day were rapidly thrust aside, for on one wall, this also dotted in places by dried blood, was the answer that I sought. I hurried to the granite facing, and I ran my fingers gently across the message that had been hastily scrawled with the jagged tip of a stone.

My beloved Ro-lan:

I write these words in the language of you and my grandfather, yet I hesitate to even hint at my as yet unknown destination, for *he* will soon return, and who can say for certain what he knows? His powers diminished before he could take me back, and his image faded, though not before he vowed to again find me. I must leave quickly, for I fear him more than I fear death itself. In my heart I know that you still live, that one day we will again be together. Come, Ro-lan, come and find me, please! I love you and, as I swore, I will wait for you always.

Your Adara

I fought against the tears that welled in my eyes as I continued to stare at her message, and not until I felt Denny's hand on my shoulder did I shake free of the spell. Then, as I came to grasp the reality that she had escaped the terrible fate ordained for her by the Master, I laughed uproariously, the joyful sounds echoing from the cavern walls.

"She cheated the devil!" I roared. "How I wish that I could have seen his twisted face when he realized that he had been robbed of his pleasure!"

Denny smiled sadly as he shook his head. "It's been a long time, Rollie. Anything could have happened since then. Even if the madman didn't find her, what would the odds be against her surviving the dangers of Boranga? I apologize for my pessimism, but—"

"She's still alive!" I stated emphatically. "I know this, Denny, just as she knew that I would one day read these words. We *will* find her!"

"But where do we begin?"

I indicated the dark tunnel through which we had just come. "Right here," I replied.

CHAPTER SIX

THE SILENT CAVERN

The sea: the taunting, cryptic medium that had first wrested me from the world I once knew, and upon whose waves I had been borne to this deadly land, to a fate that had long been predestined for me. With the waters of the ebbing tide barely reaching my ankles I stood at the mouth of the seaward opening and gazed wistfully across its glistening expanse, now calm, but capable of altering to an unrivaled fury in an hour or less, depending on the whims of the moody gods who ruled it. I cannot say for certain why I remained thusly for long minutes—though likely it had something to do with the more than real possibility that, considering the challenges before us, I might not ever look upon its waves again.

I was suddenly aware of Denny standing at my side, and I noted his puzzled expression as he stared at me. "What are you thinking about?" he asked.

"Nothing, really," I replied with a smile.

Not wishing to intrude on my thoughts, he too faced the ocean. "You know, Rollie, I've been curious about something. You told me all that happened since we last saw each other in Mogara, and I recall most everything subsequent to the Mogars finding me on the beach. But now that I think about it, I have no idea of the fate of the *Maui Queen*. I—I remember her striking a rock; then I fell, and . . ."

"She's dead, Denny," I replied sadly. "I saw her go under and, worse, I found her wreckage on the shore the next morning. I'm sorry, pal. I know what she meant to you."

He gnashed his teeth. "Come on, let's get the hell out of here."

A few steps took us out of the water, and we strode purposefully toward the narrower tunnel. But before quitting the cavern Denny paused, and he indicated an oddly formed outcropping of jagged rocks at the base of the wall opposite Adara's message. "Rollie, what's that?" he exclaimed.

Months in the Borangan forest had sharpened his vision, for at first I saw nothing. I followed him to the spot, where he knelt down and fumbled amidst the stones for a minute, twice cutting his fingers. Finally he extracted a small piece of tattered cloth, which he handed to me. Its color was faded by long exposure in the open chamber, though there could be no doubt that it had once been blue. This fact, coupled with the few diamondlike stones still clinging to it, identified the shred as part of the sheath forced upon Adara in Sekkator, the garment that she had worn throughout our escape. I fondled it lovingly for a moment before thrusting it into my pouch, and I nodded at Denny, who did not have to question its origin.

During the first uneventful hour that we negotiated the damp tunnel, I thought about the countless satongs that awaited us at the far end. Surely Adara had pondered the same thing, for she was more than aware of their existence, the pursuit of the bestial killers the cause of our entering Peter's cave in the first place. Only the fear of returning to Sekkator could have induced her to again penetrate their deadly nest; but what weapons, other than her superior wit, could she have employed to reach the comparative safety of the forest? Even there, the predators of the night, as well as the other manifold dangers, would have heightened the odds against her survival. Had she endured? Would I ever learn the answer, one way or the other?

These tormenting thoughts were soon driven from my mind, much to my relief, by an unexpected discovery. Not having exited this cave before I couldn't have known of the fork in the tunnel, for the passage on our left was little more than a crevice dissecting the dark wall, and it was well camouflaged when approaching from the other direction. I stared at it reflectively, as I know Adara must have months earlier, and I tried to match my thoughts with hers over the expanse of time.

"What do you think?" asked Denny.

I pointed down the main tunnel. "Knowing what lurked at the end of this one, I would have opted for the other. Should we give it a try?"

He nodded his agreement, and we squeezed through the opening into the passage, which for the first hundred yards or so was barely a few feet in width. Then it broadened, and the jagged ceiling, which at times had required us to walk bent over, lifted to a height that ranged between fifteen and twenty feet. In all respects this granite burrow was twice the size of the other—though traversing it was hardly easier, due to the vast quantity of shifting rubble that dotted the floor. We each stumbled more than our share of times, and after an hour or so of marginal progress I began to question our choice.

This time it was I who made the find, and my hand trembled as I reached for the bit of cloth, which had been torn loose by the tip of a large stone projecting upward at a severe angle. I showed the jeweled patch, which had retained much of its azure tint, to Denny, who grinned broadly as he pounded me on the back. It then became necessary for him to restrain me, albeit playfully, from racing on ahead too fast, lest I fall headlong and carve open my skull, for I now knew that I walked the same path as the woman I loved!

The dark passage began to twist and turn dizzily and, when it finally straightened out, we hadn't the least idea of the direction in which it led us. Of only one thing could we be certain: the tunnel now sloped upward, at times so sharply that the rock-strewn floor caused us to concede up to half of the distance that we so painstakingly attained. Our efforts became more strained, our fatigue excessive, though not solely from this change. We realized that, in the midst of this perpetual blackness, there was no way of telling how much time had passed since we first entered Peter's cave: twelve hours, a day, possibly longer. With this in mind we cleared away a quantity of the shattered stones, and after a Spartan repast we settled in for a less than comfortable period of sleep.

We slept again, then a third time, during the countless hours that followed, and not once did the difficulty of the ascent lessen. On the contrary, the slope became increasingly severe, while the tunnel narrowed to little more than a shaft through which our bodies could barely squeeze. Our last period of slumber was undertaken in just such a cramped space, and to me, who loathed confinement of this nature, it was no different from being entombed alive. The visions spawned there were by far the worst in many days, and only the diligence of the light-sleeping Denny prevented me from smashing my head against the low ceiling during the many times I was jarred awake.

Finally, as if emerging straight upward from a stone-lined grave, we pulled ourselves free of the shaft. We now stood at the perimeter of an immense cavern, the sight of which caused us to stare in dumbfounded silence for long moments. Branching veins of silver, impregnating much of the walls, illuminated the chamber, and they reflected brilliantly from the elongated, dripping stalactites, icy wands that hung from a granite ceiling more than fifty yards above. The slightly terraced floor, as much of it as we could see before a range of slender outcroppings shielded our view, was a blood-red shale, and it glimmered like a crimson sea in places where the huge droplets of water had fallen. Clusters of dazzling gems abounded upon the surface, as did—quite unbelievably—plants: small, ovoid shrubs whose numerous tiny leaves were of an unnatural saffron. This splashing of colors, impossibly beautiful to behold, was a subterranean landscape that the most skilled painter would have found hard to duplicate, even had his easel stood where we now did.

Still awed, we negotiated a few yards of the cavern unconsciously before pausing. My palms extended before me, I turned to the wide-eyed Denny and said, "Can you believe this?"

We raised our hands to our ears simultaneously, both realizing that we had heard the same thing. Every syllable of my words reverberated a hundred times, not necessarily from the surrounding walls, but within the recesses of our respective brains. It was an eerie, dizzying sensation, and I reflexively sought to shake free of it, though in vain. Denny, who had attempted the same thing, now stared at me, and while the thought went unsaid we came to realize that the key to this enigma would doubtless never be revealed.

Both hands cupped over his mouth for no apparent reason, Denny asked, "Rollie, can you understand what I'm saying?" Though flinching at the echoes, I nodded. "Then tell me, where do we go from here?" His arm described a broad arc.

I glanced about the kaleidoscopic chamber for a minute, and when I finally answered him it was not verbally, for I found the echoes an irritant. Instead, I pointed a shaking finger across the heart of the cavern, for in truth I could come up with nothing better. Denny also studied the nearby walls for some sign of egress, but like myself he saw no break in the illuminated facings. With a shrug he nodded his assent, and we began traversing the shale floor, the reverberations of our slapping sandals causing me to gnash my teeth.

The gem clusters, which we soon wound between, proved to be delicate ice crystals, these shattering into microscopic pieces at our touch, if not our approach. But the plants were no illusion, and as we neared the first of them I wondered how such a thing of beauty could thrive in so dark and cold an environment. Denny, who also found them fascinating, knelt down to examine one up close, his hand reaching for one of the brightly foliated branches. It was at that moment I noticed the countless tiny thorns along each stem, and, not certain if he too was aware of them, I thought it best to warn him.

"Denny, be careful!" I cried, or so I thought that I had—for the words, while still reverberating, were distant, barely intelligible. He glanced up at me, though not in response to my warning, for he too had heard only remote garble. I shook my head as I pointed at the shrubs, and he quickly guessed my meaning, for he rose to his feet. Then, with the mystery of this phenomenon deepening, we resumed our trek across the cavern floor.

The natural cold of the chamber was soon no match for the gelid chill that pierced my flesh, and I felt as though the warmest of furs would offer minimal protection, even if I had possessed them. My level of anxiety was raised to its extremities, as was that of Denny, who shuddered slightly while casting furtive glances about him. As we approached the thin formations that we first noticed from a distance, I came more and more to understand the cause of these numbing sensations. The falling globules of water, which earlier had sounded like cascading waves, were no longer audible, nor was the scraping of our sandals on the shale. We were engulfed by a pall of silence, a fact which I was unwilling to accept, until I forced myself to call my friend's name. Two, three, times I formed the word, but there emerged *nothing!* No sound, no echo; only a deathlike stillness in an oppressive vacuum.

I touched Denny on the arm to get his attention, and in this I succeeded beyond my expectations, for he spun wildly about, his face contorted in horror as he glared at me. A barrage of angry words poured soundlessly from his mouth, the ghostly sight further heightening my own creeping terror. But I set aside my emotions for the minute as I motioned for him to calm down, and soon he had regained some marginal semblance of control. We then cast rapid glances all around the rainbow cavern, as though seeking some visible sign of what was happening to us, and only after realizing the futility of our efforts did we hesitantly resume our journey along the noiseless path.

One who is born deaf, or one who loses his hearing at some stage in life, develops other senses to a keenness that partially offsets the impairment. But to us, being thrust so suddenly into a world of silence was far more than we could have been prepared for, and as our terror mounted we became our own worst enemies. A droplet of water from the cathedrallike ceiling became a towering, angry wave as it fell upon my arm; a small flying insect was a deadly menace ten thousand times its size as it hovered noiselessly before Denny's face. We flailed wildly at each imagined assault, and once, after brushing lightly, we went for each other's throats, our eyes bulging with horror. Not until we rolled about on the hard, gritty surface, where we left more than a few shreds of bloodied skin, did we come to our senses. We separated, and I rose to my feet, as did Denny, who brusquely refused the hand that I offered.

Silence! Crushing, deathlike *silence!* I began to run, and I did not know if Denny remained at my heels, nor did I care. Through upreaching stone fingers and over brambled shrubs and ethereal ice clusters I ran and ran. For hours, days, months, until my lungs verged on bursting; but still I ran, for I could not hear my own breathing, and I continued to deny the agony. Then, with my vision clouded by rivulets of perspiration, I stumbled over an unseen impediment, and I fell headlong to the shale, the impact stunning me. There I lay, victimized by the stillness, and no longer caring.

A faint, unintelligible sound suddenly penetrated the recesses of my tortured mind. I glanced up, and I saw Denny racing toward me, his lips moving animatedly. His concern overshadowed his previous terror as he sought to assist me, but I quickly forgot the pain as I scrambled to my knees, for I now realized that the distant noise had come from him. I motioned for him to stop, and I cried out something that I cannot even remember. He first cocked his head, and then his puzzled look turned to one of excitement as he nodded vigorously.

The walls on the other side of the chamber were about two hundred yards away, beyond what was by far the most treacherous range of jagged formations yet encountered. We negotiated these carefully, despite our anxiety, and once past them we quickened our pace. One hundred and fifty yards, then one hundred, until the echoes of our slapping sandals were again audible. I looked at Denny hopefully, and I said, "Can you hear me?"

He flinched, but he nodded as he cupped a hand to an ear. "It still sounds awful, but I'm glad the worst is over. Where to now?"

I scanned the silver-streaked wall, until I noticed a small, semi-circular opening along its base, previously hidden by a huge boulder strewn in our path. We strode toward it purposefully, finally stopping about ten yards away. There we turned, and once again we looked out over the deceptively beautiful world of horror through which we had just passed.

"Rollie, about what happened back there," said Denny, his words clear and crisp. "I—"

"Forget it," I shrugged. "My own actions were enough to turn my stomach. It's over now, and we survived, which is all that matters. Let's go."

We squeezed through the narrow adit—the scraping sounds of our efforts, at other times irritating, now welcome as we quit the silent cavern.

CHAPTER SEVEN

DWELLERS ON THE MESA

The low tunnel that we now traversed offered little challenge initially, for in addition to it being flat and relatively free of rubble, it was well lit by veins of silver not unlike those in the chamber. Then, as it began to angle upward almost imperceptibly, we paused for a period of sleep, for the fatigue that we had denied in placing so many yards between ourselves and the cryptic cavern finally overwhelmed us. We partook of a meager repast, which we washed down with limited sips from our rapidly dwindling water pouches—this a growing concern to us since the last time we had rested.

Shortly after resuming the trek the passage inclined sharply, and once again our progress was slowed, though not for any length of time. After careening wildly for a few hundred yards, the narrow tunnel straightened, and we were assailed by gusts of frigid air that poured into the cave mouth before us. Here at last ended this part of the journey, a fact that did little to cheer us, for we could not guess at what lay beyond the opening, nor could we say for certain that we were still on the right path.

We made the grisly find about forty yards from the mouth of the tunnel, and we looked at one another in disgust. On the floor of the cave was the half-eaten remains of an animal, something that appeared to be kin to a mountain goat. A few black beetles scurried across the flesh, which in the icy tunnel had not yet begun to decompose.

"What do you suppose did this?" asked Denny.

I shook my head. "Whatever it might be, it appears that we're trespassing in its den. Look!"

Starting about five yards before us, a carpet of bleached bones stretched almost as far as the opening. The majority of them, most still in one piece, were similar in form to the creature at our feet. But there were a few that neither of us could identify, tiny figures with disproportionately large skulls. I stared closely at one of these for a moment, while Denny began wading amidst the haphazardly strewn piles.

"Whatever calls this hole its den is hardly concerned with cleanliness," he stated. "Or perhaps it saves these as trophies. In either case, don't you think we ought to get out of here before it comes back?"

Still puzzling over the skeletons of the small creatures I fell in behind Denny, and we stepped gingerly toward the mouth of the cave, until we were past the final heap of bones. They were quickly forgotten as we turned our attention to the oddly shaped opening, which was shrouded by a dense fog that wafted in and settled below our ankles. We could see nothing past a few yards, though we were certain that somewhere above the vapor the killer sun of Boranga now hovered. It might have been two hours past dawn, or perhaps an hour before sunrise; but whatever the case we had shed our stone-walled tomb for the first time in many days, and despite our earlier insensitivity we admitted to some relief as we walked out into the heavy, chilled air.

We became instantly alert as the strange sound permeated the vaporous stillness. Our eyes darted to and fro, but we could see nothing through the shroud. The noise, a series of rapid clicks punctuated by a brief groan, was distant at first—though each time it was repeated it grew louder, until it was accompanied by a scraping sound, as if something heavy was being dragged along the ground. Denny raised the barbed spear, which he had retained throughout the tedious journey, while my fingers tightened around the haft of the Mogar ax, and we stood shoulder to shoulder as the inconceivable horror emerged from the fog.

The ovoid, scabrously plated head of the massive thing before us resembled that of an arachnid, though the elongated, limbless trunk that propelled it awkwardly atop the hard earth seemed to be reptilian. A pair of wriggling feelers—these emanating from atop two reflexively snapping, savage mandibles—guided the path of the twelve foot long torso, which, save for the tip of the tail and the swiveling neck, was thicker than the bole of an elm.

111

Its lidless eyes, one on each side of the bony pate, were coal black, and neither appeared to be focused in our direction, though there could be little doubt of the creature's goal as it snaked toward us purposefully.

"Separate, quickly!" cried Denny. "Maybe that will slow it down!"

We placed about fifteen feet between us, our unexpected diversion, as Denny had guessed, causing the thing to halt in its path while its miniscule brain sought to conceive of a subsequent course of action. But this was not long in coming, much to our surprise, for the grotesque creature, again emitting its strange sound, bore down upon me. Reacting quickly, I hurled the ax at its head as it neared to within yards; but my aim was poor, for the weapon did little more than chip away a small piece of the armorlike material before caroming away in the fog. The speed of this onrushing engine of death was hardly altered by the blow, and, though ignorant of what was behind me, I was forced to retreat further.

I was suddenly aware of Denny angling toward the clattering horror, his spear poised. Before the dripping mandibles could close he drove the tip of the weapon into the thing's neck, and just as deftly he withdrew it. The creature recoiled as the pain registered, and it whirled about quickly to face its tormentor, its lashing tail catching me squarely in the chest. I was hurled against a granite facing about five yards from the cave mouth, the impact seeing me crumple to the base. My vision further clouded, I could only sit by helplessly while the provoked monster sought after my friend.

For what must have been minutes the thing

112

pursued Denny, and I lost sight of them at least three times as they disappeared in the dense fog. Utilizing all of his jungle skills, Denny managed to keep the snapping thing at bay with his thrusting javelin, his nimble feet disallowing the predator any chance of ensnaring him. Finally, as it came to realize the futility of its efforts, the creature turned its attention to a far less resistant goal: me! It began to crawl in my direction, its whiplike tail purposely swinging in a broad arc to hinder any attack from the rear. Denny, at first frustrated by the instinctive maneuver of the thing, quickly realized that its approach was slowed by its defensive action, and he reacted accordingly. Circling around its sphere with as much speed as he could summon, he positioned himself firmly between myself and the creature, which again paused as it eyed him. Thus did the two unlikely foes stand, the erstwhile engine-room mate from Nebraska and the mindless atrocity from a primitive dawn, both aware that this time there would be an end to the confrontation.

Neither moved for endless seconds; then, disdaining its earlier aimless charging, the thing reared high on its tail, and from the folds of its underbelly a tubelike spinneret was revealed. With an almost inaudible hiss it spewed forth a dark red cloud—a strange, sticky substance that Denny, unable to leap from its path, eyed curiously as it gathered about his legs and clung to them, hardly a strand falling elsewhere. At first I thought that this was some kind of web meant to trap him, but as Denny sidled away cautiously, his eyes again glued to his monstrous adversary, I realized that this was not so, for it did not

113

appear to hinder his movement in the least.

The thing, rather than loosing more of the stuff, lowered itself to its original position, and it too shuffled to one side, until the pair was parallel before me. Then, without apparent cause, Denny fell to his knees, and a mask of terror covered his face as he stared at me.

"Rollie, my legs!" he cried. *"I can't feel them!"*

Sensing its victory, the creature emitted a chilling moan as it snaked slowly toward its fallen enemy, its mandibles clattering loudly. In desperation, Denny hurled the barbed spear at the obscene head, the effort causing him to topple forward to the hard surface, where he lay helpless. The missile glanced harmlessly off the scabrous plate, landing a few yards away, and the triumphant horror, assured that there would be no further resistance, began to narrow the few yards left between them.

Shrugging off my own torpor I forced myself to my feet, and I denied the pain that wracked my body as I staggered toward my doomed friend and his would-be executioner. I gathered up the javelin, and with no time for thought I leaped atop the slimy trunk, this only an instant before the dripping mandibles tore at his flesh. The thing, unaware of my approach, hissed loudly as it reared high, and I was nearly hurled to the ground, but I was able to maintain my hold by utilizing the antennae as reins. This further disoriented the horror, which began to turn slow circles, and the relative easing of movement enabled me to study the armored plate that covered its skull. Amidst the crusty layers I discovered an unprotected patch, where I positioned the tip of the spear. I released the feelers, and with as much strength as could be mustered I drove the deadly point deep into its brain. Its hissing now altered to a shrill, bone-numbing scream as the impaled thing began to thrash madly, while I leaped from its back and rolled away, my chance path carrying me alongside the fallen Denny. Together we watched the squirming monster beat the ground wildly in its death throes, the loud claps melding with the hideous shrieks. Then they abated and the horror, after a last reflexive shudder, was dead.

I turned my attention to Denny, whose face had whitened in horror as he absorbed the reality of his unexpected affliction. Avoiding contact with the red substance, I rolled him over carefully on his back and made him as comfortable as possible atop the hard earth. I then withdrew the barbed spear from the skull of the fallen creature, a task made even more difficult by my own fatigue. After gathering up the ax that I had earlier thrown, I returned to my friend and knelt at his side, my puzzled eyes transfixed upon the strange matter that encased his legs.

"Rollie, what are you going to do?" he asked, his tone anxious.

"I'll see if I can scrape this junk off. Don't move. . . ."

He managed a grin, despite his fear, while I sheepishly diverted my attention to the job at hand. I tried to remove the substance with the shaft of the spear, and I discovered, to my relief, that the translucent stuff clung tenaciously to the wood. It peeled off easily, and within a minute I was able to remove every shred. I deposited it five yards away, and once certain that it would not be blown back by a stray gust of wind I glanced at Denny, who had raised himself to a sitting position.

"Do you feel anything?" I asked hopefully.

He shook his head. "It might take hours for the effects to pass. I just hope—Rollie, listen!"

I heard the sound, too, and I immediately recognized it as being identical to that of the horror I had recently dispatched. It was distant, and there was always the chance that its perpetrator bore no interest in what had transpired here, though I was of little mind to wait and find out. I lifted Denny in my arms, his dead weight proving a considerable burden. Upon legs that were less than steady I staggered blindly through the fog, and for a few moments, as the cry of the dead monster's kin grew louder, I feared that it might cross my path. Then it faded, and once again I dared to breathe, though not before I had traversed nearly a quarter of a mile did I cease my headlong flight. I deposited Denny on the ground as gently as I could, and I fell breathless alongside him, my previously unfeeling arms now throbbing mercilessly.

Minutes passed while I lay there, the overwhelming fatigue twice thrusting me near the rim of darkness. Denny's voice then pierced the stillness, and this, more than anything, lifted me from the grasping lethargy.

"Rollie. Rollie, are you all right?"

I muttered something unintelligible as I raised my head, which now throbbed beneath the assault of a thousand hammers. "We—we've got to get out of here," I gasped, my tone less than forceful.

116

"Are you crazy?" he snapped. "You're not going anywhere like that!"

I pointed feebly in the direction from which we had come. "Still—too close!" I forced myself to my feet. "Mustn't stop now; I'll be . . ."

My protesting legs buckled, and once again I fell in a heap, my hands clutched tightly to my head in meager defense of the thunder that assailed it. Long minutes later, when this finally abated, I found myself again able to reason, and I knew that Denny was right. Whatever the potential danger we could go no further, at least for now.

After regaining my wind, I asked Denny: "Has the numbness passed?"

He glanced at the members, and for a moment it appeared as if he was attempting to will them to life; but his efforts were fruitless, and his expression marked his disgust as he shook his head. "Nothing," he stated bitterly. "I'm sorry about this, Rollie, but—"

"Sorry?" I roared. "You saved my life back there! I'm the one who should apologize for getting you into this mess."

"You didn't bring me, pal; I came. Let's not discuss it any more." He glanced all around him. "I wonder where we are. This blasted soup!"

We noticed the change simultaneously, and I was amazed that we had not been aware of it previously. The fog had begun to lift, though as yet the visibility was limited to about fifteen or twenty yards. Then, as if a curtain had been pulled open, we saw the blue sky before us, and floating in this azure sea was the fiery orb called Ama, which hovered just atop an as yet undetermined horizon. I rose tentatively, and I walked toward the breach in the haze, where I quickly learned the answer.

Ever since departing the scene of the creature's attack we had paralleled the rim of a sheer cliff, one which towered majestically over a spreading emerald carpet: the steamy forest of Boranga. We were high above the hills in which the satongs dwelled—too far to make out their hulking forms amidst the outcroppings near the base, an exercise that demanded little of my attention. I must admit to a sense of awe as I gazed across the gleaming expanse, although the natural beauty of this land was diminished in my estimation by the ever-present image of the depraved monster that ruled it. Only by ridding Boranga of the devil called Ras-ek Varano could I feel that my purpose in being summoned to this world was fulfilled, that . . .

Realizing that my thoughts were drifting, I backed away from the edge of the vertical wall and returned to Denny. I told him of what I had seen, my words being absorbed silently. We then watched the crimson ball as it sank beyond the curvature of the land, a spectacle that, even in light of our tenuous situation, we found breathtaking.

The fog continued to lift, and before darkness was total we were afforded a clear view of our surroundings. We were atop a broad mesa, one dotted with huge boulders, as well as the skeletons of towering trees that apparently had once flourished here. To the north, it extended beyond our range of vision; but to the east, about three miles, it terminated at the base of another granite wall, the upper elevations of this mountain not visible in the clouds overhead. I had believed our present perch to be lofty, but the thought of what the world must look like from atop the giant before us was staggering.

Denny's brows suddenly knitted as he focused on one particular area of the mountainside, and he wagged a finger excitedly in the general direction. "Rollie, do you see that?" he exclaimed.

I shook my head. "What is it?"

"Here, look!" he said impatiently. He steadied his arm, and I squinted as I followed the invisible line. Then I too saw it—though not until I had stared at it for awhile did I recognize it as a path, a well-defined trail hewn from the side of the mountain. It vanished frequently as it wound upward, always to reappear, until it too penetrated the clouds, its destination shrouded in mystery.

"What do you think?" asked Denny, his eyes still glued to the spiraling path.

"Only man could engineer something like that, for only man would have use for it. If Adara made it this far, then she must have reasoned the same thing. If nothing else, at least we know where we're going from here."

"Where *you're* going," he corrected.

"If the paralysis doesn't pass quickly, then I'll carry you up that mountain! Whatever the case, I'm not going to leave you here. Now, we'd best take turns on watch, in case one of those things is on the prowl. Are you up to it?"

Knowing that it was futile to argue with me, he nodded his head. "I'll take the first—"

"*I'll* take the first watch, while you get some

119

sleep," I interrupted. "But before that, let's see what we have left to eat."

We had little, and even less with which to wash it down. In the brief time that it took to finish the repast we were engulfed by blackness and, as it had been when the fog sat atop the mesa, I could not see past a few yards. I ordered Denny to sleep, and I turned my back toward a chilled wind that had begun to blow as I settled in for the early hours of night, my sole wish being that the weariness I felt would not cause me to unintentionally shirk my self-assigned duties.

Silence dominated the mesa for what I approximated to be an hour; then a shrill scream pierced the deathly stillness, its source so close by that Denny was jarred instantly awake. I leaped to my feet, my weapons raised, and I darted glances in every direction; but I could not pinpoint the perpetrator of the unnerving sound, which rose to ear-shattering proportions as it continued unbroken.

A second began, then a third, finally so many that it became impossible to separate them. The din was maddening, but I refrained from covering my ears, as did Denny, for we were more concerned with defending ourselves against whatever new horrors chose to torment us, something that did not take long to discover. A small, dark object emerged from the night, and it launched itself at my face so quickly that I was unable to impede its shrieking flight. It clung to me, and I was overwhelmed by a fetid odor as I dropped my weapons and tried to tear it free. This I was able to do, though not before it had sunk its teeth into the lobe of one ear. I cried out in pain as I dashed the thing to the ground at my feet, where it lay stunned. Then, as I bent down quickly to scoop up my weapons, I chanced a hasty look at my attacker, and I was astonished by what I saw.

The tiny creature, hardly more than two feet in length, had a pencil-thin body, equally slender limbs, and a long, prehensile tail that lashed reflexively as it sought to shake off the effects of the blow. Its features were identical to those of a tropical spider monkey, save for its outsized head—this three times what it should have been. Other than the blunted nose, and the small, lipless mouth in which gleaming cuspids were bared in a perpetual snarl, the face appeared unnaturally human. A tuft of unkempt, reddish hair atop the ivory white skull contrasted the layers of coarse brown fur that covered the rest of its body. Its eyes, which glinted cruelly in the dim light of the recently risen Zil, were blue. The cheeks were sunken and, had it not been for the menacing fangs, its expression might have been described as puritanical. Its presence now dispelled any questions in my mind regarding the skeletons that we had noticed earlier in the cave.

They spewed forth from the blackness, scores of the small, screaming devils, and I lost sight of Denny as a foul-smelling cloud of fur encased my body. I impaled a couple, but the barbed tip would not allow me to shake them loose, and I was forced to discard the now useless weapon. With ax and knife, with bare hands when necessary, I fought off the onslaught of the tiny creatures, whose teeth found my flesh more times than I could count. Once, after a particularly savage bite on my arm, I heightened my frantic defense in driving them from me, and for a few moments I could see the Borangan sky beyond the rim of the cliff. But another wave of the monkey-like things launched themselves at me, and I was again blinded.

How long the assault lasted was impossible to tell; but as quickly and unexpectedly as it began, so did it end. The small creatures, as though summoned, relinquished their tenacious holds and vanished into the night, leaving me to stand ankle-deep in a bloodied pool of those that I had destroyed. I chose to ignore my own countless wounds as I waded through the gore toward Denny—who despite his affliction had acquitted himself well, judging by the many small carcasses that surrounded him. But before either of us had a chance to speak I stumbled over one of the sprawled forms and fell headlong to the hard earth, about a yard from my friend. His concerned voice, and the diminishing screams of our erstwhile attackers, were the last sounds I heard, for the blow, on top of all else that had occurred, was enough to drive me into the blackened realms of insensibility.

CHAPTER EIGHT

A FEAST BY THE RIVER

When I awakened, or to be more precise, came to, I discovered that the night had passed, that the dense fog again swirled about me. Denny was gone, as were the innumerable carcasses of the nocturnal creatures, the former revelation making the other seem less than important. I absorbed this fact slowly at first, ensnared as I was by my own torpor. Then, as the reality became more lucid, I shook off the remaining webs and rose unsteadily, the pain that wracked much of my body momentarily forgotten in light of my concern over Denny's well-being.

"Denny!" I shouted. "Denny, where the devil are you?"

"Right here, pal," he replied, emerging from the fog behind me and nearly scaring me to death. "I was looking for water."

I smiled as I indicated his mobile legs. "When did

that happen?"

"Not long after you fell. It took a while, two hours or more, but when it passed it was as if it hadn't even happened. The first thing I did was to hurl the remains of those things over the side of the cliff, in case the others came back for them. Then, after checking you, I began the search, though at no time was I more than twenty yards or so from this spot."

"And did you find any?"

He shook his head. "Nothing but rocks, dust, and dead tree limbs. We've got to keep moving, Rollie. Are you well enough to continue?"

"I was going to ask you the same thing. *You* were the helpless one, remember?"

"Things change quickly here. What do you say?"

"Let's get going."

"Look at this first." He indicated the ground. "I drew this arrow before the fog rolled in. It's pointed straight at the mountain trail. I can't say for certain how long we'll remain on the right path, but at least we can embark with assurance in the desired direction."

We set off into the fog, and before a few minutes had passed I could not even tell if we were headed back toward the rim of the cliff. But Denny seemed to know where he was going, and I chose to trust his judgment as I walked alongside him, our silence shattered only occasionally by the kicking of a loose stone. Then, as we neared to within a mile and a half of the rock wall, the heavy fog began to lift, and I saw that his training in the Borangan forest had served him well, for the mountain trail was still directly ahead of us.

124

"Well, what's this?" I suddenly exclaimed as I noticed something about twenty yards distant.

"It looks like one of our problems is solved," said Denny, hurrying on ahead.

The source of our conjoint pleasure was a thin, rapidly flowing stream, its churning water the most welcome sight that we had known in days. It cascaded down the mountain along a flumelike rock bed, and once at the base it slowed, for there the tributary widened considerably. After about half a mile it narrowed, and in this guise it poured through a nearly circular opening, disappearing into an unseen conduit within the bowels of the mountain.

After sipping the icy water tentatively and finding it pure, we gratefully satisfied our heretofore unquenchable thirst. Then, letting our feet dangle in the rapid current, we rinsed days of grime from our bodies. Further along, where it was gentle, we might choose to bathe more thoroughly; but for now this was sufficient, and we could not be blamed for luxuriating in it for what seemed an excessive period of time.

We followed the stream for the most part as it wound toward the mountainside, though not until we were less than half a mile from our objective did we notice something that had previously been concealed from view by boulders. Scores of circular shafts, all in evenly spaced rows, pocked the surface for more than a square acre. Their purpose at first eluded us, until we chanced to gaze into one of the wide openings along the perimeter. Standing upright in the eight foot deep hole, its bony fingers positioned high above its head, was a human skeleton, its bleached death mask leering wickedly at us. A second hole revealed a similar grisly find, as did a third, and every one subsequent to these—save for five or six, which were empty. Though I could hardly guess at the kind of people responsible for this, I had little doubt that the part of the mesa we now negotiated with tentative steps was a vast graveyard!

"It's becoming more and more evident that this mountain is, or at least was, inhabited," stated Denny, gazing at the barren land that surrounded us. "But by whom?"

"I don't know; but I can assure you that they're still here."

"How can you be certain?"

I indicated a particular skeleton, one with knots of cartilage, bloodied bits of flesh, even hair still adhering to the bones. "This fellow has been deposited here within the past month."

Denny stared at it for a few moments, before turning away in disgust. "You're right," he nodded. "Come on, let's get out of here."

During the half hour that ensued we threaded our way slowly through the strange, vertical cemetery. Our preoccupation with the tenuous footing along the narrow strips of ground that separated the holes made it impossible to avoid noticing the leering inmates below—this further stretching our already taut nerves to their limits. Once we tried to follow the now calmer stream, but the chilled water, which was surprisingly deep, forced us back to land, and we continued along our original path.

The funereal shafts finally began to thin, the last of

them falling behind us about one hundred yards from the base of the foothills. After drinking one last time from the tributary, and filling our water pouches to brimming, we set off in the direction of the trail that wound toward the summit. But before we had traversed a fraction of the short distance we were brought to a sudden halt by an unexpected noise, one that pierced the deathlike stillness of the mesa and drove us instinctively into a nearby cluster of rocks. The sound, which seemed to emanate from far overhead, resembled the crashing of cymbals. It was repeated five, six, times clearly, until the heightening reverberations melded the individual strikings into a terrible din. I feared that the side of the mountain would tumble downward from this racket; but only a few small stones were loosed—these clattering harmlessly to the base, where they disappeared amidst countless others that had fallen over the years.

The last echoes faded, and silence again dominated the mesa. For long seconds we listened, but there was nothing. Satisfied, I began to rise from our place of concealment, when I felt Denny's hand grasping my arm tightly.

"Rollie, get down!" he hissed.

"What is it?"

"Over there!"

He indicated a large outcropping to the right of the mountain trail, where a form was emerging from an almost imperceptible fissure. At first it appeared to be a man, an illusion that was quickly dispelled as it broke free of its erstwhile place of confinement and shambled away from the base of the hills. Though stooped, it was clear that the two-legged creature stood at least a head above six feet. Its arms, which swung apelike before it, were narrow, elongated, and no digits were in evidence at the end of the stumpy hands. The neckless head sat atop a broad chest, neither displaying even a tuft of hair; nor was any in evidence over the rest of its body. Its face, a pulpy mass of layered tissue, was featureless, save for a broad slash of a mouth that contained rows of long, savage teeth. But above all this, its most disquieting characteristic was the gelatinous texture of its bluish, translucent flesh, which quivered obscenely with each heavy footfall that it chanced. It seemed as though the thing would decompose while it walked, but it did not, and each deliberate stride brought it closer to where we hid.

"What the hell is *that?*" Denny exclaimed beneath his breath.

"Only an angered or depraved Nature could have conceived of such a thing," I replied. "Let's just hope that it doesn't find us."

Its intitial path carried it straight toward us, and I visualized an unwanted confrontation. Then it veered away toward the river, and we breathed a sigh of relief as, once along the bank, it turned and faced the towering mountain. For more than a minute this translucent horror stared at the lower hills, until the object of its rapt attention was revealed.

From each invisible crevice, from every minute fissure they poured: ten, fifteen, eighteen of them by our most accurate count, all formed from the identical mold as the first. The silence of these hulking monstrosities as they approached the tributary was unnerving, more so than any cacophony of bestial sounds might have been. We wanted to run, but we could not, for they would have spotted us immediately; and we were of no mind to test their agility, despite the sluggishness that they displayed at the moment.

The last of them joined its brethren along the bank, and their well-concealed eyes now turned conjointly to the higher elevations of the mountain, more specifically to the snaking river, which bore an as yet unidentifiable object with it on its downward journey. Our own attention became riveted there, and we watched as the bobbing thing dissected the narrow flume. For more than a minute it disappeared under a broad layer of shale, and when it again emerged it was much nearer to the bottom, although we were still unable to see what it was. Then, with a churning thrust, it was deposited into the becalmed portion of the tributary near the base, where it rose high above the surface twice before settling. In those few moments we saw it clearly, and we looked at one another in disbelief as we realized that the object anticipated by these silent horrors was a pallid human corpse!

Silence again reigned as the body began floating downstream toward the waiting horrors, whose gelatinous frames now undulated obscenely as they leaned expectantly over the water. The corpse, that of an adult male, drifted to within ten yards, then five, before two of the creatures broke loose from the quivering mass and plunged into the river. They intercepted the body, and they hurled it to the bank through a rift made by their hovering brethren. It rolled over twice, finally coming to rest face up.

Then, before we were given the chance to examine its features, the blue horde fell upon it, and there ensued a ghastly symphony of slavering, sucking noises that left little doubt as to their incomprehensible designs.

For the greater part of an hour the creatures fed, while we tried vainly to deny what was happening only a short distance from our place of concealment. Our sole desire was to quit the scene of this atrocity, but in spite of their preoccupation we deemed it best to stay put. We sank deeper into our stone sanctuary, and not until the foul noises had begun to subside did we peer hesitantly over the rim.

One by one the horrors rose from their feast, and by the dim light of the fog-covered mesa we were able to discern the dark blotches through the folds of their translucent flesh, these denoting the fact that each had partaken of its desired portion. They shambled to the river, and they washed down the repast with great quantities of water—while we stared in disbelief at the now abandoned source of their pleasure, a blood-soaked skeleton with little more than a few shreds of skin hanging from it.

The fully sated creatures stretched languorously as they emitted low gurgling sounds, the first we had heard from their foul throats. One of the grotesque pack then stepped forward, and it gathered up the bulky skeleton in its long arms as though it were weightless. Under the watchful gaze of its brethren it bore the remains toward the vertical shafts behind us, its path leading it to within a few yards of our refuge. Despite its awkward appearance, the thing negotiated the cemetery with relative ease, and it did not pause until it stood over an empty hole—where it entombed the grinning skeleton carefully, almost ceremoniously.

Minutes later the creature had rejoined its fellows, and this marked the end of the grisly ritual. They set off toward the foothills, where they manipulated their cumbersome bodies through the narrow fissures from which they had first emerged. The last of them soon vanished, leaving only a tuft of white hair and a few spots of blood near the edge of the river to denote the site of their mindless perversion.

We rose simultaneously upon legs that were rubbery, and we stared in dumbfounded silence at the base of the mountain. Denny then turned toward me, his quaking voice penetrating the deathly stillness that had once more engulfed the mesa.

"What now, Rollie?" he gasped. "What now?"

I indicated the spiraling trail alongside the stone sentinels that had swallowed the flesh-eating horrors, and as I stepped from our sanctuary I told him: "Let's see how much of that we can put behind us by nightfall."

He leaped forward and grabbed my arm. "But Rollie, what about—?"

"Can this be the same madman who I followed across a carpet of slumbering satongs to reach Peter's cave? What is so different here?"

"The satongs had been asleep for hours, while these things returned to their lairs only minutes ago! They might be watching us right now!"

"In that case they already know that we're here. I'd rather take the chance now, than wait until after dark. Come on!"

We walked boldly toward the base of the mountain, our eyes glued to the fissures. Twenty yards, then fifteen: each footfall, every kicked pebble sounded like a clap of thunder amidst the silence. But the glutted monsters chose not to emerge, and we reached the path without incident. Disdaining even a single glance behind us, we began the ascent along the side of the stone titan that rose high above the plateau of terror and death.

CHAPTER NINE

THE ENDLESS WALL

During the first few hours the mountain trail inclined gently, and we were able to place a considerable distance in our wake. Then we penetrated the clouds, and our progress was slowed, for the denseness of the moisture-laden air was such that we did not know if our next step would carry us over the rim of the ofttimes narrow path to a jagged death below. After what seemed an eternity of minimal gain we decided to stop, for in addition to our weariness we were cognizant of the fact that darkness was beginning to descend.

It had been cold on the plateau, but at this elevation the air sliced through our flesh like gelid knives, and our worn garments were hardly enough to protect us. We traversed a few more yards in an effort to escape the full force of the wind, and we huddled together for warmth. With our bellies rumbling from hunger, we sought the merciful sanctuary of sleep as a means of denying our incomprehensible fatigue and discomfort.

I cannot begin to guess why, but on that night the terrible visions of recent months, which had troubled each of us at differing times since our being reunited, chose to assail our overtaxed minds simultaneously. Throughout the hours of darkness they passed before us, and we were barely able to calm one another in the midst of our individual torment. Slumber came in broken stretches that could be measured in minutes, the sum total hardly worth considering as dawn approached. Ravenously hungry, exhausted almost beyond caring, we resumed the trek, our sole wish being that it would soon end.

How far above Boranga we now walked was impossible to tell: ten thousand feet, twelve thousand, perhaps more. The continuously thinning air at times left us gasping for breath, and because of this we spoke few words during the seemingly endless day, which eventually terminated in much the same manner as the previous one. Our chances of survival diminishing, we fell to the sloping, rock-strewn surface, the numbness that we suffered in both mind and body our only defense against the frigid gusts that battered the mountainside.

Denny, who had seemed far the worse for wear during the latter part of the day, somehow managed to raise himself to a sitting position. Through a crimson haze I noticed him staring at me with sunken eyes, and I saw that his lips had turned a ghastly shade of blue. They parted with much effort, the muted words that he spoke barely audible through the howling wind.

"If . . . your Adara . . . survived this, then . . . she must be . . . quite . . . a woman."

"She is. I know that she endured, just as I'm certain that you and I will do the same."

My words, uttered in a tone that was less than convincing, fell upon deaf ears. Thrust to the limits by his efforts, Denny's eyes became blank. He fell back, his breathing heavy and sporadic. I wanted to help him, but I was unable to move. The haze darkened before me, and as I became cloaked in an ebon shroud, I grudgingly conceded victory to the mountain.

Misty daylight penetrated the dim recesses of my brain. It might have been morning, or afternoon: there was no way to tell. I lay torpidly for minutes, until the reality of the situation became lucid. Even then it required excessive time and effort to sit upright, my numbed members at first rebelling against my will. I noticed that the savage wind of the past night was nonexistent, this greatly lessening the severity of the still frigid air that dominated the upper reaches of the stone titan.

Denny was still alive, but barely. His flesh was pallid, and his breathing came in short, labored gasps. That he had survived the night was little less than a miracle, though the chances of him knowing another hazy dusk were limited. It was this fact, above all else, that prompted me to rise upon legs that were anything but steady in an effort to restore their circulation. I achieved this after about a minute of pacing the limited confines of our aerie, the throbbing pain of the returning life causing me to gnash my teeth.

After repositioning Denny on the hard earth I began massaging his arms and legs vigorously. The frozen appendages began to thaw quickly, and his breathing seemed more even; but in spite of this marginal success I was forced to curtail my efforts, for my overwhelming fatigue temporarily drained me of whatever strength I had been able to summon. I resumed my ministrations just as soon as I could, the results being no different. Panting heavily as I knelt alongside my friend, I knew that this was not the answer. But what was?

Not until my own breathing had become less labored did I sense that something was different, for only in the silence could I discern the unmistakable sound of rushing water nearby. More than likely this was the mountain stream that had borne the sacrifice to the horrors on the mesa, for in the lower elevations it had occasionally wound to within a few yards of the trail. Its proximity at first elicited little reaction on my part, for our supply of water was ample, and I could not think of any other way in which it might avail us. But my friend was dying, and with no other options I decided to have a closer look.

Seven tentative steps through the encompassing fog brought me to a narrow ledge, its width barely enough to accommodate my sandals. I traversed it with the utmost caution, and for the first time I was gratified by the presence of the clouds, which prevented me from seeing what awaited a single misstep. Beads of perspiration appeared, despite the chill, and only after I reached the edge of the flume did I realize that I had not dared to breathe for minutes.

The river, about a yard across, coursed rapidly on its journey down the mountainside, its present force possibly the result of a recent rain on the summit. Along the opposite edge, quite surprisingly, the topmost branches of a long dead plant emerged a few feet above the churning surface. The thickness of the gnarled boughs gave me an idea—one that, despite the risk involved, I believed to be worth a try. I straddled the angular walls of the slippery flume, at first employing a firm grip on the branches to maintain my balance. Severing the trunk near the waterline proved a difficult task in my awkward position, but I eventually succeeded; and after a breathless moment that nearly saw me tumble into the river I again established firm footing on the near bank. I secured the prize with a length of rope, and I slung it over my shoulder. Though bulky, it did not hinder my return along the ledge, and I soon found myself at Denny's side in about half the time it had earlier taken to negotiate the same distance.

Following a brief respite, I broke off one of the branches and began carving away the outer bark, which as I had guessed was saturated from its countless years of exposure. But the core of the solid wood was dry, this reinforcing the hope that I had discovered usable kindling. I stripped all the branches, a total of six, and I stacked them carefully next to the still unconscious Denny. Igniting them proved difficult, especially with nothing to use as tinder, and initially I wasted three of the precious matches that I had brought with me from the *Winged*

Messenger. But finally a few splinters began to burn, and within minutes I had manufactured a fire that, while hardly a raging inferno, was enough to begin dispelling the chilled air of the mountainside.

After warming my hands over the blaze I returned to the flume, which I straddled in much the same manner as previously. I inched my way upstream through the fog, and before long I came across another of the ancient plants—two of them in fact, the second only a few yards beyond on the same side. I chopped the branches from the nearest one, and after negotiating a dangerous turn I carried it to the intersecting ledge. But before reaching the spot, I chanced to notice something moving beneath the surface of the river. I could not tell what it was, but I did perceive it as a potential source of food. I stored this information for later use.

The flames were still dancing when I returned to the campsite, and I noticed that a reddish hue had replaced much of Denny's deathlike pallor. He had not yet regained consciousness, but his breathing was far stronger than before, and I felt sure that the warmth he continued to absorb would eventually wrest him from the black pit in which he had been held. Relieved by this knowledge I carved more of the kindling from the soggy wrappers—a laborious task that, when piled atop my growing cairn of exhaustion, threatened to drive me toward the rim of the same well from which my friend was emerging. But I managed to finish what I had started and, with half of the new pieces added to the blaze, I reclined alongside it, my damp, chilled body gratefully soaking up the life-giving heat.

Denny's eyes soon blinked open, though at first they stared upward dully. Then, as awareness returned, he glanced curiously from the fire to me, and he proffered a pained smile as he gasped, "I won't even ask how you managed it. Thanks, pal. . . ."

He was asleep before I could reply, the meager smile still creasing his face. Despite my own weariness I found slumber elusive, for the realization that we would again resume the search for Adara was more than sufficient to tap a flow of adrenalin that I did not believe existed. Rather than sit idly by, I decided to channel this energy into something productive.

I returned to the flume, the hazardous journey along the ledge now almost second nature to me, even with the lengthy Borangan spear in one hand. Once positioned over the torrent I stared downward, my vigil being rewarded within minutes by the appearance of a slow-moving, shadowy form similar to the one I had noticed earlier. I lowered the barbed tip into the water, and I proceeded to impale a huge, multi-legged crustacean—its frantic wriggling, coupled with its weight, nearly causing me to lose my balance. But it perished quickly, and I carried it to our encampment with a minimum of difficulty, where I deposited it atop the fire.

The aroma of the broiling crab soon caused Denny's nostrils to flare, and the crackling sound awakened him from his peaceful slumber. He stared in disbelief at the prize, his head shaking as he sat up.

"When I saw the fire earlier, I thought that I had died," he stated. "Now I'm sure of it!"

The repast, which we attacked ravenously only minutes later, could not have been topped by the finest seafood restaurant in New England. Despite its size we consumed every edible portion of the crab, and I don't doubt that we could have found room for more. But the gnawing pangs abated, and the returning strength provided by the nourishment was quite gratifying.

Night began to descend as we finished, and we turned in alongside the amply fueled blaze. We slept peacefully, and were well rested by the time we arose at dawn. The first thing that we noticed, surprisingly, was the lessening of the heretofore choking mist. Our visibility was unhindered as far as the river, and for the first time I was struck with the precariousness of the almost nonexistent ledge that I had negotiated so often during the previous day. Denny also stared at it in disbelief, for it did not take him long to deduce where the life-saving fuel and food had come from.

"You walked across *that?*" he exclaimed.

Nodding, I told him: "I intend to do it one more time before we go."

"But why?"

"I know for sure that there's more wood, and with any luck I might be able to spear another one of those things. Wait for me here."

Leaping to his feet, he exclaimed, "Not on your life! Why should you have all the fun?"

I did not argue with my rejuvenated friend, for I knew better. We traversed the rim separately to avoid placing unnecessary weight on it, and we chose not to gaze below at what was a smooth, nearly vertical facing. Once at the flume I traipsed upstream for the plant I knew to be there, while Denny, his spear poised, stared into the tributary for some sign of life. But he found none, and after sharing the fruitless vigil for a brief time we returned to the encampment with nothing more than the saturated wood, which we stripped quickly. Though unnecessary, I extinguished the remaining embers of the fire with the toe of my sandal, and neither of us looked back at the place where we had almost perished, as we resumed our trek up the formidable mountain.

Within a half hour the steepening path terminated, and from the base of a rugged granite cluster we stared at what appeared to be the rim of the summit some twenty-five feet above. We could not be certain of this, though we did know that we would find out soon enough, for our choices were nil. Denny was the first to begin the dangerous ascent, myself close at his heels. We utilized every niche, each grudging handhold, and despite the cold the perspiration flowed freely as we struggled for precious inches. The last five feet were by far the most treacherous; but Denny, with a teeth-gnashing effort, was able to haul himself over the edge. He denied his weariness for a few moments longer, until he had lifted me safely to his side.

Minutes passed while we lay breathless on the hard surface. The numbness in my arms and legs was quickly displaced by waves of throbbing pain, and for a time I wrestled with consciousness. Then it subsided, and I urged myself to a sitting position. My attention now turned to the still supine Denny, whose eyes were open.

"Are you all right?" I asked.

"Yeah," he groaned, pushing himself upright with obvious agony. "I just hope we don't have to subject ourselves to any more of that!"

"I don't think so. Look."

Our view across the level, rock-strewn plateau upon which we now sat was unimpeded for more than twenty yards. What lay beyond the perimeter of the fog was anyone's guess, though somehow I sensed that no more peaks loomed and that we were indeed upon the summit. If so, then the realization that we had nearly succumbed within the very shadow of our goal was more than my already troubled brain could comprehend, and I sought to deny it as I scanned the lifeless terrain.

"Do you see the river?" Denny asked. "That would be the easiest path to wherever the body came from."

The snaking flume had veered away from the trail minutes after we broke camp, and I had not noticed it since. For all we knew it could have disappeared into the side of the mountain; but then again it might be only a hundred yards or less from where we sat. Whatever the case it would be worthwhile to seek out the tributary, for Denny's idea, considering the unknown nature of our destination, was better than anything that I could come up with at the moment.

Upon sore, protesting legs we paralleled the edge of the plateau, but we did not intersect the river, and after about a quarter of a mile I concluded that it had indeed penetrated the granite titan further down. I motioned for Denny to stop, and I indicated the hovering fog toward what I approximated to be the east.

"Instinct and luck have guided much of our journey until now," I said. "Let's see if it can work one more time."

Hardly of a mind to argue, Denny matched my strides toward the core of the plateau, and within minutes the rim had vanished behind us. Our progress was slow but steady, and by the time the swirling mist again closed around us we had traversed at least three miles. Now our headway was indeed minimal, for the fog seemed denser than at any time before, if such were possible, and we were wary about even our next step. The increasing cold was also a hindrance, the bone-numbing chill of the vaporous fingers leaving me to ponder whether I would ever be warm again. I toyed with the thought of igniting a fire to ward off the moist, frigid air; but I knew that our limited fuel would be better utilized after dusk, and so we endured the cold stoically as we forged ahead through the soup.

The wall loomed before us quite unexpectedly, its presence a mystery until we stood barely two feet from its base. It was a fabricated barrier rather than a natural one, as evidenced by the smooth, uniformly cut stones that were joined together with a dun-colored mortar. Its height could not be judged, nor its length, though this seemed of little importance in light of a more eye-opening revelation: this fog-enshrouded wall, which I touched with a trembling hand, was man-made. Beyond it were people, and more importantly—if miracles were in order upon this enigmatic island—my Adara!

I gazed at Denny, who seemed to sense my unspoken anxiety as he examined the barrier. "We've got to see

143

what's on the other side of this thing," he stated forcefully. "Let's start looking for a gate or something."

Nodding, I pointed to our left. "This way's as good as any."

My excitement was ill-concealed as I took the lead and strode rapidly along the base of the wall, Denny close at my heels. Five hundred yards fell to our rear, a thousand, then twice that; but no doorway, not even the smallest aperture, dented the smooth granite blocks. Once, likely as much in frustration as curiosity, we hurled smaller stones toward the uppermost reaches of the cloud-draped wall in an attempt to ascertain its height. But our many grunting efforts were fruitless, for none of the missiles cleared the top, all instead ricocheting back to the hard earth. We grudgingly acceded to the reality that we would not be scaling this towering barrier, and with no additional effort expended we continued along our original path.

A few hundred yards further along we came across a skillfully constructed corner, the stones at this junction nearly twice the size of the other mortared blocks. With a shrug of resigned acceptance we altered our own path, and for a distance of two miles, perhaps more, we paralleled the endless wall. Then, as our hopes ebbed to a low point, we discovered a hardwood door of average height and width—a knobless portal that seemed a part of the wall itself, so precisely did it fit. We pressed our shoulders against it and pushed inward, but it did not give even a fraction of an inch. Nor could we learn if it opened toward us, for there was nothing to grab hold of, and

144

we were unable to wedge our knife blades between the wood and the jamb. Finally we backed away a yard or so to mull over our next course of action, though not before the red-faced Denny had loosed an angry kick at the barrier.

"Damn thing," he growled. "What do we do now?"

Drawing my ax, I replied, "I don't care if we have to hack it into kindling, but somehow . . ."

The words caught in my throat as I heard the muffled noise that emanated from behind the door. I looked at Denny, who had instinctively drawn his Mogar knife, and I knew that, like myself, he had already identified it as the sound of a bolt being drawn through its brackets. Someone on the other side, alerted to our presence, was opening the door!

"Rollie, let's get out of here!" hissed Denny, grabbing my arm.

I shook my head as I stared at the oaken portal. "After coming this far, we might as well see what we've found. What do you think?"

His silence was his answer. With a look of grim determination he faced the barrier, and side by side we listened to the purposeful sound of the sliding bolt, which terminated only seconds later. The heavy door creaked loudly as it swung toward us, and when it was fully opened we were afforded our first look at the mysterious gatekeeper.

The large, shadowy form that filled much of the doorway appeared to be human, the considerable bulk denoting a male. His features were indistinguishable, encased as he was by the dense fog. For more than a minute he stood there mutely, the oppressive tension of this silent standoff causing my fingers to whiten as they squeezed the haft of the ax. An elongated arm was then lifted, and twice, three, times we were curtly bidden to enter. He then stepped aside, leaving us to ponder the invitation.

I was the first to stride forth, Denny following less than a yard behind, and together we passed within the shrouded walls of this cryptic place perched high atop Boranga.

CHAPTER TEN

KHARITH

Despite the bitter cold, the hulking, dark-skinned figure that was momentarily preoccupied with forcing the heavy bolt into place wore only a scanty breechcloth, one fabricated from a single strip of leather threaded through a patch of tan fur. Once done with his task, which he performed without any hint of strain, he drew himself to his full height of nearly seven feet and turned toward us. It was immediately evident that there was not a trace of hair anyplace on his body, not even eyebrows. His sleek, muscular body contrasted his bland face—an emotionless mask of two dull eyes, pinprick nostrils in the center of a flattened nose, and an impossibly small, O-shaped mouth. He was unarmed and did not appear hostile, a fact that hardly lessened the anxiety I felt as I lowered the ax in an attempt to exhibit our peaceful intentions.

Stepping forward slowly, I asked, "Who are you? What do you call this place?"

My queries were at first met with silence; then, as if oblivious to our presence, the huge fellow deposited himself cross-legged on the ground, his back against the door. This frustrated both of us, but especially Denny, who stormed forth a bit less than cautiously and dropped to his knees before the giant.

"We've come a long way!" he snapped. "We're cold, tired, and hungry. Can you or your people help us? We would be willing to work for whatever you can offer."

The outburst elicited no response from the silent gatekeeper, who continued to stare blankly past us. Rather than pursue what now appeared to be a futile exercise, I motioned for Denny to rise. "Let's look for his kinsmen," I said. "Maybe they'll be more cooperative."

After casting a last hopeful glance at the statuelike fellow, Denny joined me. Once again we penetrated the fog, no less thick on this side of the wall, and in seconds we had lost sight of the portal and its enigmatic guardian. Initially we were silent, each absorbed in his own thoughts, my own centered about the shrouded land into which we had so willingly strode. Was Adara truly within these walls, or had the dangerous mountain trek, which nearly cost us our lives, been undertaken in vain? And what of the inhabitants of this place? Were they, like so many others on this hostile island, to be feared and mistrusted? Doubtless we would learn the answers before long, though until then the uncertainty would prove the cause of much anxiety.

A subtle change snapped us simultaneously from our reverie, and we turned our attention to the surrounding terrain, which was becoming more visible as the fog lifted. For thirty yards, then fifty, we were afforded a clear view of the dismal landscape, which appeared no different from the long stretch of rugged plateau that we had crossed outside these walls. Two, three hundred yards, until we could see the many fissures that split the surface—these snaking outward in a weblike pattern from its hub, a small rift not far to our left. But still we witnessed no sign of life, not even a brittle shrub, and so we continued on without any knowledge of where we were headed.

The biting chill that dominated the lofty plateau began to lessen in its severity, this curiously proportionate to the increasing visibility. Soon the air, though still damp, was warm, and I found myself perspiring under the heavy poncho, a revelation that hardly troubled me in light of what we had endured. We discarded the once invaluable wood, now useless, as we continued toward the source of the pulsating heat, which appeared before us only a few minutes later with a suddenness that we had scarcely anticipated.

From the lip of a broad, craterlike depression we gazed across a mile of an uneven lava floor at a city, this sprawling conglomeration of buildings occupying more than a third of the bowl. The uneven rows of structures, which ranged widely in size and shape, appeared to be constructed from the same white stone as the surrounding walls. Along one side of the metropolis, enigmatically situated amidst the black stone bed, was a rippling amber meadow, where herds of creatures that we could not identify from such a distance grazed with apparent contentment. Their shepherds were likewise indiscernable, though no more so than the tiny specks that flitted before the backdrop of the albescent city.

"During the time I had spent with Ter-ek and the Homarus, I heard of nothing like this," I told Denny. "What about the Mogars? Did they ever speak of such a place?"

He shook his head. "I was about to ask you the same thing. Shall we wait until nightfall before going down?"

"Whether you wish to admit it or not, we're at the mercy of this strange mountain world and its inhabitants. Why delay the inevitable? Besides, I have a hunch that we're expected."

Denny appeared incredulous. "How can that be? The only one who saw us was that dullard at the wall, and I'd be willing to bet that he's still sitting where we left him. You can't believe that *he* advised the others of our presence!"

"Who can be certain how these beings communicate? Maybe he did, maybe he didn't. Whatever the case, I believe that they know we're here and have known for some time. Call it a gut feeling, or anything you want; but I don't think that we need trouble ourselves with stealth when we're so close to learning the answer to that which has brought us this far. Are you coming?"

I stepped off the rim onto a gentle declivity, and Denny, with a resigned shrug, did the same. The descent was accomplished with relative ease, save for the last twenty-five or thirty yards, when the angle of the slope altered severely. Despite all attempts at caution I stumbled on the shifting gravel, and I rolled headlong to the base, the rough stones tearing loose a few inches of skin. Denny, who had negotiated the same distance without incident, voiced his concern as he assisted me to my feet; and only after I had convinced him that I was none the worse for wear did we set off across the lava bed toward the gleaming city.

The solidified molten floor, doubtless the result of some ancient upheaval, proved difficult to walk upon, especially in light of the fact that we had long since been footsore. We might have paused to rest, but the distance before us was short; and this, coupled with the first hints of dusk above the cloud-filled sky, was enough to urge us onward at a steady, if slow, pace. Once I leaned over to touch the lava, which, as I had guessed, was quite warm. I checked this odd phenomenon three more times along the path to the city, but I found the heat to be no more intense, not even when we stood ten yards from the entrance to an alleyway that dissected the outermost buildings.

We had not encountered any of the city's denizens during our journey across the floor of the depression, and initially we came upon none as we penetrated the city along the narrow, winding passage. Though alerted to their inevitable appearance, we were afforded a few moments to glance at the structures that we passed. The ivory blocks from which they had been fabricated were, as I had earlier assumed, the same as those of the unending walls—the only difference here being the mortar, this compound, spread more thinly between the stones of a less contrasting bluish tint. There were no doors facing the alley, and few windows, those in evidence little more than slender apertures. One thing that struck me about the buildings, which varied haphazardly from a single level to as many as four, was their cleanliness—as though they had recently been scrubbed. Even the lava path was devoid of dust, refuse, or anything else that would not have ordinarily seemed out of place here. Whatever the nature of these inhabitants, they were clearly meticulous.

The alley, after a sharp turn, intersected a wide avenue, and we pulled up short as half a score of figures were suddenly revealed. All of the hulking men, exact replicas of the gatekeeper, were preoccupied with one bustling task or another, and our appearance was hardly noted, despite the fact that they could not help but see us. Most were engaged in some sort of cleaning activity, either with mops or long-handled brooms. The only exception was the giant who strode purposefully down the center of the path, his massive thews rippling beneath the weight of something that appeared to be a side of beef. Two others, following in his wake, frantically mopped up the dripping blood, and somehow they managed to stay within five yards of the bearer, who soon disappeared around the corner of another intersecting road.

Emerging hesitantly from the alley, we confronted a trio who were mechanically sweeping the almost dust-free street. "We would appreciate your help," I told them loudly. "Please, can you stop for a minute?"

They did not cease their labors, nor did they even look up, this irritating both of us. I proceeded to address them in snatches of four different languages, but the result was no different.

"Listen! The fool talks to the horriks! Did you ever hear of such a thing? Ha!"

"Perhaps it is his Pleasure to give amusement. If so, then I am surely amused!"

Our weapons poised, Denny and I whirled about to face the source of the voices. We saw two people, a man and a woman, emerging from a doorway about ten yards distant. The grinning pair, both slight of stature, were fair skinned—the man's sandy hair closely cropped, that of his partner pale blond and lengthy. They were garbed almost identically in shapeless sackcloths, their feet shod in thick-soled sandals. Neither bore any weapons, and this fact, coupled with their cheerful demeanor, saw us resheath our own blades.

Though standing only inches before me and staring at my face, the young woman's words were addressed to her companion as she said, "I have been to the houses of all the Givers, and never before have I seen this one. What about you, Swekon?"

"Not this one, not the other," replied the man, who stood before Denny. "Besides, Malba, have you ever seen a Giver dressed thusly? This is not even Evirian garb!"

"I suppose you're right," the woman called Malba sighed. "But the way he made us laugh! Perhaps Ventoth, the Giver of Amusement, should know—"

"Wait a minute!" I roared, my outburst causing

them to back away slightly. "I don't know what the devil either of you are talking about. As for saying anything funny, I can assure you that I didn't!"

"But you *did!*" Swekon insisted. "You spoke to *them!*"

"Who? These men?" I indicated the huge laborers.

"Men! The horriks!" Malba exclaimed, and the pair broke into uncontrollable peals of laughter, while our own frustration grew. Denny, his teeth bared, lifted Swekon a few inches off the ground and shook him, this lessening the small fellow's glee only slightly.

"Listen to me, you idiot!" he bellowed. "We're not going to stand here and play games with you. If you can't give us some straight answers, then steer us to someone who can. Where will we find the ruler of—what did you call this place? Evirian?"

Malba's chortles began anew, while Swekon, desperately trying to stifle his own mirth, replied, "This city is Kharith. *We* are Evirians. But I don't understand what it is you want. What is—ruler?"

"Ruler!" Denny hissed, as he struggled with himself against throttling the irritating fellow. "Leader, president, chief, boss—the one in charge!"

"In charge," Swekon nodded. "I think I know what you mean. There is a formal triumvirate, but they meet infrequently, and it's anyone's guess where they might be in between. Here, put me down!" Denny complied, and Swekon continued, "You should try the house of Deklus. He is the Giver of Knowledge, and there is little that he couldn't tell you."

"Where will we find this Deklus?" I asked.

Malba, again under control, pointed down the broad avenue. "On the right, forty or so buildings down, a large house among smaller ones. Now, we must go, for there is a grand feast commencing at the house of Obbor, the Giver of Sustenance. Maybe later we will see you there."

The pair scurried off along the avenue, stopping about fifteen yards distant. For a few moments they whispered amongst themselves; then, as they glanced back toward us, they again began to laugh uproariously, the echoes of their merriment lingering long after they had disappeared around the same corner as the huge fellow who had earlier journeyed that way with his dripping burden. Still incredulous, I gazed at the workers whom Swekon and Malba had called horriks, noting that none evinced the least bit of interest in what had transpired here. I then turned toward Denny, who was still shaking his head.

"If you happen to see a white rabbit carrying a pocket watch, please don't tell me about it," he said mirthlessly.

"Don't worry, I won't. Let's see if we can find this Deklus."

We followed the ebon lane for about three hundred yards, and we maintained a cumulative inventory of the structures that we passed. Along the way we saw many more horriks, though as previously these silent titans ignored us as they went about their menial labors. We also encountered a few Evirians of varying sizes and complexions—all of whom, while barely breaking stride on their way to some unknown diversion, greeted us cheerfully. Sniggering comments were made behind our backs about our garb, as

155

well as our haggard appearance, but we refrained from thrashing the perpetrators, which at the moment I believe I would have enjoyed.

Nearly four dozen alabaster houses on our right fell behind us before we came to the dwelling of Deklus. As the woman called Malba had said, it was by far the largest house in the area, half again the size of some, twice the height and breadth of most. From the oddly shaped, doorless entranceway a line of about fifty Evirians, all of whom appeared to be awaiting ingress, snaked along the side of the building. We chose to ignore them as we approached the portal, our actions disturbing a few, who waved their arms animatedly as we passed.

"Here, where do you think you're going?" snapped one.

"We've come to see Deklus," I replied.

"Haven't we all?" said a shrewish woman. "Get in line and wait your turn!"

"Yes, what's your hurry?" questioned another. "More than likely you'll be seeing one of the apprentices, and not the Giver himself. Do as she says!"

I glanced at Denny, who had already unsheathed the Mogar knife. "I'll be damned if I'm going to wait for—!"

"Put away your weapon, young man!" a voice commanded in a harsh, authoritative tone.

We turned toward the entranceway, where a smallish, wizened man in a dusty gray tunic was waving a gnarled finger in our direction. His face was a scowling mask, though I could discern the curiosity that burned in his eyes as he stared at us.

"I am Deklus, and I intend to grant you an immediate audience," he rasped as he shuffled across the few yards that separated us. "I thought that you would come looking for me."

"Then—you knew we were here?" I exclaimed.

Ignoring me for the moment, he said to the knife-wielding Denny: "You've not yet done what I asked." My friend, snapping free of his brief lethargy, complied with the request of the elder, who then went on: "That's better. Now in answer to your question, it is hardly a secret in Kharith when either of the two gates along the outer walls are opened, since it is an infrequent occurrence. Who else but strangers would enter? And in their confusion, they eventually wind up here."

"We have a lot to ask you," I admitted.

His demeanor softened, and I thought that I even detected a hint of a smile. "I too have questions, but come! I don't conduct audiences in the streets! We'll go inside, where it's comfortable." He faced the line of mumbling Evirians, one hand upraised. "The apprentices will get to all of you in time, and you will have their undivided attention."

His words hardly placated the crowd, though he did not seem to care. He strode toward the portal, and he motioned for us to follow, but at first we did not move. Then, knowing that there was only one way to learn the answers, we set off in his wake—a few lengthy strides carrying us through the ovoid portal into the gleaming house of Deklus, Giver of Knowledge.

Along either wall of the broad, low-ceilinged hallway that we now traversed, scores of Evirians sat

157

by small, utilitarian tables and interacted with considerable animation. Those who mostly listened were young men in dull robes, undoubtedly the apprentices of Deklus. The echoing din was such that I could not understand a single word being uttered, though the puzzle of what transpired here was quickly solved by the perceptive Deklus.

"A Giver of Knowledge would have nothing to give without first taking," he explained. "In this hall my predecessors and I have *taken* the knowledge of all—*all* that has transpired in Kharith since its inception. There are few details, no matter how insignificant, that are not absorbed and recorded for posterity. This is a considerable task, when you realize that more than twenty thousand dwell within Kharith's walls. Normally the line outside is five to ten times as long, and it is only because of the waning day that there are not any more. But we have learned to deal with it, especially during my tenure, for I have more willing apprentices than any before me."

Denny shook his head. "You record—everything? But that's impossible!"

"Is it?" said Deklus, pausing before a large door at the far end of the corridor. "Observe!"

He flung open the heavy portal ceremoniously, and we followed him into an immense room of about three hundred square yards. Stark shelves lined every inch of the lofty walls, these stacked high with leather-bound volumes of uniform thickness. At two elongated tables, intense acolytes penned the latest news of Kharith into fresh journals.

"There are two other rooms in the building identical to this one," Deklus announced. "We have commandeered the houses on either side, and they too are full. Soon we will be near bursting once again, and additional space will be required."

"Why do you do this?" I asked, staring at the countless stacks.

"Because I am the Giver of Knowledge!" he stated indignantly. "I am of the Elite, descended from among those closest to Cuhram, founder of Kharith. I exist only to impart my knowledge to others, as Obbor exists to provide food, Ralzon to give slumber, and so on. It is my predestined labor of life, but it is also my greatest Pleasure."

"I still don't know what you're talking about," Denny shrugged.

"I don't expect that you do," replied Deklus. "Ah, but I'm probably getting ahead of myself. Follow me to my private quarters, and I'll spend a brief time satisfying your most basic curiosity regarding Kharith. I won't detain you for long, for I suppose that you're tired and hungry. But know this, strangers: more than anything I yearn for knowledge of the outside world, and those who dwell in it. You must return soon, so that I might learn everything about you. Do I have your word?"

We nodded vaguely, and this seemed to satisfy him. With a new lightness to his step he led us back into the corridor, and we passed more than a dozen pairs of conferees as we journeyed to his chamber at the far end of the building. This room, while not large, was opulent, especially when compared to the starkness of the rest of the house. Tapestries lined the walls, thick furs the floor. The divan, where Deklus motioned for us to sit, was luxuriant, though no less so than the plush hassock upon which he perched.

"Now then, let me tell you about the place and the people within whose sphere you have stumbled," he said, this beginning an almost mechanical, monotonic recitation that he had doubtless made more than a few times before. "We are the ancestors of those who came here a century past from Eviria, a land far to the northeast of Boranga, and many times its size. Led by the revolutionary named Cuhram, this hardy band of four thousand journeyed to these shores to escape unimaginable persecutions in the land of their birth, and they sunk the special ships that had carried them across the waves, lest any return and reveal their new homeland. The only thread that bound them to Eviria was their name—which, for whatever reason, they chose to retain and which we have inherited.

"From a Mogar that they had chanced to take prisoner during their trek across the hostile land, Cuhram's people first learned about the one called Ras-ek Varano. As the vision of his terrifying reign unfolded, the Evirians panicked, for they feared that their precious freedom would again be wrested from them. Had they not sank their vessels, they would have immediately sailed in search of another land. Cries arose to begin building new ones, but Cuhram reasoned that in the length of time it would take, the risk of so large a group being discovered by the Master was considerable. Most eventually concurred.

"The mountains were reached not long after, and they found their way to the summit of this particular one, though the price that they paid was considerable. Here, amidst the thin, cloud-choked air, they

160

carved the city of Kharith, so named for Cuhram's woman. It took twelve painstaking years to build, but it was well worth the effort: for it gave them a home far from the Master's sphere of influence, or at least his interest, and in the ensuing decades it served our people well."

"Even twelve years seems like a relatively short span of time," I interrupted, "considering how few able-bodied workers Cuhram must have had. Was this the first occasion that your people had to utilize slaves?"

Deklus appeared taken aback. "Slaves? The Evirians have never kept slaves, not then, not now! Whatever gave you the idea—?"

"Do you think us ignorant, blind, or both?" Denny roared. "We've seen scores of ridiculed menials wandering the streets of your city! What do you call *them?*"

"You don't mean the horriks?" asked Deklus incredulously.

"That is how others referred to them."

He shook his head,' and his perpetual scowl was nearly turned into a smile. "A slave is someone kept against his own free will, wouldn't you say?" We nodded. "Then the horriks cannot be slaves!" he exclaimed. "They have no will; they are mindless, soulless. Their life is not life as we know it, but rather directed animation. They are—creations!"

"Creations!" I hissed. "Of what?"

"Not what, but whom. Cuhram, genius that he was, fashioned the first of them. They were improved upon through the years, and a level of near perfection has been achieved by a descendant of Cuhram, the

161

one called Kobuld, Giver of Wonders. He would be well pleased to know how much you were fooled by his exquisite toys."

"I don't believe this!" cried Denny. "How could the horriks be *made?*"

"Kobuld once related the entire process to me," said Deklus seriously. "Perhaps you'd like me to read it to you . . . but of course you don't. All right then, let me tell you about the Givers, and we'll hold the rest for some more propitious time.

"Our forebears were dedicated to a total fulfillment of life's Pleasures—their pursuit of these goals one of the principal reasons for the animosity of their peers upon Eviria. Cuhram's circle, the first Elite, had far surpassed all in attaining their greatest individual joys, and when Kharith was established they were aptly dubbed the Givers. Cuhram became the Giver of Wonders; Tummoro, my own ancestor, the first Giver of Knowledge. Let me see, then there was—"

"You don't intend to name them all, do you?" I said curtly.

He proffered a crooked smile. "My apologies, but imparting knowledge is *my* Pleasure, and I find it difficult to be brief. We won't concern ourselves with the old ones for now, and as for the current Givers, you'll have ample time to learn of them. But let me finish what I have begun, so that you will have some inkling of what to expect beyond the portals of my house.

"As was the dream of Cuhram, the people of Kharith live only for Pleasure. They do not expend themselves in menial labor, especially now that the

162

horriks have been developed so superbly. You will encounter many Evirians who appear hard at work, such as my own apprentices; but this is what they desire to do, and therefore it is not work, but Pleasure. The masses, far less refined than the Elite, happily take from all who give, and their lives are greatly enriched. Are you beginning to understand?"

"It sounds like a stimulating, progressive society you have here," said Denny dryly.

"Do not seek to judge us!" Deklus snapped. "It is the way we choose and it is right for us. Remember too that we did not ask you here." He indicated the door. "Go now, and learn how hospitable the city that you scorn can be to strangers! Ah, but come back soon, for there is so much that I wish to ask. Perhaps you know more of the Homarus and the Mogars, of the assault undertaken by the former as a means to achieve peace between them. You may even—"

"Wait a minute," I interjected. "That was a comparatively recent occurrence. How did you know about it?"

"From our last arrival, a young woman."

I found it difficult to restrain my emotions as I absorbed his words. While trembling with anticipation, I asked, "What was her name?"

Deklus shook his head. "I don't remember. Oh, she was a beautiful thing! Let me withdraw a journal, and—"

"Never mind. Is she still in Kharith?" He nodded, and in a rasping voice brought about by the dryness in my throat I said to Denny: "My girl made it! She survived that miserable ascent, and she's here, *now!* Let's go, pal: we've got to find her!"

As we raced from the room, Deklus called after us: "Why the haste? You'll find her soon enough."

"The quicker we're reunited, the quicker we can bid farewell to your city of sloth."

"That, my young friends, will not be possible."

We ceased our headlong rush, and we turned slowly toward the elder, whose demeanor did not hint at jest. "What do you mean?" I asked icily.

"Your woman already knows, and she will tell you: since its inception Kharith has admitted a few; but never have its two gates permitted egress, not even to its citizens. You will not see the outside of Kharith for the remainder of your lives!"

CHAPTER ELEVEN

THE GIVERS OF SUSTENANCE
AND LOVEMAKING

For a few minutes we were too stunned to respond to the words of Deklus, who eyed us impassively as he rose from the hassock. Then, as our bewilderment turned to anger, we stormed the elder, who shrank before our purposeful approach.

"Please, think of what you are doing!" he cried.

"What I'm thinking of doing is tearing you apart!" roared Denny, as the two of us halted only inches before him. "But first, we're going to find out what you meant by that!"

"I was not prepared for such an outburst," said Deklus haughtily. "Why did—?"

"You pass a life sentence on us, and you think that we should accept it calmly?" I snapped. "Who are you to decide our fate?"

"I did not decide your fate," he countered, "I only

advised you of what had been decreed a hundred years past. Any Evirian you ask will tell you the same thing. The laws of the first Elite have guided our people well, and they cannot—*will* not—be changed!"

Denny thrust a finger at the old man's face. "Do you expect us to stand idly by and allow ourselves to be taken?" he challenged.

"You are already *taken*," replied Deklus. "The two gates are now guarded by three horriks each, though one of the invincible creatures would easily suffice to prevent you from escaping. The walls, as you more than likely discovered, are unscalable, unless you can somehow take wing. There is no other way out, my friends, so you might as well accept Kharith as your home."

"Our prison, you mean," said Denny dryly.

"If that be the case, then we Evirians are all prisoners. Yet there are none, nor have there ever been any, who have desired egress, not even the handful from below who have found their way to the City of Pleasure over the decades."

"That's a lie, Deklus!" I snapped. "There's been one among you for months who, even though she arrived here of her own volition, cannot be satisfied with this captivity, whatever its guise."

"And now there's three, old man," Denny added. "Aside from a few basic needs, this place has *nothing* to offer us."

Nodding, I asked, "What purpose can you have for keeping everyone within these walls?"

"You, who come from the surface of Boranga, should know the answer to that. Besides, I hinted at it earlier."

"The Master!" Denny exclaimed. "You're afraid of Ras-ek Varano!"

Deklus nodded. "As I told you, our ancestors came to these mountains in the hope of removing themselves from his sphere of influence, and they succeeded, though every day they dwelt with the fear that he would find them. This dread, I assure you, has been passed down through the years. Our freedom is everything, and we cannot chance our existence being revealed—which could happen, inadvertently or otherwise, by one who finds his way to the surface. That is why the horriks are conditioned to destroy anyone, *anyone*, who approaches within ten yards of either gate. You see, we know far more about the Master than any of you, and we—"

"Wait a minute," I interrupted. "How can you make such a claim? Your people have never been confronted with the horrors of Ras-ek. All you have to go by are the superstitious prattlings of a terrified Mogar, and the words of a few other natives. From experience, I've found their knowledge regarding the Master to be less than adequate."

"Nonetheless, what I say is true. During the latter years of the first Elite, a Homaru of superior intelligence found his way to Kharith. Utilizing various means, Cuhram—ah—persuaded him to detail everything he knew regarding the one called Ras-ek Varano. As the sordid tale of the Master and his powers unfolded, it struck an at first dim chord in the mind of Tummoro, my grandfather. He hastened to his house—where, after spending hours thumbing through immense journals, he found what he wanted in a volume of ancient Evirian history."

167

"What was it?" asked Denny irritably, as Deklus paused.

"Simply this: from entries made in the old text, Tummoro and his peers came to learn about the source of Ras-ek Varano's powers."

We gazed at one another in disbelief and then stared at the wrinkled Giver. "You—*know* what the source of his obscene powers is?" I gasped.

Deklus smiled. "Ah, so I've piqued your curiosity, have I? Yes, there it was, in the scrawl of someone long dead. Then, more than previously, was the fear of this entity harbored by the Evirians elevated to heights above the realm of reason. Cuhram's original decrees were reinforced tenfold, and the tasks of the horrik guards were altered drastically from peaceful detention to . . ."

"Understanding this power, couldn't your ancestors—or you, for that matter—utilize such knowledge in destroying the Master?"

The elder shook his head. "I said that we knew of the source, not that we understood it. I suppose that it gave us some minute advantage over the rest of Boranga's enslaved minions—though this did not mean very much, for there was little that we could have done. You will realize this too, when you hear the words of the journal."

"Will you—tell us what it said?" I asked expectantly.

Deklus rubbed his palms together as he grinned broadly. "In time, my friends, in time. I am not the old fool you perceive me to be. You would not have come back to talk to me, as you promised. But now I possess information that you desire, and this places a different light on the matter. You will return to my house, yes, you *will* return! Oh, I would sit up throughout the night to exchange thoughts with you . . . no, I must not be tempted! Go, now; seek out your woman, partake of food and rest. I will await you here—not patiently, mind you. Then, once you have paid the small price I require, you will learn the secret of Ras-ek Varano!"

He guided us back into the corridor, now nearly deserted, and he led us along its entire length, the footfalls of our slapping sandals on the stone floor the predominant sound. At the oddly shaped portal he bid us farewell, and we strode out into the crisp night air, which we hardly noticed as we attempted to meld the jumble of bewildering thoughts that had overwhelmed us in the house of Deklus.

Kharith proved to be a strange spectacle after dark. The avenues were lined with silent horriks, each holding a dazzling, phosphorescent torch. Scores of carefree Evirians hurried along the well lit, intersecting roads, most turning onto the broad thoroughfare along which we traveled. We were greeted cordially by all, but especially by the women, the majority of whom were impossibly beautiful. Their sultry smiles, their words of welcome as they ran their tapered fingers along the contours of their exquisite, lightly clad forms—these left little doubt regarding their desires, though this hardly seemed to disturb their male companions. One of the Evirian females, a stunning blonde, inched her way closer to us as we walked, and she ran her fiery tongue across her lips in a successful attempt to catch our eyes.

"I'll be at the house of Oghis within an hour," she

whispered, her darting, emerald orbs giving no clue as to the object of her interest. "You'll look for me, won't you?"

She sped off without awaiting an answer, while we stared at one another with something that, in spite of our predicament, hinted at amusement. "If that's what Kharith is all about," said Denny, "I can almost understand why no one wants to leave."

I nodded as I indicated the well-used path before us. "Do you know where we're going?"

"Beats me. I guess we just follow the crowd until we get there."

As we continued to dissect the gleaming structures, each again consumed with his own thoughts, it occurred to me that we had as yet said nothing of what had transpired in the house of Deklus. But then, what was there to say? Here was an individual who could matter-of-factly reveal the secret of the Master's powers, possibly the key to his destruction! I felt like turning back and confronting the old Giver once more, perhaps even throttling him, until he told me what I wanted to hear. But Adara's well-being remained foremost, and I knew that I would not return there before assuring myself that she was indeed the woman who had come to Kharith months earlier and before she again was walking at my side.

For one not yet accustomed to it, the climate in the heart of this crater city was indeed odd. The natural stone floor continued to give off warmth from an unknown source below, the layer of dry heat hovering more than a foot above the surface. Sitting atop this was the chilled night air of the summit, which in light of the tattered condition of our garments was barely tolerable. I was surprised to note that the Evirians, most clad in the flimsiest of garb, appeared unaffected by their environment. Undoubtedly the wonder of evolution had altered their chemistry, despite the relatively brief span of a few generations, for in addition to their tolerance of the cold they sped about with ease in the thin air of the mountain. From recent experience, I knew that such movements on our part in this rarified atmosphere would see us gasping for breath within minutes.

The ceaseless wave of Evirians carried us further into the city, where the dimensions of a few of the gleaming structures altered drastically. Though they rose no higher than the others that surrounded them, the depth and breadth of three stone edifices appeared at least five times greater than the rest. Broad steps inclined about a third of the way up, terminating before wide entranceways that, like the one at the house of Deklus, were doorless. Evirians streamed in and out of these buildings, the largest number of them upon the stairs of the one closest to us, on our left. For want of a better destination we turned toward this bustling center of activity, and we learned its ill-kept secret long before reaching its base.

"Can this be anything but the house of Obbor, Giver of Sustenance?" I heard Denny mumble, as we eyed the scores of Kharith natives who emerged from the structure with armloads of food, the portions ranging from small platters to enormous, steaming beef joints.

Nodding, I asked, "Are you hungry?"

"No, just famished! What are we waiting for?"

We mounted the stairs, paying little heed to the grinning Evirians who hailed us as we climbed. The mass of pasty white bodies seeking ingress accompanied us to the top, where we were brought to a halt by the overpowering, albeit delectable, aroma that emanated from the house of Obbor. Individual smells were not distinguishable amidst the melding of so many—though this hardly lessened the wafting, almost visible, enticement. Driven by our own hunger, urged on by the many behind us, we allowed ourselves to be drawn within the walls of Kharith's Giver of Sustenance.

A wide, abbreviated corridor, its walls literally draped with moving rows of Evirian men, women, and children, led us to a wide portal, its thick double doors held open by two robed apprentices of considerable girth. From the opening, where we were forced to pause for a few moments while the anxious throng was greeted individually by the smiling acolytes, we gazed across a chamber of impressive dimensions. It was a nearly perfect square, each muraled wall approximately fifty yards across. The ceiling rose to the full height of the building, at least thirty-five feet. In the center of the hall, below a chandelier of countless tapers, was the junction of four lengthy wood tables, these laid out in a perfect X. There, sitting regally atop an ornate chair, was an individual whose appearance could scarce be believed. Of average height, this grinning, repulsive fellow weighed no less than four hundred pounds. His folds of flesh rippled obscenely as he alternated between devouring a massive piece of beef and downing a pitcher of something that resembled ale.

The scores of Evirians who lined the sides of the tables, themselves partaking of food and drink from the unimaginable heaps before them, gazed reverently at the benign fat man, who paused briefly between noisy gulps to address his guests.

"Eat well, my friends, eat well!" he roared, his voice resounding through the chamber. "No one wants for sustenance in the house of Obbor!"

The assemblage acknowledged his words, which were anything but empty, with loud grunts and belches as they continued stuffing themselves voraciously. My own attention was diverted from this unimaginable orgy of gluttony to the many towering horriks in the hall, these muted beings appearing from barely visible nooks in the far wall to replenish the victuals that disappeared from the table at a dizzying rate. I was certain that they had prepared this feast, and that they would be cleaning up after the Evirians many hours past the termination of the night's activities. In watching them toil I found that, despite what Deklus had told us, I could not help but feel a twinge of compassion over their mindless plight.

"Come on, let's get this over with," muttered Denny disgustedly, his words snapping me from my thoughts.

"I'd just as soon turn around and get out of here," I replied.

"So would I; but I don't think we'll find food anywhere else in Kharith unless we took it from someone, and our hosts won't appreciate that. Besides, it appears that much of the populace is gathered within these walls. With any luck our search could end right here."

Denny's words altered my feeling of revulsion to one of hopefulness, and I proffered a meager smile as we began forging a path into the banquet room of Obbor. With heightened anticipation I glanced from face to face, form to curvaceous form, but nowhere in the eager throng did I see my incomparable Adara. By the time we elbowed our way alongside the nearest table I had forgotten about food, and only the urging of an impatient Evirian to my rear forced me to mechanically gather up an ample quantity of meat, bread, and water on a stone platter. I then followed in the wake of my friend, and we made our way to the base of one ornately painted wall, where we were free from the crush of bodies.

Opting to utilize our time to our best advantage we strode along the outer edge of the anxious Evirians, who continued to elbow their way toward a share of the mountainous repast. Three times we circled the great hall as we downed the food that we had taken, our eyes darting hopefully amidst the crowd for some sign of Adara, but in vain. What we did see, however, would surely have sufficed, had we not been starved, to extinguish our appetites.

One Evirian, a slight fellow of middle age, sat with his back against the wall, a heaping platter of food on the floor alongside him. We could only guess at how much he had already eaten—though it must have been considerable, for his belly was distended and sagged obscenely atop the stone surface as it anchored him there. But in spite of this he was not yet done; with a trembling hand he raised another chunk of meat to his lips, and he uttered mewling sounds of ecstasy as he thrust the entire piece within. He chewed it slowly, and then he tried to swallow, but he could not, for his limits of consumption had long since been surpassed. He gagged loudly, this discharging the piece, and then he swooned, a dreamy expression forming on his face in only seconds. No doubt his thoughts were of his next gluttonous orgy, by my guess at least a week away.

Some yards further along, a boisterous trio drank their dinner. Each hefted a pitcher of ale in one hand, a smoked glass bottle containing either wine or liquor in the other, and there were ample reserves all around them. They shouted suggestive obscenities at the women who passed within their sphere, and they invited some of the sleek beauties to join them, but none accepted. This enraged the drunken three, and they stumbled to their feet in order to pursue the objects of their desire. But the effort proved too much for the bloated revelers, who simultaneously began to puke out all that they had consumed. A nearby horrik raced toward them, the moplike contrivance in its huge hand indicating that it had been positioned with just such a purpose in mind. It set about the disgusting task mindlessly, but even before it was finished the grinning trio, again roaring at all passersby, returned to their store of spirits to start anew.

Scenes similar to these were repeated over and over, until we could take no more. Our own hunger satisfied, our hopes of finding Adara in this place all but crushed, we quickened our steps to the exit; and we were less than gentle with the few Evirians who chanced in our path. At the portal of the huge hall we

175

paused, for in spite of our revulsion we could not help but glance behind us one more time at the mountain of flesh called Obbor and his engorged minions. We then quitted the house, and not until we were far past it did we pause to suck in the cool night air of Kharith.

"Is *that* what we have to endure every day to get food?" I gasped.

"It looks that way," Denny replied. "Maybe we can train one of these horriks to bring it to us."

"Maybe we can get the devil out of this city before too many more days pass!"

He appeared tired and defeated, as I know I must have. "I hope so, Rollie, I really do," he stated unconvincingly. "Where to now?"

The choice might have been simpler to make, had we not stood equidistant from the remaining two large buildings. I glanced from one to the other, noting that the maw of each was accepting a like number of Evirians. For no particular reason I indicated the house on the side opposite that of Obbor, and we began our ascent of the broad stairs amidst more than a score of citizens, most of them dreamy-eyed couples who walked arm in arm.

"Welcome, welcome, good friends. Come in and enjoy yourselves. Yes, enjoy your Pleasure in the house of Oghis."

These words were repeated over and over by the man and woman who stood just outside the first doorway, their purpose to extend an individual greeting to all who passed within. Unlike the robed apprentices of Deklus and Obbor, each of them was garbed quite uniquely. The handsome young man

176

wore a skintight garment of black, this accentuating his finely muscled frame—a fact hardly unnoticed by the women, escorted or not, who swayed past him. His stunning counterpart, who stood nearly a head taller than most of the Evirian women we had seen, was encased in a tightly drawn crimson sarong, her ample breasts threatening with more than marginal success to break free of their confinement. Her natural beauty was apparent, even through the heavy makeup that she wore. A fragrant aroma wafted from the small white flower that she wore amidst her cascading ebon locks—the pleasing scent growing stronger as, after issuing the customary welcome, she leaned closer to us.

"Wait for me inside, either of you, or both, if you wish," she whispered, her enticingly parted lips barely moving. "I'll be finished soon."

Her attention turned to those behind us, and we were not obliged to offer a reply. Shaking off her spell we penetrated the house, its difference from the previous one immediately striking us. The floor of the hallway was covered with a plush carpet, its hue a gaudy violet. Scrolled sconces depended from either wall between the many rooms—each skillfully cast holder containing half a score of incense candles, their heady aroma at first overwhelming. The cubicles, of uniform size, were also carpeted. In addition every one, or at least those with open doors into which we glanced, were adorned with luxuriant furs and pillows. We still remained a bit vague regarding the precise nature of this house, though additional clues were not long in coming.

Indicating one of the sealed portals, in the

majority for the first twenty-five yards or so, I told Denny: "Let's see what the mystery is here."

He nodded, and without hesitation he cast open the door. There, atop the furs, lay a man and a woman, the latter moaning ecstatically as she writhed beneath her partner. That we startled the pair was obvious, for the young Evirian beauty gasped loudly, while the man, his urgency altered to rage, rose to confront us.

"What do you mean by this?" he bellowed. "You should know better!"

The equally surprised Denny slammed the door in his face, and we retreated down the corridor. We expected him to emerge and set off in pursuit of us; but the door remained closed, and after half a minute it seemed safe to assume that the pair had resumed their interrupted lovemaking.

"I'm beginning to get the picture," said the red-faced Denny. "Why don't—?"

"Ah, there you are!" a voice behind us said. "I thought you'd never come!"

The subdued lighting of the corridor could not conceal the identity of the girl, the same one who had approached us in the streets of Kharith shortly after we had departed the house of Deklus. She had just emerged from a room about ten yards distant, and she had left its door, which appeared to be half again the height and breadth of any other, slightly ajar. Muffled sounds emanated from deep within, these rendered even less distinguishable by the words of the unclothed goddess, who now came toward us.

"They've already begun, but of course there is still plenty of time," she stated, curling her arm around

178

mine. "However, if you would prefer one of the private cubicles . . ." She winked slyly.

"They would not!" a new voice insisted. "This is their first time in the house of Oghis, as you should well know. Seeing how they have honored us so, they should be afforded nothing but the best!"

The statuesque apprentice, her duties apparently completed, joined us, and she grasped Denny's hand with her own tapered fingers. She had already loosed the knot of her garment, and although she had not shed it entirely, it did little to conceal the full extent of her charms. The first girl shrank before her purposeful gaze, though she did not relinquish her hold on me.

"Of course you are right, Naori," she said sheepishly. "But they are so different, so—beautiful! Don't you agree?"

"Indeed," replied Naori huskily. "I cannot wait to share the furs with one of them in a private cubicle. However, this night we must place their own Pleasures before ours. Come now, quickly; Oghis will be pleased to welcome them."

Before we could voice a protest we were whisked down the corridor. Our panting escorts paused before the larger door, and Naori, without disengaging herself from Denny, thrust it open.

"Behold," she announced, "the ultimate Pleasure to be offered in the house of Oghis, Giver of Love-making!"

The low-ceiling room, many times the size of the other cubicles, was carpeted by an undulating wave of naked Evirians. Eager, red-lipped beauties writhed atop the cairn of furs, some crying out in their ecstasy, others sighing softly as the heights of their urgency were scaled. Those who probed the ill-concealed charms of the desirable women grunted loudly as—one by one, their own flood of passions were loosed, their sweat-soaked bodies thrashing wildly in compliant surrender to the moment. Our presence in the doorway went all but unnoticed by the participants in this wanton revelry; but they seemed to relish the proximity of those engaged in like pursuits, as if this was part of their own personal gratification. Hands often wandered outside their sphere to explore the flesh of one nearby, and it was not unusual to see a woman, her lust as yet unsatisfied by her spent partner, hasten to join her neighbors. The most hardy Evirian men shared their furs with two, even three, willing lovemates and, while all paused at intervals for a respite, it was clear that they could scarce have enough.

Indicating the far wall of the chamber, Naori said, "See there: Oghis acknowledges your presence!"

Along the base of the tapestried wall was a large bed, the sole piece of furniture in the room, Five, no, *six* tantalizing women, most too enraptured by their own desires to notice our existence, lay atop the luxuriant spread. In their midst we could discern a head, a grinning, lecherous face beneath a shock of curly hair. A hand emerged from the glistening flesh, the fingers wriggling meekly. Such was our abbreviated greeting from Oghis, Giver of Lovemaking, before he was once again engulfed by the pulchritudinous sea of sensuality.

"Let us not stand here like this," the aroused Naori gasped, as she shook off her garment and hurled it to

180

the floor. "Come, quickly!"

"Yes, oh yes-ss," the other girl hissed, tugging my arm. "I must have you. *I must!*"

I tore loose from her grasp, and I gazed at Denny as I retreated into the corridor. "We won't find Adara in—*there!*" I snapped. "You can do whatever you please."

He eyed the incomparably beautiful pair, who swayed alluringly before him in their heightening lust, and I saw that his own body was trembling. Then, casting off the heady net that had briefly ensnared him, he turned toward me.

"Let's get the hell out of here," he said.

CHAPTER TWELVE

THE GIVERS OF SLUMBER
AND AMUSEMENT

We hastened along the plush corridor of the house of Oghis, leaving the two women to find another means of satisfying their urgency, something that I knew they would have little trouble in doing. The aroma of the clinging incense began to dissipate as we descended the steps, and by the time we reached the base it was gone. When we paused to catch our breath it was for more reasons than one.

"I'm sorry that I could not reach you sooner. Perhaps the house of Oghis would not have been such a shock had I prepared you for what to expect inside."

A smiling Evirian in the robes of an apprentice strode toward us, his palms extended. His unexpected appearance at first startled the high-strung Denny, who unsheathed his knife as he whirled around. The fellow shrank back in terror, but he quickly reassumed his pleasant demeanor as Denny, noting the absence of danger, lowered his weapon.

"Who are you?" he snapped at the slight figure.

"I am Pahmun, an apprentice to Deklus," the other replied. "I saw you both when you visited him. As an afterthought, the Giver instructed me to follow you and offer any assistance or information that I could. I was unable to find you in the house of Obbor, but I did see you climbing these steps. You passed within before I could catch your attention, and so I waited. For newcomers the houses of Kharith are often a jolt at first. I hope that this was not the case."

"Don't worry about it," I told him. "If you're supposed to help us, then tell me where we can find Adara."

"Adara?" he asked, puzzled.

"The woman who arrived here some months ago," I replied impatiently.

"Ah, of course! We are not certain of where her assigned quarters are, but we are still looking into the matter. Perhaps by tomorrow we'll have an answer."

"Big deal," said Denny disgustedly. "Can't you even offer a guess as to where she might be tonight?"

"Why?"

"Because we intend to keep looking for her!"

Pahmun shook his head. "That will not be possible."

"What do you mean?" I roared.

"After the designated hour, no Evirians are to be found walking the streets of Kharith. We must return to our quarters, or remain in whatever house we have chosen for the night. Most of our people opt for the latter. Obbor's feast will continue long past day-break, as will the activities in the house of Oghis, and—"

"Wait a minute," I interrupted. "What is the purpose of this curfew?"

Scratching his head, Pahmun replied, "I'm really not certain, though I know that Deklus, if not myself, could look up the answer for you. It is one of the laws decreed by the first Givers, so it is unquestionably valid. By my guess, it was formulated as an additional measure of preventing anyone from leaving Kharith. Hm, now you've stirred my curiosity. When I get back I must—"

"How is such a restriction policed?" asked Denny.

"Policed? Ah, I understand! Specially prepared horriks are released into the city after the signal has sounded, their task to detain, injure, or destroy anyone they find, depending on the nature of resistance. They—listen, there it is now!"

A gong was struck twice in some other part of the city, the resultant sounds echoing softly through the crater. The few Evirians remaining on the street scurried away, as did nearly all of the torch-bearing horriks, leaving the three of us to stand in blackness.

"There's no more time to talk," said Pahmun. "Since you have not yet been assigned quarters, you must make your choice from among one of these three houses. As you must already realize, you will be welcome in any of them."

Knowing what to expect from those we had visited, I indicated the one across from the house of Oghis. "What's in there?" I asked the acolyte.

Pahmun grinned broadly. "Our standing here was indeed fortuitous. That is the house of Ralzon, Giver of Slumber. It is his Pleasure to provide the facilities for restful sleep, nothing more. Considering how weary you both look, I know that you'll be pleased with what awaits you there. Now, you must go quickly!"

"What about you?" Denny asked.

"As an apprentice, I am allowed to move freely for half an hour after the signal. I will be in my quarters at the house of Deklus with little time to spare. I'll return in the morning, after I've gone through the applicable journals, and with any luck we'll find the girl you seek. Sleep well."

The robed figure vanished into the night, while we stared at one another in disbelief. "You know," said Denny, "this place is reminiscent of an asylum, with walls and everything."

I nodded. "The problem is that everyone's an inmate. But 'when in Rome . . .' and all that. If we keep our noses clean, at least until we find Adara, then we should be all right. Let's go."

We hastened across the deserted street, and we did not deny our overwhelming fatigue as we trudged up the steps, for we knew that we would soon be afforded an opportunity to rest. At the door of the house of Ralzon we were greeted by a single apprentice, like most of his brethren a slight fellow. He guided us along the narrow corridor, one which was also plushly carpeted, though its hue was a more pleasing beige. After utilizing the communal toilet, which was shared by those of either sex, we were led to a chamber about half the size of the largest room in the

185

house of Oghis, though no less ornate. Sleeping places were clearly defined by the organized rows of soft furs and pillows, each situated a comfortable distance from those who surrounded it. Save for a handful of children, who slumbered peacefully, the other diverse occupants sat cross-legged and stared at the door, our entrance eliciting little interest from any of them.

"What are they waiting for?" I asked the apprentice as he motioned us toward a pair of unused spots about fifteen feet from the portal.

"A personal word of greeting from Ralzon," he replied solicitously. "The Giver will be here shortly. Now, are these places comfortable enough for you? Do you need more furs, more pillows? You may ask anything you wish of me, before I depart."

We assured him that everything was all right, and he left the room with a broad grin creasing his face. Then, before we could speak, another robed figure filled the doorway, and from the low murmur that began around us we felt reasonably certain that the new arrival was the much anticipated Ralzon. The smiling elder, of medium build, extended his arms toward the assemblage, as if preparing to offer benign benediction, and he nodded three times before he spoke.

"Dear friends, it is my Pleasure to offer you the ecstasy of slumber. May you rest well, your dreams serene and untroubled, until the morning."

The gesticulating Giver retreated, and the door was drawn shut by one of his apprentices. The final click served as a signal to the Evirians, who fell supine to the furs as a single entity. Their eyes remained open, and they stared dreamily at the ceiling, while we looked at one another incredulously.

"I don't know how much more of this lunacy I can take," said Denny, shaking his head.

"You'd best be prepared, because I don't think we've scratched the surface of Kharith." I indicated those around us. "Just what are we supposed to? . . ."

The words caught in my throat as a bluish vapor began pouring into the chamber from a thousand heretofore unseen niches in the walls and the floor. An ecstatic sigh was loosed conjointly by the Evirians, who nestled themselves more firmly in their beds as the mist engulfed them. We tried to rise, but the first faint whiffs of the narcotic smoke had already numbed our senses, and we quickly found ourselves on our backs.

"Damn . . . this place—!"

The vapor penetrated more deeply, and within seconds we plunged unwillingly into the induced blackness proffered by Ralzon, Giver of Slumber.

My head throbbed mercilessly, and it took nearly a minute to ease myself up on one elbow. The room was empty, save for the still sleeping Denny, the door wide open. I tried to call my friend, but no words came, for my throat was dry. Biting my lip against the pain I struggled to my hands and knees, but before I could crawl to his side a smiling apprentice glided into the room.

"Ah, so one of you has finally rejoined us," he said cheerfully. "I trust that you slumbered well. But now we must awaken your friend, for those who seek the

187

Pleasure of this house during the morning hours will soon be here. Of course, if you wish to remain I see no reason—"

"Let us . . . out . . . of here!" I gasped.

The apprentice's grin broadened as he withdrew a leather flask and a pair of stone goblets from a pocket inside the folds of his robe. He filled a third of one vessel with an amber liquid, and he handed it to me. Under his watchful gaze I downed the unknown concoction, which was tasteless and odorless. The dryness in my throat was immediately dispelled, and seconds later I felt a surge of strength coursing through my veins. My head ceased pounding, and the fog that had hindered my vision lifted.

"What's in this brew?" I asked, returning the goblet.

The apprentice shook his head. "Only Kobuld, Giver of Wonders, can answer that with any authority; unless, of course, it was recorded by Deklus, Giver of Knowledge. You might look in one of his journals." He filled the second goblet to overflowing. "Here, get as much of this into your friend as you can."

I lifted Denny's head and put the vessel to his lips. Some of it spilled to the furs, but a goodly amount managed to find its way inside, and soon he was sputtering loudly as the strange potion wrested him from blackness. I instructed him to down the remainder on his own, and he complied. An instant later he scrambled to his feet, his eyes clear and alert, and I was gratified that he did not have to endure the hangover that had accompanied my awakening.

"Are you ready to go?" I asked him.

"You know it! Let's—wait a minute, Rollie; where are our weapons?"

His senses were far keener than mine, for in spite of having been awake longer I had not yet noticed this obvious fact. I flipped over some of the rumpled furs in the hope that our invaluable arsenal had fallen beneath them, but I quickly realized the futility of my efforts. In my ensuing anger I glared at the acolyte, who smiled knowingly.

"You call this hospitality?" I growled. "Why did you take what belongs to us?"

"Do not be angry," he replied placatingly. "There is no need to bear arms in Kharith, for we are a nonviolent people. You'll more than likely discover them in the house of Ventoth, Giver of Amusement, who occasionally finds use for such things in the arena. They are yours to retrieve whenever you so desire."

Denny began striding toward the apprentice. "You little bastard!" he roared, reverting to our native tongue. "I ought to—!"

I grabbed his arm. "Let it be, friend. Hurting him won't do us any good."

"Come on then, let's go," he hissed, pulling free. He stormed toward the open door, and I followed at his heels. The Evirian, seemingly unruffled by what had transpired, smiled benignly as we passed, and I too found it difficult to refrain from smashing his teeth.

"Is there perhaps some message you wish to leave with Ralzon, your host?" he called after us as we reached the portal.

Denny whirled about. "Yeah, tell him to go—!"

"Tell Ralzon that we appreciate the use of his house," I interrupted, admonishing him with a glance. "We're glad that we had somewhere to stay for the night."

"Ah, the Giver will be pleased!" he nodded, his grin broadening. "Please come again. You will come back, won't you?"

I nodded vaguely, while Denny gnashed his teeth. I then dragged him into the corridor, and I addressed him quietly but firmly as we walked toward the main entrance.

"Don't you remember what I said last night? You can't blow up like that again!"

"Yeah, but Rollie, these Evirians turn my stomach! Their overindulgence, their warped values! How much of this can we take?"

"As much as necessary, at least until we find Adara. Please, Denny—"

"You're right," he replied sheepishly. "I'll try, Rollie, honest. But I swear that some day, before we leave Kharith, I'm going to crack a few skulls together!"

"Count me in," I told him, and we laughed knowingly as we passed three more of the dumbly grinning apprentices. We strode into the hazy daylight of this enigmatic cloud city perched high atop Boranga and, as we descended the broad stairs, we encountered half a score of the earliest arrivals for Ralzon's next session of drug-induced sleep. Ignoring these fools we hastened to the lava-topped street, where we were immediately confronted by Pahmun. Initially I rued his presence, though this quickly changed.

190

"I've been waiting for so long!" he stated with considerable animation. "All the others emerged nearly an hour ago. Ah, but no matter. Here, I brought you warm garments to replace your rags, and food from the house of Obbor, so that you would not have to wait with the others. I trust that you'll find the clothes a reasonable fit."

We grunted our thanks to the doting Evirian, and without reservation we tore loose the remaining shreds of our once useful garments. After donning the loose-fitting waistcoats, breeches, and ankle-high boots, all fabricated of thick fur, we plunged into the ample repast provided by Pahmun. The crisp mountain air heightened our appetites, and we ate well, though we were careful not to down any quantity of the heady beverage that accompanied the meal.

Between gulps I asked Pahmun: "Did you learn where we might find Adara?"

The apprentice glanced apologetically at his toe. "I had hoped you would not ask me that," he said. "So seldom has anything like this happened in the house of Deklus. Two journals, those documenting assigned quarters for the period during which the woman arrived, were not in their place last night, and their whereabouts were still unknown when I left this morning. But they'll show up, this I promise. They always do."

"When?" I challenged.

"Another day or two," was the reply. "Until then—"

"Until then we keep looking," Denny snapped. "Come on; we can eat the rest as we walk."

191

We strode away from the steps of Ralzon's house, while four horriks that had been scrubbing the street nearby converged simultaneously to clean up what we had left there. The houses of the three Givers fell away behind us, until we were again surrounded by comparatively small structures of nearly uniform size. Pahmun, who had initially balked at our insistence to continue the search, now strode happily before us, and he prattled without pause about matters of little importance. Noting his willingness to talk, I thought that I might try something.

"Pahmun, what can you tell us about this Ras-ek Varano, the so-called Master of Boranga?" I asked innocently.

The acolyte grinned. "Deklus warned me that you might attempt to probe this matter, and this was one of the reasons why he chose me as your guide. You see, I don't know the precise story that you desire about the Master. Even if I had heard it before I cannot recall it, so you will not even be able to elicit it from me by threats. I'm truly sorry, though I can understand the Giver's motives."

"Damn his motives," Denny mumbled under his breath; then he asked Pahmun: "Where are you leading us now?"

"The nearest house is that of Ventoth, Giver of Amusement. Activities abound there during the day, and many Evirians gather to enjoy them. You'll have more than your share of faces to look at, I assure you."

"That sounds like an acceptable choice," I said, nodding.

"For more reasons than one," Denny added.

"Since you are strangers, you must be alerted to one thing," Pahmun told us. "Those who enter the house of Ventoth do so with the understanding that they may be chosen to participate in any of the activities planned for that time. Such a request by the Giver or his apprentices cannot be turned down, though no one would even consider such a thing, for the Pleasure can only be enhanced by taking part. You'll remember that, won't you?"

We nodded our assent, though to what I could not even guess. With Pahmun again prattling meaninglessly we continued along the broad avenue of Kharith, and we were joined by scores of others from intersecting paths during the couple of hundred yards that ensued. Then we saw the house of Ventoth—which also dwarfed its immediate neighbors, though even more so than the last three. We elbowed our way to within thirty yards of the main entrance—where the crush of the throng, among which were many smiling apprentices, slowed us considerably.

"Ah, see the unshaven ones! These can be no one else but the two strangers that we have heard about. How honored we are to have you here. Come, come and participate in the Pleasures of Ventoth. Oh, he will be so pleased!"

A hand encircled my arm, a second one Denny's, and we were led through the crowd by a pair of ecstatic acolytes. Many praised our good fortune as we passed, but we chose not to acknowledge them, for we were more concerned with maintaining our balance, lest the hasty actions of the apprentices see us deposited on the ground beneath hundreds of anxious feet. We angled toward the steps, but away from the entrance, and when we finally reached the base there were few Evirians to hinder us. A glance behind revealed that the gasping Pahmun had somehow managed to stay close at our heels.

"I have been assigned to the strangers," he told the others breathlessly, "and would prefer to accompany them within."

"All right," nodded one. "But you cannot join them in the arena, as you well know."

"Ah, the arena today," Pahmun sighed wistfully. "What are the activities?"

"Come inside and see," said the second impishly.

We did not mount the steps, but instead penetrated a narrow doorway near one corner of the building. The apprentices of Ventoth led us down a long, dimly lit corridor to a drafty chamber of considerable size, where other acolytes, chosen citizens, and towering horriks intermingled. We were greeted warmly by two of the factions, our escorts then conferring with an individual who might have been their superior.

"How well you have done!" the white-haired elder exclaimed as he gestured in our direction. "Ventoth will praise you for finding the strangers. Oh, we must let them have the first Pleasure!"

"I suggest you let them wait a turn or two," said Pahmun, stepping forward. "They are just learning our ways, and should at least have a chance to observe the Pleasures before participating."

"Why not leave that up to them?" He looked at me. "What do you and your friend say?"

"We accede to the wisdom of our guide," I replied,

194

my sardonic tone noticed only by Denny, who struggled to suppress his laughter in the face of this ludicrous situation.

"Then it is decided!" said the old man emphatically. "Follow me, and I'll show you where the activities may be observed."

He led us across the hall to another door, a heavy affair that opened with a groan. The light from outside momentarily blinded us, but we recovered quickly. From the confines of a small balcony we gazed into the arena, a many-tiered amphitheater that was the hub of Ventoth's enormous house. Thousands of high-spirited Evirians sat expectantly atop the hard benches, though at the moment there was nothing for them to observe on the dirt floor.

"See there!" cried the senior apprentice suddenly, indicating a box on the opposite side. "Ventoth is already here. It will not be long now before the activities commence."

He waved excitedly at the Giver, and the greeting was returned by the distant figure, whose face I could barely discern. In fact, the position of the overhang prevented us from seeing nearly all who sat within our immediate sphere, and I was irate at being disallowed the chance to scan the assemblage for Adara.

A stone door hewn from the facing of the ten-foot wall that ringed the floor clanked open, and five smiling Evirians strode jauntily to the center of the arena. The crowd voiced their approval over the appearance of the armed quintet, who brandished their longswords and javelins in acknowledgement. Then, from the same opening, a pair of huge horriks emerged, and the din barely lessened as they approached the others, the door closing behind them. Each of the humanoids carried a deadly looking scimitar, held in its meaty hand like a penknife.

"What's going on here?" I stated suspiciously to no one in particular.

"Observe, and you shall know," replied Pahmun. "The Pleasures of this house begin!"

The five Evirians, whooping like boys in a playground, raced toward the horriks, their weapons flailing awkwardly. Freezing before the assault, the creatures at first allowed themselves to be set upon by their unskilled foes, who managed to land some telling blows. Chunks of thick, gelatinous material flew across the arena, though nothing even remotely resembling blood gushed from the gouged flesh. Then, responding to some unheard command, the horriks raised their gleaming blades simultaneously, and the roar of the throng intensified as they began slashing methodically at the stumbling quintet. The arm of one hung by a mere ligament, while the head of another rolled grotesquely in the dust, the spurting gore from the crimson stump of the neck causing the spectators to cry out in ecstasy.

It was a short-lived encounter, for the remaining Evirians, inexplicably still wearing grins, chose not to retreat in the face of the carnage. One of them, a bit more fortunate than his fellows, was able to sever the leg of one horrik, this only seconds before nearly being carved in half just below the waist. He fell amidst a pool of gore, though it was impossible to tell whether it was his own or that of another, for the

196

lifeblood of all had melded into a single stain nearly five yards in diameter.

"Is *this* what you call amusement?" I roared disgustedly at Pahmun, the apprentices of Ventoth too far enraptured by the grisly scene below to respond.

"It looks more like murder to me!" Denny growled.

"Please, watch what you say," the apprentice whispered. "You are honored guests in the house of the Giver."

"Honored, huh? Is this the kind of *Pleasure* that we're to experience?"

"Yes—or something similar."

"Then we decline, and I don't give a damn *who* we offend!"

Pahmun shrugged. "As I told you before, that won't be possible."

We glanced past him at the door, which was now flanked by two horriks, each eyeing us impassively. There were others just inside the chamber, their number undeterminate—though this hardly seemed to matter, for we would have been mad to attempt an escape that way. After glaring at the serenely smiling apprentice we peered hopefully over the edge of the balcony, but this potential avenue of flight was immediately negated by the distance to the crowd-choked tiers below—a fall that would have seen us knocked senseless, or worse.

"Rollie, we've got to get out of here," whispered Denny, his voice barely audible. "What if we took this geezer hostage? Maybe we could—"

"Such an action will not avail you at all," interrupted Pahmun, seemingly reading Denny's lips. "The horriks will fall upon you as soon as you chance a questionable move, and your holding of any Evirian will have no bearing on what they'll subsequently do to you." He proffered a broad smile as he indicated the arena. "Here, continue to observe the activities, and you will soon come to understand, even desire the Pleasures of the house of Ventoth!"

Our attention, as well as his, returned to the floor of the arena, where the bloody spectacle was all but finished. Three of the hapless Evirians were unquestionably dead, while the remaining pair, each minus a limb or two, writhed atop the darkly stained dirt. The two horriks, their blades lowered, stood by docilely as half a score of robed acolytes poured into the arena. They scurried to the scene of the carnage, where they began to gather up the severed members and wrap them carefully in what appeared to be a malleable paper. All but one engaged themselves in the grisly activity—this fellow methodically tending to the survivors. He applied a bluish clotting powder to their bleeding stumps, as well as to the countless other wounds, and this seemed to work in a matter of seconds, though not without an unnerving chorus of shrieks from the recipients of his ministrations.

"What—is going on here?" I asked disgustedly.

Pahmun smiled. "The apprentices of Kobuld, whom you see before you, take their fellow Evirians, *all* of them, to the house of the Giver of Wonders." He paused as another wrenching scream arose from the floor.

"What for?" Denny growled.

"To be—should I say?—reassembled. I'm not

certain of the exact procedure, but it is well documented in the house of my own—"

"*Reassembled?*" I exclaimed incredulously. "No! You can't mean that these—parts are put back together!"

He nodded. "It is nothing novel, for Kobuld's ancestors, even prior to Cuhram, were capable of the same thing. Those two will have new limbs before nightfall, and within a month they'll be functioning as well as or better than before. From the remains of the three a single Evirian will be restructured, while anything that is left will be preserved for future use. In this way, a part of each individual lives on. This is why participation in the Pleasures of the house of Ventoth is so cherished, for all know that they cannot really die. Can you now understand why you have no cause for trepidation?"

"Would *you* willingly participate in that?" I challenged, indicating the floor of the arena.

He peeled back one sleeve of his robe, and he proudly displayed the narrow scar that encircled his wrist. "I was fortunate enough to be selected a few years past, before I decided to devote my life to the giving of knowledge. As an apprentice I am no longer allowed this honor, and I accept the fact, though on occasions such as this I find myself a bit regretful. Ah, so be it! I'll just have to take solace in observing your own Pleasure after you are called."

"Pahmun!" Denny roared. "Why can't you understand—?"

"Forget it!" I ordered. "He couldn't help us even if he wanted to. We'll have to fend for ourselves, like we've done from the beginning."

A clamor arose suddenly from the core of the arena, and the crowd, which had stilled after the early bloodletting, once more became vocal. The horrik with the missing leg, heretofore ignored by the busy acolytes, now spun wildly about on its remaining member, its extended blade immediately slicing through the other horrik and the nearest of the unsuspecting Evirians. The robed figures began to scatter as the thing hopped about uncontrollably—though one of them, in his confusion, ran right into the arc of the steel—and the price of his action was excessive.

While the throng screamed ecstatically, two more of the dark creatures emerged from the side and raced toward their frenzied fellow. The foremost of the pair paused within ten feet of the lethal dervish, and it doused the latter with a clear liquid from a pail that it held. Then, as the dripping thing slowed its gyrations, the second one hurled a torch in its direction, and the ensuing blaze, more than substantially fueled by the highly flammable liquid, engulfed the doomed creature instantly. Reddish smoke wafted high as it burned, the unimaginable stench assailing my nostrils despite the distance that separated me from the source. But this was short-lived, for within half a minute the flames had died, and all that remained of the horrik was a charred lump in the dirt alongside the still glowing scimitar.

The grisly harvest resumed as if nothing had happened, though now there was even more to gather. Once again the din of the crowd subsided—while the apprentices of Ventoth, for the first time since stepping out on the balcony, turned their attention to us.

"We must go now," said the old apprentice cordially. "The second activity will be over by the time you are prepared. Then, honored guests, it will be your turn to know the Pleasures of the house of Ventoth!"

CHAPTER THIRTEEN

A FIGURE IN THE THRONG

With silent horriks paralleling our every step, we were marched back across the vast hall to the corridor through which we had first been led. On the opposite wall was the entrance to a smaller room, containing scores of weapons. There were swords of varying shapes and sizes, javelins, knives both elegant and utilitarian; and in the midst of the formidable arsenal were our own weapons, as the apprentice of Ralzon had predicted. In the brief time out of our possession they had been carefully polished, and now they were comparable to the gleaming steel that surrounded them.

"The majority of these loathsome things were brought here by the first settlers of Kharith," Pahmun explained, "for the ways of their warlike brethren on Eviria still touched them. Others are more native to Boranga, as I'm sure you already perceived. Are your own weapons among them?"

Ignoring his query I said, "Those who were mur—who participated in the arena carried only one weapon each. Is this all that we're allowed?"

He shook his head emphatically. "You may take as many as you can carry, for it only adds to the Pleasure!"

We gathered up our own weapons, supplementing these with some of the fine steel in the armory. Denny added a barbed Homaru spear, while each of us hefted a well-honed Evirian longsword. The possession of these arms momentarily imbued us with a feeling of invincibility, and we believed ourselves capable of slashing our way out of this room, out of Kharith itself. But the self-assured warnings of Deklus, coupled with the appearance of a dozen armed horriks in the corridor, quickly dissuaded us from any foolish action, and we were much subdued as we rejoined our waiting hosts outside.

"Ah, you have made some fine choices," the elder crowed. "Let us hurry now, for the second activity is nearly concluded."

The twelve horriks lagged behind as we hastened down the corridor, though the unarmed ones that had accompanied us from the balcony continued to dog our every step. Finding this odd, I questioned Pahmun.

"Are those horriks back there not part of our guard?"

"Your escort, you mean," he corrected. "No, they are specially prepared to participate in the arena activities, like the pair you saw earlier."

"How many of the devils do we have to face?"

asked Denny.

"All of them," was the matter-of-fact reply.

"*All?*" I roared, my voice resounding through the hallway and startling the flanking horriks, who eyed us suspiciously. "What—?"

Denny clamped a hand over my mouth as we continued to walk, and the creatures lightened their surveillance. He then glared at Pahmun and hissed, "You're going to pit two against twelve? Tell us now, Pahmun, that our execution has not been decreed! Don't lie to me or I'll cut your heart out, and the consequences be damned, considering that we're going to die anyway!"

Though taken aback, the apprentice managed to laugh. "This is not an—execution, did you say?—but a Pleasure of the house of Ventoth. It is quite different from the one that you observed. Here, let me explain.

"All but two of those particular horriks are incapable of inflicting injury, unless you choose to stand idly by and allow them to accidently crush you. In fact, their sword arms are virtually immobile. The others are well-trained fighting machines. But they will not immediately reveal themselves, so you must be on guard against every one until the last possible second. Can you not see the intricacies of this encounter, one of the most popular ever conceived by the house of Ventoth? Oh, the two of you are indeed fortunate!"

"Feel free to take our place any time, Pahmun," I stated dryly.

The passageway, which bustled with activity, began to slope downward at a severe angle, and it terminated only a few yards after again leveling. A stone portal leading to the arena floor was ajar, and through it passed the participants of the most recent activity. Two Evirians, both grinning broadly, were virtually unscathed, while four others, these bathed in blood, writhed grotesquely under the care of countless chattering apprentices. I could only hazard a guess at how many more there might have been, but I know that the number was considerable, for the many sacks slung over shoulders bulged substantially. There was only one horrik, a pathetic, legless thing that dragged itself along in the wake of the rest. Considering the numbers that *we* would have to face, it was apparent that the Evirians' sense of fair play was not tilted toward favoritism.

The remnants of the second activity were soon gone; new apprentices with empty sacks appeared, and we had little doubt for whom they awaited. Our dark opponents, who had fallen further behind, were not yet in view, though this did not deter the ebullient senior acolyte from proceeding with the ceremony that all gathered there seemed to anticipate.

"These two have been chosen to take part in the Pleasures of the house of Ventoth, Giver of Amusement," he intoned. "It is an honor for them, and it is an honor for us—an even greater honor in fact, for they are strangers to the walls of Kharith. They have journeyed a long way to share the remainder of their years with us, and I know that I speak for Ventoth when I say that we are gratified, nay, ecstatic to offer them the Pleasures of this house so soon after their arrival. Let the activities begin!"

He pointed us toward the door, while the beaming Pahmun nodded his approval. For the last time I gave thought to hacking my way back through the corridor, and my hand tightened on the hilt of the sword. But Denny, whose own short temper had been displaced by reason as an offsetting measure against my own rising frustration, stepped in front of me, and I found it difficult to meet his reproachful stare.

"Don't be a fool, Rollie," he whispered sternly. "If we make a break now we're as good as dead, and you know it. We might die out there too, but then again we could survive. Just remember what we've endured since I found you in the Haghr village. Besides, you have to admit that we're a bit more capable of fending for ourselves than these wretched Evirians."

I managed a meager smile as I eased my grip. "You're right, pal. Let's—"

"Hurry now, hurry!" the elder urged. "Word has already spread through the tiers, and all look forward to seeing you. Hurry!"

With the rest of the apprentices exhorting us on we stepped into the arena, the ensuing din caused by our appearance immediately rising to proportions that were earsplitting. The assemblage rose to their feet as we walked purposefully toward the heart of the ring, and their outpouring did not lessen for many minutes after we reached the appointed spot. We gazed impassively at the rolling sea of indistinguishable faces, until the uproar finally subsided.

My own attention was now diverted toward the open door, and I felt my muscles grow taut as I waited for the horriks to emerge. When Denny grabbed my wrist I nearly disemboweled him, so intense had I been on awaiting our foe. I started to berate him, but immediately backed off when I noticed that his normally flushed face had turned a ghastly shade of white.

"Rollie, look—over there," he stated softly, pointing behind us.

I whirled about, and I quickly perceived the object of his interest. There was a figure in the throng about fifteen tiers up, quite clearly a woman, her lengthy raven hair cascading down upon the shapeless Evirian sackcloth that she wore. I was unable to see her face clearly amidst the many others, nor could Denny, though it was quite evident why her presence had warranted his attention. Unlike the many thousands gathered there, all perched firmly atop the hard benches, this woman was on her feet, and the intense manner in which she gazed at us bespoke something more than the idle curiosity of those around her. In fact, her actions were beginning to vex her neighbors, who urged her to regain her seat so that the activities might commence.

"Rollie, is it? . . ."

"Adara?" I called hopefully, striding toward the far side of the arena.

"Ro-lan! Oh, my Ro-lan!"

The cries of my Homaru goddess echoed through the amphitheater, and for the moment they silenced the bewildered Evirians. She began descending the tiers, and she thrust aside those before her as she forged her purposeful path. My heart sought egress from my chest as it pounded rapidly, and for long seconds my legs were leaden weights that refused to obey my will. But Denny, now grinning broadly, shook me from my torpor, and I cast my weapons to the ground as I raced across the arena. Adara was already lowering herself off the top of the encircling wall when I reached its base, but I was able to grab hold of her before she fell to the dust.

"Ro-lan, my Ro-lan," she cried, covering my face with fiery kisses. I tried to respond, but her lips found mine, and for a fleeing iota of time I denied the existence of the world, *both* worlds, as we became lost within the quintessence of one another. Then it was over, and we reluctantly reemerged into the reality of the situation.

"Oh Ro-lan," my tear-streaked beauty sighed, "I knew that you did not die. I heard the words that you spoke as your boat drifted from the cave, and I believed them. I—I would even have endured Sekkator again to await you, though I praise everything holy that such was not the case. Now we're together again, and I cannot begin to measure the joy that I feel in my heart!"

"My beloved Adara," I said softly, my arms encircling her. "I've endured an eternity for this moment. Hear me now, and once more believe what I say: never, *never* again will we be separated! The cryptic void between the worlds of our birth was not enough to deter me, for I would have penetrated a thousand voids to find you. My life begins anew as of this moment, for once more I am whole."

Joyful sobs racked her body as I held her tightly to me, and I stroked her long hair gently as I luxuriated in its natural scent. Then, as she wiped her reddened eyes, she chanced to notice Denny standing quietly above five yards distant. With a soft kiss she disentangled herself from me and walked toward him, her arms outstretched.

"You're Denny McVey, of course," she said knowingly. "I am gratified to see that you survived your ordeal in Mogara."

"Adara Summers," he replied with a wink. "It has such a nice ring to it. I would have known you anywhere, Adara, for I've heard you described a thousand—no, five thousand times!"

They embraced warmly, and I beamed proudly as I gazed upon the two people who meant as much, no, more to me than life itself. With broad smiles they beckoned for me to join them, and I willingly complied. But before I reached them the assemblage, which had remained mute during the unanticipated reunion, loosed a deafening roar, and I did not even have to look across the arena to know that the horriks were emerging from beneath the house of Ventoth.

"Adara, quickly!" I cried. "Let us boost you back into the tiers!"

"Not on your life!" she replied haughtily in English. "You'll find it a difficult matter to get rid of me now, husband!"

She sped gracefully toward the weapons that I had temporarily discarded, and despite our predicament I could not help but grin broadly as I watched her. "That's my girl," I told Denny.

He nodded. "She's worth everything we went through to find her. Now come on!"

All but three of the horriks had emerged when we again stood in the center of the amphitheater. Denny, who had retained his weapons throughout, eyed the creatures carefully as the two of us gathered up the javelin and longsword from the dirt, but their actions were so torpid that initially they posed no threat. I offered Adara her choice of arms, and she opted for the wicked Mogar spear. She also accepted the ax, which I insisted upon, while I kept the gleaming knife and the ancient sword. Thus prepared, we turned to face our would-be aggressors.

The twelve now stood shoulder to shoulder before the portal, which creaked shut behind them. Still they did not approach, but instead stared at us blankly as they remained riveted to the dirt. Each held a curved scimitar in its right hand about waist high and, try as we might, we could perceive nothing different about any that would have enabled us to separate the deadly pair from their docile kin. Then they began to move, not toward us, but rather along the base of the ringing wall: six in one direction, six in the other. Their deliberate steps were uniform, and we were still unable to tell one from the rest.

"Adara, have you seen this kind of thing before?" I asked, my eyes darting back and forth between the rows.

"Yes, more than once," she shuddered.

"What the devil are they doing?"

"They will encircle the arena, and once equidistant from one another they will begin to tighten the ring around us."

"And they expect us to wait for them here?" Denny exclaimed.

"That is what the Evirians do, the mindless fools! Often I wondered why they did not take the offensive and eliminate the horriks one by one, rather than allow themselves to be trapped in their midst."

"My thoughts exactly. Rollie, you and Adara take that row; I'll tackle the ones over here."

"Denny—!"

He was off in an instant, Adara's firm grip on my arm preventing me from pursuing him. "Denny is right, Ro-lan," she insisted. "Come quickly now, lest they gain even the slightest advantage."

"All right," I conceded. "But no heroics, woman; you stay with me!"

She stuck out her tongue while nodding her agreement, and I could not help but laugh out loud as we raced across the arena floor to an uncertain fate. Then, as we neared to within a few yards of one horrik, my demeanor was transformed to fierce intensity, and my knuckles whitened around the hilt of the finely honed Evirian blade. We wasted little time in engaging the towering creature, which offered no resistance during the brief seconds that it took to drive it to the dust, where it squirmed mutely.

The roar of the throng elevated as we whirled to face the next one, which stood only yards away. In fact, the other four were not a considerable distance from us—all having abandoned their preordained course of action in light of this unexpected development, something I had believed them incapable of doing. This horrik, like the first, eyed us dully; but when Adara sought to probe at its throat with the lengthy javelin it leaped to one side, and with a powerful swipe of one meaty hand it tore the weapon from Adara's grasp and propelled it more than ten yards distant. Its arcing scimitar then whistled through the thin air as it strode toward us, while we discreetly backed away.

"At least we know where to concentrate our efforts," I offered in consolation.

"No, Ro-lan; just because they split in half, we must not take it for granted that only one of the pair is among them. Look out!"

Our retreat had carried us within the sphere of another, and only the fact that it was not the second aggressor saved us from having our heads sheared off. We placed the torpid horrik between ourselves and our pursuer, this affording us a moment's respite.

"Denny! Can you hear me?" I shouted across the arena. "Are you all right?"

"Yeah!" was the booming reply. "I've already put away one of them, but I'm not bragging, mind you, for the damn thing didn't fight back!"

"We've got one of the attackers over here. Let me know if you come across the other!"

"Check!"

The killer horrik thrust aside its useless fellow, and once again it approached us methodically, its blade singing. Aware that we could not dodge its purposeful designs for long I bent over and gathered up a handful of the gritty dirt, which I launched at its face. Now blinded, the horrik pawed frantically at its eyes, while I sought to press our advantage by thrusting the blade at its broad chest. But the dark skin was tough and leathery, and despite my grunting efforts I was barely able to make a dent. In the meantime Adara had retrieved her javelin, which lay nearby, and her attempt to drive the multi-barbed tip into the thing's throat met with far greater success. My hands joined hers on the hardwood shaft, and we steadied ourselves against the horrik's flailing as we pushed it further in. No blood gushed forth from the O-shaped mouth, nor did it utter a sound; but it was mortally wounded, of that we had no doubt, and the scimitar fell from its nerveless fingers as it staggered about. Its unseeing path carried it toward the first horrik we had dispatched, and there it stumbled headlong to the dust. For a few seconds it thrashed wildly, and then it stilled, its subsequent quivering more than likely reflexive.

The crowd screamed ecstatically over our unexpected triumph, while we sought a moment's breather before engaging any of the remaining horriks. We then felled two more, neither resisting in the least, and only the sound of Denny's voice as it cut through the din saved us from additional unnecessary effort.

"Rollie, quick! I found the second one!"

We sped across the arena floor—noting as we ran that Denny, who was anything but skilled in swordplay, was locked in close combat with the deadly horrik. So far he had been able to defense the mighty blows, though each time the curved blade fell he was driven further back, and the speed of his silent attacker was such that he could not reestablish any kind of firm footing. And to worsen matters, the non-aggressive horriks that remained had begun to ring the combatants—those directly behind Denny, which of necessity he was forced to ignore, posing a definite barrier to his already limited avenues of flight.

I drove my shoulder flush into the back of the nearest horrik as I reached the scene, and despite its bulk the creature, which had been unaware of my approach, toppled headlong like a felled tree. It collided with its lethal brother, the dusty cloud raised by the pair as they struck the ground momentarily concealing them. Wasting little time in savoring his reprieve, Denny raced toward the pair and separated his erstwhile attacker from its blade by severing the thing's arm just above the elbow. We quickly joined him, and after rolling aside the other horrik we unleashed the full force of our steel upon the flailing thing, our atavistic assault serving as a release for the pent-up emotions of hatred and rage we felt toward those who observed us. Soon the creature succumbed soundlessly, without expression, though not until it had been hacked beyond recognition did we pause to savor our victory in the arena of Ventoth.

CHAPTER FOURTEEN

AN INTERLUDE IN HELL

The faceless throng of Evirians, which had sat in stunned silence for the past minute or so, now sprang to their feet in unison, and the roar that they loosed fell upon the floor of the arena like a flowing sonic tide. We chose to ignore this mindless adulation as we struggled to regain our breath, nor did we pay heed to the grinning apprentices that poured from the now opened door and scurried toward us.

"Adara, Denny, are you two all right?" I asked with much concern.

"A few bumps and scratches, nothing more," was Denny's reply, to which Adara nodded her agreement.

"And what about you, Ro-lan?"

I rubbed my left shoulder, which throbbed painfully from coming in contact with the rock-hard creature. "The same," I winced. "Here, let's keep an eye on the rest of these devils. I don't want a repetition of what happened during the earlier encounter."

My fears regarding the potential rebirth of the other horriks were unfounded, for the huge creatures, after rising to their feet, dropped their weapons in the dust and began plodding mechanically toward the opening. It almost seemed as if they had been summoned conjointly, though by what or whom I could not begin to guess. They strode past the puffing acolytes, some of whom stumbled comically over their own robes in their haste to reach us. As I watched the grinning Evirians approach I was struck by a wave of revulsion, and for a moment I contemplated wading in amongst them with slashing steel, for the tension of the recent fray still gripped my body. But a reprimanding look from Adara, who sensed my thoughts, caused me to stay my hand, and her subsequent smile melted the tautness.

"Oh, how wonderful you all were!" crowed Pahmun, who led the robed pack. "Not in many years have we been treated to an encounter such as that! Yes, you people of Boranga's surface are so reminiscent of our warlike ancestors. But tell me, did you not experience the ecstasy, the Pleasure of participating in this activity?"

"We're so beside ourselves, Pahmun," I answered dryly, "that we can't wait to—"

"Ro-lan!" Adara snapped and then, in hushed tones said, "Please don't say it, my love, for the Evirians are a literal people."

Nodding my understanding, I told Pahmun: "We want to get out of here, *now!* Our obligations have

216

been fulfilled, haven't they?"

"What is this? They wish to leave?" cried the old apprentice, only now arriving at Pahmun's side. "How unfortunate, for Ventoth would so like to meet them." He indicated the Giver of Amusement, who waved vigorously from his elegant box.

"Are we allowed to leave this house?" I demanded.

"Why of course, but—!"

"Pahmun, show us the way out."

"But at least acknowledge the presence of Ventoth!" the elder whined. "After all, he did provide you with such memorable Pleasure."

"I'd like to recognize him with this!" growled Denny, brandishing his blade.

"Denny, Ro-lan, please!" Adara implored firmly. "What the apprentice asks is the custom here. Do as he says, however repugnant it may be to you, and our continued existence here will be far less troubled."

We turned toward Ventoth, and we bared our teeth in a bestial grin as we raised our swords high. This again set off the crowd, until we could take the deafening crescendo no longer. We strode toward the doorway, Pahmun close at our heels, and none dared to remain in our purposeful path. Along the way we noticed a few apprentices of Kobuld, their empty sacks dangling limply in their hands, and I nearly laughed out loud over the wistful manner in which the ashen-faced ghouls stared at us.

With the good wishes of Ventoth's acolytes resounding off the walls, we followed Pahmun along the seemingly endless corridor, which mercifully terminated at the base of the stone steps. It was impossible to judge the time of day due to the absence of the sun, though by my guess it was early in the afternoon. The broad thoroughfare was surprisingly devoid of life, save for a few horriks performing menial tasks. It was a tranquil scene to be sure, a far cry from the one still in progress behind us.

"Where might I take you now?" asked the solicitous Pahmun, his words shattering the silence that had momentarily predominated.

"You will no longer be needed, apprentice," Adara stated with authority. "I am well versed in the ways of Kharith and would be pleased to assume their indoctrination."

"But Deklus himself assigned me—!"

"The Giver will understand, and he'll be pleased to see you hunched over your journals once again. Trust me, Pahmun."

"Very well then," he grumbled. "But what about quarters? They have not yet been assigned any."

"I live on the fourth street of the north central sector, not far from here. The house is the nineteenth, my cube the fourth. Theirs will be the same for now."

"But that is impossible, as you should know!" he blustered. "Everyone in Kharith *must* be assigned individual quarters!"

Adara sighed peevishly. "The third cube is vacant, as is the eighth. Enter those as belonging to Ro-lan and Denny respectively. There, does that satisfy you?"

"You'd best hope that no others have decided to change quarters in the past few hours," warned Pahmun as he began walking away. "Farewell for now, fellow Evirians. I'll be back to look in on you, this I promise."

The conscientious little apprentice of Deklus' glanced over his shoulder more than a score of times as he departed, and just before dropping from sight he paused to eye us. Then he was gone, and once again we were left on our own in the streets of Kharith. But despite the realities of what we had already endured and the uncertainties of what might still lie ahead, I found that I did not care. The woman whom I loved beyond the perimeters of reason, the woman whose mere existence had seen me thwart the grasping fingers of Death itself was again at my side, and at the moment nothing else seemed to matter.

Her one hand interlaced with mine, the other encircling Denny's arm, Adara guided us past the house of Ventoth to a narrow, intersecting path, where we turned to the right. Despite the thousand questions we had she advised us not to speak, for our labored breathing indicated that the rarified air of the mountain city, coupled with our recent exertions, was beginning to tell. In fact, I was surprised that it had not weakened us sooner than it did. Perhaps we had adapted to it more than I'd realized during our climb, though in truth we had probably denied its effects in light of the deadly situation into which we had been thrust unwillingly. Whatever the case it was evident that we needed to rest, and I was relieved to find that Adara's house was nearby, as she had told Pahmun.

The gleaming structure, which stood only two levels high, was one of the smallest I had yet seen in

Kharith. There were six medium sized rooms, or cubes, on each floor, all similarly decorated with thick, overlapping layers of plush furs. Few other amenities were visible in any of them, save for an occasional chair or table, and none were occupied.

"Seldom will you find Evirians in their assigned quarters," Adara explained as she led us down the abbreviated hallway. "They leave the doors ajar so that the horriks can enter and tidy up. Here is your 'assigned' cube, my love, and Denny, yours is on the next level, second on the right."

The fatigued redhead began striding toward the narrow stairway at the end of the corridor, but Adara stayed his designs by refusing to relinquish her hold on his arm. She guided us into her own cube, and she motioned us to the furs, an invitation that we could hardly refuse. Then, as we struggled against our weariness, she walked to the table on the opposite wall and gathered up a tray of fruits, as well as a pitcher of water.

"I always keep food and drink here," she stated as she placed the welcome repast before us, "so that I can avoid any more trips to the house of Obbor than are necessary."

"We can sympathize with that!" said Denny, scowling disgustedly.

Adara sat cross-legged before us as we downed our food ravenously, and the gentle smile that lit her radiant face reflected my own inner tranquility over our long-denied reunion, this despite the dubious circumstances in which we found ourselves. Emotions withheld and dormant for an eternity began to surface as I gazed at the incomparable form of the only woman in two worlds that I would ever love, until I found it expedient to douse these flames with the rushing currents of reality. Doubtless there would be a more propitious time later, considering the fact that the duration of our undesired sojourn in Kharith appeared to be limitless.

Kharith! Now that we were again together, how were we to escape the fog-enshrouded walls of this loathsome place, which the Evirians revered as their City of Pleasure? Had the resourceful Adara, whom I knew would not willingly exist in such an environment, sought out a means of egress during her months here? If so, had she been successful? And if not, then what chance had we of continuing our quest to rid Boranga of the monster that ruled it, the unspeakable devil that had caused us so much grief? If Deklus, who I did not believe inclined toward boastfulness, had spoken the truth, then this walled city was to be our prison—*forever!*

Adara, whose own look of yearning had altered to one of thoughtfulness, was the first to break the silence as we downed the final remnants of our meal. "I so greatly wish to hear all that has happened to both of you," she said. "But common sense dictates that I speak first, for you are still short of breath. Here, let me tell you of all that occurred since you and I, Ro-lan, were last together in the cave of my grandfather."

We nodded conjointly, and she began: "I stood helplessly and watched your boat as it drifted beyond the horizon, this thrusting me to the very limits of my sanity. It was then that Ras-ek, whose laughter had echoed through the cavern without pause, suddenly became agitated. 'Enough of this!' he bellowed. 'We must return to Sekkator *now!*' And with these words the swirling red mist encircled me. I cast up my will against it, futilely I thought, but when my vision cleared I found that I was still in the cave. A second time it engulfed me, though for only seconds, and with the same results. Ras-ek's powers had been expended, and he was helpless.

"'Await me here,' his fading image ordered. 'Do not leave this cave, woman, for I will seek you out wherever you hide, and your punishment will be beyond your conception. Heed me, for I do not jest; heed me!' And then he was gone.

"Despite my momentary stupor I was able to surmise the following: Ras-ek's powers were first used up after he transported us from the lair of Tomo Raka to the forest. Truly were we on our own then, Ro-lan. Not much time had passed when he again found us, and in light of what subsequently transpired I believe that his replenishment was only partial. Oh, how helpless he is at times! But how to get to him?

"Wild thoughts raced through my head, like diving into the water and swimming after you. But if the sun had not destroyed me, then one of the dark shapes that occasionally broke the surface about thirty yards from the cave mouth surely would have. I scrawled the note to you, and with a last wistful glance at the sea I returned to the darkness of the tunnel.

"I need not relate in detail what transpired

222

immediately thereafter, for in all probability my experiences were much like your own. According to a journal in the house of Deklus there is only one path leading to the summit, the one that led the ancestors of these people here, the same one that you and I ascended. Suffice to say that somehow I endured, and I found my way starved and frozen to the walls of Kharith. The Evirians took me in, and I was cared for in the house of Kobuld, Giver of Wonders, until I recovered. But my gratitude was soon lessened by the realization that I was their prisoner, and it was further diminished by the briefest exposure to this degenerate society. But my options were negligible at the time, and so I've lived among them during these months, each week, each day dragging like a decade.

"I've lost count of the times since my arrival that I explored Kharith in the hope of finding some way to escape. I—I'm sorry to tell you that if one exists, then it has so far remained elusive. On two occasions I even went as far as the walls, though each time the thought of a killer horrik possibly standing only yards away in the clouds drove me back to the city. Anyway, I've since learned that the foundation of the barrier sits far below the surface, and that the ground is as hard as stone. There is no chance of tunneling our way out.

"Life in Kharith, as you have no doubt discovered during your brief time here, is intolerable. The ways of these indolent Evirians can scarce be comprehended, much less endured. Sometimes I find myself sinking in this languid mire, but I combat it by constant utilization of my mind. I read the journals in the house of the Giver of Knowledge, the majority of these dwelling on the history of ancient Eviria as far back as six centuries; I observe the apprentices of Kobuld as they heal the sick, and sometimes I assist them. Only on rare occasions do I force myself to endure the degenerate ways of these people, so that I might never forget where I am, and how much I desire to leave. Today was such a day, and that is why you found me where you did. The spectacles in the arena of the Giver of Amusement are among the worst . . ." Her voice trailed off, and she shuddered.

"But above all that I have mentioned," she continued, "stands one reality: never, *never* have I stopped thinking of you, my Ro-lan. I believed that you survived the horrors of Ras-ek, and I believed that you would find me atop this mountain. Even had I been free to leave I would more than likely not have done so, for I concluded that the chances of your finding me would be heightened if I remained in one place. Not once did I abandon my dreams, and now you have fulfilled them; even more so in fact, for Denny is with you. I could not be happier, and for this hour, this day, I will not allow the specter of our surroundings to intrude upon my joy."

Adara fell into my arms, and I held her tightly for long seconds while she sobbed softly. After wiping her tears she resumed her original position on the carpet of fur, and she listened intently as the two of us related our experiences. Silence then prevailed as we concluded our respective narratives, for we were content to bask in the proximity of one another, and when Denny finally broke the stillness it was like the report of a rifle.

"I suppose someone has to say it," he offered

hesitantly. "From all that we've gathered it appears that we're destined to spend the rest of our lives in Kharith, though I'll be damned if I'm going to let that happen! Rollie, Adara, *how do we get out of here?*"

"You and I have not been here long enough to judge the probabilities," I told him. "Adara, are you certain that you've exhausted every possible avenue of escape, even ones that entail some degree of risk?"

"I once conceived of a plan, but I quickly abandoned it as ludicrous, for there was no way of my initiating it alone. Even with the three of us it is no less insane, and I hesitate—"

"Tell us, Adara, please!" Denny exclaimed. "It has to be better than anything we've got at the moment."

"Very well," she shrugged. "Did you witness the earliest encounter today in the arena of Ventoth, when the horrik had to be destroyed?"

"Yes," we nodded simultaneously.

"Then you should be able to guess what I had in mind."

"Of course!" I exclaimed. "We could incinerate the devils at the gate with whatever the apprentices utilized!"

"How disgustingly simple," Denny added. "A wonder we couldn't see it then, or since."

"It's not as easy as either of you may think," Adara warned. "I've had much more time to dwell on it, so listen. The killer horriks that guard the portals of Kharith are quick, cunning stalkers, though you may find this hard to believe in light of the torpidity of the one that afforded you ingress. They will not stand idly by and await our approach, which somehow they can sense. We won't know from which direction they will attack, and because of the dense fog they will remain invisible until the last possible second."

"What about their numbers?" I asked. "There was only one when we entered. Deklus advised us that three of them guarded each gate, but aren't there times when this is not the rule?"

Adara shook her head. "The guard was doubled after I entered Kharith, and only recently was it lessened. Nearly five months passed before they accepted me without question as an Evirian."

"But if we become a willing part of their lunacy, at least to all appearances, then won't they ease their vigil sooner?" Denny asked.

"From the manner in which the two of you described your interview with Deklus, I'm afraid that he'll see right through such deceit. Besides, I have read of outsiders who succumbed within days to the lure of this place, until they would not have left by choice. But still the increased guard stood for almost five months, the length of time decreed by the first Elite. We will have to wait at least that long."

"Five months!" Denny exclaimed. "There's no way that I'm going to remain in this degenerate hell-hole for five months! I'm for getting out of here now!"

"I'm afraid that I have to agree with Denny," I told Adara apologetically. "Even if this place were tolerable, which it hardly is, I wouldn't remain any longer than necessary. We have much unfinished business beyond these walls."

Adara smiled as she placed her hand atop mine. "You needn't apologize, my love, for I desire nothing more than the chance to be at your side when we flee this wretched place. I only wished to present the facts to you as they truly exist. Yet even here I've been remiss, for there's one thing I omitted."

"What's that?"

"The tirr oil used by the apprentices to douse the horrik is not a commonplace thing in Kharith, but rather something conceived of for just such a purpose by Kobuld. It exists in limited quantities, and accordingly it is well guarded in the house of the Giver of Wonders. Nor is it an easy task to wrest it from the apprentices, who surround themselves with killer horriks as they carry it to and from the arena of Ventoth. Obtaining it will be a severe challenge."

"Isn't there anything else we can use, like lamp oil?" Denny asked.

"Unfortunately not," Adara replied, indicating the oddly shaped lanterns that hung from two of the walls. "Kharith's light, as well as its seldom needed heat, emanates from the strange, phosphorescent stone that is mined beneath the city. More than likely you saw them utilized as torches in the streets last night. I can think of nothing else that might serve our purpose."

"Then the tirr oil it must be," I stated. "Do you have any idea where the Giver keeps it?"

"I know approximately in what part of the house it is stored."

"Then what are we waiting for?" Denny roared as he began scrambling to his feet. "Let's—!"

"No!" Adara countered sternly. "You are as stubborn and strong willed as your friend here. Both of you have had more than your share of exertion today, and this is not good, for your acclimation to Kharith must come gradually. You will rest now; tomorrow will be soon enough for us to go chasing after tirr oil."

"A couple of hours, no more," I insisted as I stretched out atop the soft cairn of furs. "We'll go to the house of Kobuld later this afternoon. Just a couple of hours, Adara, okay?"

"Sleep now, the both of you," our mother hen scolded. "I'll wake you."

I would have pressed further for her word, but I was unable to, for the shrouds of a peaceful slumber such as I had not known in an eternity quickly engulfed me, and the image of her incomparable face dissipated into blackness.

When I awakened it was nearly dark, a fact immediately evident through the small window on the opposite wall, the only such aperture in the room. Denny was still asleep, while Adara, her arms laden with food, was just entering from the hallway.

"The house of Obbor is not exceptionally busy at this time," she whispered as she deposited the load on the low table, "so I thought I'd go after our dinner while the two of you slept. I trust you're well rested, my love?"

"Adara!" I bellowed. "I told you to—!"

My outburst aroused Denny, who quickly shook free of the encompassing slumber that had held him. Then he too noticed the same thing that I had, and he waved his finger frantically as he leaped to his feet. "It's almost sunset!" he exclaimed. "Adara, you promised that you'd wake us!"

"You are both impossible," she laughed, shaking her head. "In the first place it was later than I think either of you realized when we arrived here, for you've slept barely three hours. Second, I didn't have the heart to wake you, for your slumber was deep."

I found it impossible to remain angry with her for her thoughtfulness, and I grinned sheepishly as I rose. "Very well then, you're forgiven," I joked. "Can you take us to the house of Kobuld now?"

She stared reproachfully at me as she replied, "So many endless months have passed before we could all be together, yet somehow we endured them. Now all I ask is that you be patient for a while longer, at least until morning."

"But why?" Denny insisted.

"There are few Evirians afoot after dark in the house of Kobuld, for there are no activities to entice them. We would be far less conspicuous in the morning, when people abound in the corridors. Also, . . ." she hesitated.

"Yes?"

"If we were to somehow escape tonight, then we would find ourselves on the cold and treacherous mountain path for many nights to come." She gazed desirously at me. "My Ro-lan, it—it has been so long!"

There was nothing more to be said. I took her in my arms, and together we walked to the table. Denny would have slipped discreetly out the door, but with an emphatic gesture Adara ordered him to join us. We chatted idly during the sumptuous repast, during which we partook heavily of the potent Evirian ale. It was quite dark when we finally placed the remnants in the corridor for the horriks to clean up, and this time we did not interfere with the redhead as he started to leave.

"Will you be upstairs?" I asked him.

He smiled as he shook his head. "It's been a long time for me also," he winked, "and I can assure you that Oleesha did not satisfy many of my needs. I'll be back in the morning, whenever the night curfew is lifted."

I laughed heartily as I clapped him on the shoulder, while Adara's face reddened. She then proffered a broad grin, and she whispered conspiratorially: "I've heard it said that the one called Naori is among the best."

Denny roared as he retreated down the hallway, while I chased Adara back into the cube. I bolted the door, and with a catlike leap I intercepted my laughing goddess near the table. We dropped to the furs, where we wrestled playfully for a minute or two, our faces streaked with the tears of our unbounded joy. Then the game was done, and all that pierced the subsequent stillness was the soft, albeit urgent panting of our long withheld desires. But we contained ourselves for a few minutes longer while Adara, after rising, dimmed the phosphorescent lamps to an almost imperceptible glow. She drew a dark curtain over the window, and then she faced me. Sandals were kicked free, the Evirian sackcloth discarded by the pulling of a single string. My own garb already cast across the cube, I awaited the gleaming, sensual form, which throbbed with the fires of her passion as she approached.

She fell into my arms, our searing bodies melding

as one. Her hungry lips found mine, and seldom were they apart during the night of ecstasy—a night that saw our unmatched love, our limitless desires consummated again and again.

Again . . .

CHAPTER FIFTEEN

THE BUBBLING VAT

Morning arrived quickly, though in all likelihood we would have disdained the dim light outside and pursued our lovemaking throughout the day. But a tentative knock on the door of the cube roused us from a dreamy slumber, one of many such brief interludes that we had succumbed to, and we scrambled about groggily as we sought our garments amidst the furs.

"Rollie, Adara, it's me. Hey, I'm sorry, you two, but it is another day, and there are things to be done. Are you awake in there?"

Light flooded the room as we pulled the drape and turned up the lamps. I cast open the door, and there in the corridor I saw a familiar face—not that of the tormented man with whom I had shared experiences beyond the imagination of most, but the smiling countenance of the young, exuberant mechanic who had almost single-handedly resurrected the wreck called the *Maui Queen* an eternity and a world ago. Denny's smile broadened as our eyes met, and somehow I sensed that I mirrored his rebirth, though neither of us chose to touch upon this with meaningless words.

Ignoring the rumpled state of the furs as he stepped inside, Denny said, "I don't know about you, but I'm hungry enough to devour a horse, or whatever it is that they serve here in Kharith. Even the house of Obbor sounds good!"

"Then the house of Obbor it is," Adara replied laughingly. "There is little other choice here. Besides, it is on the way to the house of Kobuld, which lies a considerable distance from where we now stand."

Indicating our cache of weapons, which we had brought with us from the arena of Ventoth, I asked, "Should we take any of those with us?"

Adara shook her head. "They will only make us stand out more, and that is the last thing we want if we are to walk the corridors of Kobuld's house with impunity."

"I don't like it," said Denny, "but I guess you know best. Tell us, Adara: can we expect any surprises from this Kobuld or his apprentices, like an invitation to participate in any of the 'Pleasures' offered there?"

"The ways of Kobuld are not unlike those of the Giver of Amusement. Many citizens are chosen by his apprentices, even more than by Ventoth. But all are doubly honored by their selection, for they revere Kobuld, who is a descendant of Cuhram. He

233

reputedly wields the power in Kharith, even above the phantom triumvirate. You will not have to worry, however, for you took part in Ventoth's games yesterday, and this eliminates you from consideration by any of the other Givers for a time."

"Why is that?" I asked.

"The fool Evirians cherish their selections as the means that elevates them to the summits of their lifelong quest for the ultimate Pleasure. Their Givers know this, and they are loath to delegate these honors lightly. No citizen will be afforded such ecstasy twice during a brief span of time. Word has already spread that the two newcomers were feted by the house of Ventoth, and therefore the apprentices of Kobuld will scarcely acknowledge your presence."

"You can't imagine how broken up we are about it," I said dryly.

"Just what kind of Pleasures are the Evirians chosen for in the house of Kobuld?" asked Denny.

"Research, the apprentices call it, perverse experiments of the body and mind that cannot be comprehended!" She shuddered. "Please, do not ask me more about them. I can only pray that we are not exposed to any, though from what I know about the house of Kobuld it seems unavoidable. Let's go now, so that we might get this over with."

We performed our ablutions in a communal toilet at the far end of the hall, and we then emerged into the overcast daylight of the cloud city. Few Evirians were afoot this early, and our passage to the house of Obbor went all but unnoticed. The apprentices of the Giver of Sustenance greeted us warmly, and they guided us personally amidst the handful of sprawling, overstuffed bodies that remained from the previous night's orgy of gluttony. Obbor was not perched atop his throne at the moment, a fact that pleased me no end, for I would have found it difficult to retain my appetite after looking at the repulsive creature. We topped our platters with food from the freshly prepared heaps on one of the tables, and we carried our breakfast to the steps outside—where all of us, but especially Denny, ate our fill.

The lava pathway that we subsequently followed to the house of Kobuld intersected the primary thoroughfare about fifty yards further along, and it twisted haphazardly amidst endless rows of smaller structures. It was a narrow street, more like an alley in fact, and the handful of Evirians who traversed it with us at first created an illusion of density. Then, as more arteries converged from various angles, it began to widen, and we were engulfed by a true flood of dully garbed, smiling citizens, all doubtless on their way to the house of the Giver of Wonders.

After what seemed hours the ebon street terminated at the base of a massive edifice, this standing along the outermost rim of the crater city. Kobuld's house was every bit as large as that of Ventoth, so much so that the tide of Evirians who had carried us there now appeared to be little more than a thin line of insects as they negotiated the steps and streamed into the maw of the structure. Initially we hesitated as we observed the activities from below, and then we too ascended, our purposeful strides quickly depositing us on the topmost level before the broad entrance-way. The grinning apprentices greeted the famil-iar Adara warmly and, contrary to what she had expected, they welcomed us cordially. This time we reciprocated in the Evirian way, and they appeared more than pleased to afford us ingress to the house of their revered tutor.

Unlike the previous houses the main portal led directly into a large room, one which bustled with activity. Here, according to Adara, was the "clinic" of Kharith, where Evirians flocked for treatment of everything from indigestion to broken limbs. Those who sat on the aseptic sheets that covered the floor awaited their turn patiently, regardless of the affliction that had brought them there, and this seemed to ease the tasks of the overburdened apprentices, who darted amidst the subdued wave in search of the more seriously ill.

"Evirians are so helpless," Adara explained, "they cannot even tend to the smallest scratch. Such is their dependency upon the Givers."

"It's no wonder their ancestors were exiled a century ago," I stated disgustedly. "Who would want such parasites around?"

"And yet this is the mire that men of intelligence, such as Kobuld, choose to wallow in. Some of his accomplishments here would no doubt raise eyebrows even in your world. But on the other hand there are things that he does for which he would be locked up, if not destroyed, anywhere else. These witless Evirians are afforded much by those whom they revere; but what they cannot possibly see is that their Givers are also takers, and what they *take* from the minds and bodies of the willing minions is far more than they could ever repay."

"Deklus referred to himself as a taker," said Denny,

"though not until now could I understand what he truly meant. Whatever their intelligence these Givers are indeed a part of this aptly named mire."

The low murmur that dominated the hall was suddenly displaced by a shrill cry, one that caused us to reach instinctively for weapons that were not there. We whirled about and faced the entrance, from where the sound had emanated, and we immediately espied the perpetrator. An Evirian male, heretofore one of the faceless throng, had been singled out by the acolytes of Kobuld for the distinction of participating in some undefined activity, and the grinning moron now leaped about ecstatically as he savored the prospect. With his peers nodding enviously the chosen one was calmed by the apprentices, who then whisked him across the hall toward one of a few doors on the far wall. We stood and watched incredulously until they were gone, and with the room again still we resumed our purposeful trek.

"If the poor fool had no conception of what awaits him," mumbled Adara, shaking her head, "then I might understand his joy. But—he knows! They all know!"

"I have no interest in trying to comprehend all this," I stated disgustedly. "All I want to do is leave it behind us!"

We reached the portal, which was not the same one that the others had penetrated. Soon the activities of the busy clinic fell behind us, and we were engulfed by the vacuumlike stillness of a lengthy, narrow corridor. We bypassed half a dozen sealed doors along the seemingly endless passageway before Adara motioned us to a halt a few yards from another of the heavy wood barriers, one which opened and closed repeatedly as small contingents of smiling Evirians passed through.

"What's in there?" asked Denny.

Her face twisted in revulsion, Adara replied, "One of the secondary research halls. I'm afraid that we'll have to pass through it to get where we're going."

"Do you know what they're doing in there?" I asked as I watched another contingent, some of them small children, pass gleefully within.

"I can only guess, and I'd rather not. Come on."

We followed the group into the stark white room, which was not as spacious as I had thought it might be. Scores of Evirians occupied the research chamber, this two-deep throng speaking in muted tones as they gazed intently at the trio of apprentices gathered near the center. The smiling citizens of Kharith appeared enthralled by the feverish activities of the robed ones, and as we made our way discreetly along the perimeter of the haphazard circle I too craned my neck to observe the thing that so preoccupied them. Then I saw it, and after grasping the reality of what transpired there I was nearly felled by a tidal wave of nausea.

A young man of no more than twenty-five years was suspended from the high ceiling by means of a harness, this secured firmly about his chest after being passed under his arms. His feet, which did not touch the floor, were secured by two lengths of rope wrapped around the ankles and knotted securely through a pair of large rings. The purpose of these bonds, as I quickly realized, was only to keep him immobilized, for he was not a prisoner. On the contrary, he wore a smile as he jabbered animatedly at the busy apprentices, and he was hardly cognizant of the gaping incision that ran perpendicular from his midsection almost to his discolored genitals. A smal pool of gore stained the floor just below him, and this was occasionally stirred by the knotted entrails that had fallen from the gash and were now dangling loosely. But at the moment no blood spilled, for two of the robed figures mechanically sprinkled a fine, iridescent powder, quite possibly an anesthetic coagulant, into the opening. In the meantime their fellow performed some sort of surgery with implements that seemed primitive, and far less than clean. He offered his procedure in a dull monotone as he worked, but I paid little attention to the meaningless words in light of the inconceivable experiment being enacted before the appreciative throng of Evirians.

Her eyes averted to the floor, the white-faced Adara said, "I didn't exaggerate, did I? Follow me, quickly!"

I tore my attention from the surgery, and we quickened our strides through the crowded room. Before long we reached another door, this leading into what appeared to be a supply chamber. The previously overpowering chemical smell of the research hall faded as we crossed the stone floor; but not so the memory of the ghastly scene, which would no doubt linger in my mind amidst the other innumerable images of Boranga for an eternity.

Other Evirians utilized the room as a means of passage, most descending a narrow stairway that began along the opposite wall. With Adara in the lead we followed the ebullient citizens of the cloud city to the next level, where we were deposited into a more austere, dimly lit corridor. Doors pocked both walls, and every so often one or two of the curious guests would disappear behind the unrevealing barrier of their choice. But we did not deviate from the purposeful path along which Adara led us, at least not until a frantic Evirian burst from a room before us and flagged down the crowd.

"It is time!" he cried breathlessly. "Oh, how well planned your arrival was! Hurry, hurry, for it is time!"

The people, those with whom we walked and those already further along the passageway, chattered excitedly as they converged on the portal where their beckoning fellow stood. Almost immediately Adara grabbed hold of our arms, and I could hear her sigh even above the din as she guided us in the same direction.

"We must go in," she whispered, "for there will be no one else in the corridor, and it is too soon for us to risk being conspicuous."

"What did this joker mean?" asked Denny. "What are they all so eager to see?"

Adara shrugged. "It is on this floor of the house of Kobuld that the horriks are—created!"

Gazing with disgust at the eagerly swarming crowd, I spat, "And this is the great attraction that none of these fools can miss? I say we take our chances and—!"

"Ro-lan, be quiet," she whispered insistently. "I've been here before, and I know what must be done."

There was no time to argue, for the throng had closed around us, and we were all but carried to the door. No apprentices waited to greet us, only the smiling Evirian who had started the commotion. Now basking in his own glory, the fellow took the place of Kobuld's assistants in welcoming his peers magnanimously, while the people, too excited to note the oversight, responded in kind. Neither Denny or I could stand to look at the idiot who had caused us this delay, though Adara more than offset our indifference by casting an alluring smile at him. Then we passed through the opening, and her smile was quickly displaced by the loud gnashing of teeth as she braced herself for whatever lay within.

We emerged onto a stone catwalk, one which extended around three sides of the large room. Evirians lined the railing in quest of a superior vantage point, but despite this they somehow managed to make room for us—the courtesy one that we surely could have done without. From our perch we gazed curiously at the scene upon the scrubbed floor some fifteen feet below. Near the center, spread out over at least a third of the room, we saw a huge vat which had been cast from a copperlike metal. An indiscernable heat source caused the liquid that filled it nearly to the rim—a dark red, viscous ooze—to bubble violently, the foul odor that wafted upward from this seething cauldron more than enough to turn our already uneasy stomachs. Four flexible, transparent tubes about four inches in diameter emerged from diverse sides of the vessel near the base, each snaking its way to a large granite block nearby. Aside from a sharply inclining wooden ramp which

241

stood alongside the vat there was nothing else in evidence on the floor of the hall, and for a moment I wondered if the grinning harbinger had not erroneously summoned the others to this cryptic scene.

One of the five diversely colored doors leading into the chamber suddenly opened, and the four apprentices who entered in unison were welcomed by the plaudits of those around us. A pair of horriks followed in their wake, the last pulling shut the red door behind it. Then, responding to a brusque gesture from an acolyte, the same creature strode quickly to the opposite side and cast open another of the heavy portals, this tinged a gaudy yellow. Its actions pleased the robed Evirian, who in a jovial voice summoned the horrik back to the side of its motionless fellow.

"Is the great Kobuld among this bunch?" I asked Adara.

She shook her head. "The Giver does not take part in such trivial matters as the creation of horriks, except when there are special circumstances. More than likely we won't see him here today."

"Who cares?" Denny growled.

A pair of apprentices now flanked one of the stone blocks, while the mute horriks stood a few yards away. The third Evirian walked alongside the tube that led to the slab, while the last knelt at the base of the churning vat. With a loudly voiced word of warning the latter twisted a valve, and the coil writhed like a serpent as the putrid stuff passed through it. While the pacing acolyte eyed it intently the ooze wended its way toward the stone and, as it disappeared within, the two who hovered there began to count. The minions joined them, until fourteen was reached, and they all stopped. Once again the valve was turned, and the flow of the slime was checked. The little that remained in the tube was forced through by the heavy sandals of the watchdog apprentice, who ignored the cheering throng as he walked skillfully atop the supple material. Then the last of it was gone, and the attention of all turned to the block of granite.

Silence reigned for long seconds, during which nothing happened; then the stone mass began to quiver—at first imperceptibly, but soon with such force that the vibrations could be felt on the balcony where we stood. The two horriks were summoned forth, and they held tightly to either end of the block, until the trembling subsided. With their massive hands the creatures raised the top third of the stone, something I did not think possible, for I had noticed no seam in the granite. As they flipped it over and deposited it gently on the floor I saw the humanoid indentation, and I knew that the thing I had tried to deny until now was true: the stone was a mold, and the sizzling, putrid blob that writhed in the bottom half, the darkly pigmented obscenity that tried to raise itself from its temporary womb, was a newly formed horrik!

The faceless, throbbing hulk began to rise slowly, and our ears were assailed by a loud sucking sound as its rapidly cooling pseudo-flesh was torn loose from the granite. All of the watchful apprentices backed away as the thing dragged itself over the edge—their places taken by the two emotionless horriks, who observed their new brother drop to the floor at their feet. Then, with the crowd screaming ecstatically, the monstrosity began to thrash wildly, its gyrations shaking free many of the thin shreds of excess matter that clung to its still less than perfectly formed humanoid body. Finally it neared the base of the bubbling vat, where it was intercepted by the other horriks. They lifted the still flailing thing effortlessly, and they spirited it off toward the door that had earlier been left open. The mindless blob was deposited into the adjoining room, the bright yellow barrier shut tightly, and the pair returned to their original positions in anticipation of subsequent tasks.

CHAPTER SIXTEEN

THE GIVER OF WONDERS

My senses still reeling from the unimaginable exhibition on the floor of the chamber, I asked Adara: "What happens to the devils in that room?"

"They are restrained by means of a stupefying gas. The apprentices then shape them properly, and they perform cosmetic work so that their appearance will not offend the populace to any degree. This is open to any who wish to see it."

"No thanks," Denny choked. "But what about their programming? How is that done?"

"Programming? You mean their preparation for specified tasks." She shook her head. "For some reason this is off limits to all, save the apprentices of Kobuld. It is a century-old decree of Cuhram, who despite his perverse ideas was certainly no fool. I imagine that it was his way of seeing that the balance of power remained tilted in his favor, which it has been for all his descendants."

"He who controls the horriks and all that," I muttered.

The excitement of the momentarily hushed crowd began to rise as the apprentices once again took their places, and soon they participated in the vociferous count to fourteen. Step by step the procedure was repeated, until another smoldering horrik fell to the floor with a punctuative thud. But as this one started to thrash the Evirians groaned conjointly, while the acolytes waved their arms animatedly.

"This horrik is imperfect!" one of the robed figures shouted. "There is obviously damage to the mold. Let us dispose of this one quickly, so that we may continue."

The cause of their consternation was evident, for the gelatinous horror that spun wildly below us had been formed without one leg. It was immediately tackled by the silent pair—who, themselves, had once been spewed forth in a like manner—these powerful creatures carrying it to the top of the ramp. With little ceremony their malformed brother was flung into the cauldron, and a loud hissing ensued as the carcass sank beneath the bubbling ooze. It rose above the surface two, three times, and on each occasion it appeared smaller than previously. Then it was gone, and the foul, agitated brew marginally settled.

As the third formation commenced I knew that I could take no more; but there seemed little choice, for the crush of bodies around us was considerable. It was then that Adara, who had been through this before, started elbowing her way through the crowd, and she motioned for us to follow.

"They are too far enthralled to care who comes or goes," she explained. "Besides, there are probably others in the passageway now on their way to various activities."

Her judgment was correct, for there were many in the corridor, some trying vainly to push their way into the chamber from which we had just emerged. We joined the flow, and we remained preoccupied with our own thoughts while negotiating another fifty or so yards of the narrow, turning passage. Soon the line slowed as the host of Evirians grew denser around us, our progress becoming almost snaillike. Then the corridor turned sharply to the left, and the reason for the delay was plain. About fifteen yards further along rose a set of immense doors, this marking the terminus of the long passageway. The dully garbed minions swarmed before it, and they spoke in muted tones, their faces creased in puzzlement.

"End of the line, it looks like," Denny sighed. "Adara, are you sure—?"

"We're in the right place, of that I have no doubt. This is the primary research chamber in the house of Kobuld. Like the others I'm surprised that it is not yet open."

"This can't be where the tirr oil is kept!" I exclaimed. "How could we hope to take any with hundreds of Evirians around?"

"This chamber, like the one above, must be traversed in order to descend to the next level, where the oil is stored. It will be difficult to achieve with so many cramming the room, but if we can do it unobserved we should be able to continue our quest with no further interference."

"Let's work our way up to the front of this bunch," Denny offered. "Any advantage we—"

The corridor became deathly still as the door swung open without warning. Then, as a trio of apprentices emerged to greet them, the throng raised their voices in joyful anticipation, and they poured into the room as fast as the smiling robed ones would permit. We were unable to push our way past more than a handful, and by the time we crossed the threshold the research chamber was jammed. While jostling our way amidst the gleeful morons, Adara indicated the far wall and, despite my inability to observe anything through the mass, I knew that this was our destination. But the distance across the spacious room was at least twenty-five yards, every inch of it carpeted with Evirians, and it was clear that our task would be anything but simple.

"Rather than force our way so boldly through the crowd, an effort that might call attention to ourselves, let's proceed slowly amongst them," Adara said. "Soon their interest will be diverted elsewhere, and our passage will scarcely be noticed."

"Yes, but at what price?" I asked. "What other perversions of this house must we be subjected to before we find what we came for?"

Shaking his head, Denny replied, "After all we've seen, what does it matter?"

"I suppose you're right. In any case, maybe we can negotiate all or most of it before the—activities begin."

We turned in the same direction as the crowd, and we sidled along inch by inch while absorbing the scene in the center of the primary research hall. There, upon an oval dais, two acolytes busied themselves with something that I could not discern. Even when one of them stepped aside I was unable to see what they had been doing, for the object of their interest—this sitting atop a tapered pedestal—was draped by a black cloth. Aside from the mysterious thing only two other objects occupied the platform. One was a large, rectangular table covered with gleaming white sheets, the second a granite cube of approximately two feet on all sides. The portent of this odd array initially escaped me.

Although packed together like rush-hour commuters, the throng somehow managed to part to afford an unusual contingent ingress. In the forefront strode a towering horrik, this expressionless creature bearing a huge scimitar; directly behind was a smiling Evirian, the same fellow whom we had seen chosen earlier at the entrance. He was flanked by two robed figures, the one on the right a striking elder sporting an unkempt shock of milk-white hair.

"Kobuld!" Adara gasped. "It is the Giver of Wonders himself! This indeed must be a momentous experiment."

The crowd echoed her amazement at seeing the revered Giver, but they did not break loose in cheers. Instead they watched with respectful awe as Kobuld and his underling mounted the platform behind the other pair, and they voiced their conjoint greeting in muted tones as the elder acknowledged their presence with a kindly nod. Then, the brief amenities concluded, the Giver uttered a few words to his assistants, who responded immediately. The one who had entered with him hastened to the side of the pedestal; another stood by the head of the aseptic table, while the last joined the Giver, who had backed toward the edge of the platform. In the meantime the chosen citizen had knelt by the stone block, and for a few moments he waved happily to some of the assemblage. Finally he rested his head on the cube, his eyes turned away from the horrik, who now hovered atop of him. Without a visible sign from any of the robed figures the creature raised the curved blade high, and it was then, only then, that I grasped the reality of what was taking place on the oval stage.

With a shrill whistle the blade arced downward and, after slicing cleanly through the knotted cords of the elongated neck, it struck the stone with a deafening clang, one which reverberated through the immense hall. The still grinning head rolled a few yards away, where it was gathered up by the acolyte who had stood alongside Kobuld. He carried the grisly thing to his comrade by the pedestal, while the horrik, after corralling the reflexively thrashing torso, lifted it up and deposited it on the table. The black cloth was then pulled away unceremoniously, and Adara, who had nearly swooned a moment earlier, cried out in horror at what was revealed. Inside a large, transparent vessel was another human head, this one bobbing in an amber liquid. Despite my revulsion I could not tear my eyes away; and after a few moments I was convinced that the mouth, as well as the eyes, were moving and that to all intent and purpose—it was alive! I knew that this could not possibly be, yet how could I deny what I saw before me? Adara, who more than likely had observed the same thing, dug her nails into my arm unconsciously, while I bit my lip against the pain in the midst of struggling with my sanity.

A transfer was effected within seconds; the head in the beaker was withdrawn and the newly severed one dropped into the liquid, which took on a reddish tinge for a few moments before changing back to its original color. The former, gasping and sputtering grotesquely, was borne to the table, where Kobuld and his aides set about the task of joining it to the stilled torso, which had been treated with the powdery coagulant to stanch the spurting. This procedure, related in a dull monotone by Kobuld, seemed to fascinate the assemblage even more than the events preceding it, and they edged closer to the stage to better absorb all that was transpiring. We had managed to negotiate more than three-quarters of the hall during the course of the unimaginable scene, and now we wasted little time in forging a path the rest of the way, for even those we jostled did not afford us as much as a glance. With the eyes of the Evirians glued to the Giver of Wonders we descended the stairway unseen, and not until we were far along the deserted corridor of the lower level, where Kobuld's voice could not reach us, did we pause.

Reality now struck with a devastating impact; Denny retched uncontrollably, Adara buried her head in her knees and sobbed, while my body trembled in the grip of the thousand gelid fingers that encircled it. But in the midst of our emotional defense against the atrocity we had witnessed it occurred to me that the time we were utilizing was a luxury—that each moment we lingered increased the chances of our being discovered in this passageway, which was generally acknowledged as off limits to the general populace of Kharith. Accordingly I denied my own anguish, and once marginally in control I spoke softly to the distraught pair.

"Come on, you two," I told them in a voice that was anything but insistent. "We can't be far from the storage room now. Let's get this over with."

Adara rose first, and after wiping her eyes she sighed deeply. Denny's torment was not as quickly resolved, but with our help he managed to regain his feet, and only after being assured that his legs would hold him did we relinquish our grasp on his arms. We then set off along the dim corridor—the masks of grim determination on all our faces indicating that, for now at least, we had successfully raised a barrier between ourselves and the mind-wrenching images of Kobuld's research chamber.

We passed a number of doors during the first twenty or so winding yards, none of these appearing to interest Adara. "As I told you before," she said, "I'm not certain of the exact location of the tirr oil. But from what I heard in the past I know that the room has to be further along this passageway. After a few more minutes we might start looking—"

From around an especially sharp curve stepped an immense horrik, its unexpected presence causing us to stand as if paralyzed. It stood only a couple of yards away, and in our current state it could easily have wrought havoc at will. But it did not attack; instead it stared expressionlessly at us for long seconds, its arms crossed. Then it pointed down the corridor in the direction from which we had come, and its meaning could hardly be misinterpreted.

"Anything you say, pal," Denny mumbled as he turned on his heel and retreated into the gloom of the stone-lined passage. We followed close behind, though not until we were beyond the thing's sphere of vision did we cease looking over our shoulder. After adding another few yards for good measure we finally paused, and for the first time in a minute or more we dared to breathe.

"Damn it, we're so close!" I exclaimed bitterly. "How are we supposed to get past that devil?"

"And what if there are more further along?" Denny added.

"I never heard mention of this level being guarded," stated Adara in a tone laced with self-reproach. "Ro-lan, Denny, please, I—"

"Don't blame yourself," I told her insistently as I managed a meager smile. "We didn't expect this to be easy, did we? The thing is, what do we do now?"

"What choice do we have?" sighed Denny, pointing above. "Come on, let's get out of here. Maybe we can devise some other way—"

"No!" I snapped, pounding my fists together in frustration. "There's got to be a way for us to reach that oil! Besides, I'm not quite ready to retrace our steps through the research chambers of Kobuld. Here, let's see what we can find in some of these rooms."

Adara shrugged. "Ro-lan is right, Denny. We have little to lose at this point."

The redhead, always game for a challenge, nodded sheepishly; and with no further discussion we approached the nearest door, a stone barrier of

253

considerable weight. I pulled tentatively on the oversized iron handle, but the door, obviously designed for use by the powerful horriks, refused to budge. The three of us then grabbed hold, and our faces reddened as we forced ourselves to the limits of our strength, until the unyielding barrier grudgingly conceded a few inches. With this success to bolster us we continued to pull, and before long the opening was wide enough to squeeze through; but only after we had regained our wind did we choose to penetrate the heretofore well-sealed room, where we quickly learned the futility of our efforts.

Swirling gusts of frigid air assailed our bodies as we stepped within, this a startling contrast to the warmth of the corridor. Metal shelves rose along the walls of the compact, seemingly natural freezer, these stacked two and three high with dismembered human parts. Larger appendages, arms, legs, even a couple of full torsos hung suspended from the ceiling, and it was Adara's misfortune to bump into one of the latter before any of us had fully grasped the truth about this incomprehensible room. She started to scream, but I clamped my hand over her mouth and bore her out into the corridor, Denny close at our heels. For long moments I wrestled with the wide-eyed beauty, while Denny, driven by the forces of horror, placed his shoulder to the stone barrier and closed it by himself. It was this definitive sealing of the room that seemed to wrest Adara from the mindless terror that had held her, for she ceased her struggles, and when I uncovered her mouth she did not cry out.

"Are you all right?" I asked, concerned.

Nodding, she gasped, "Come on, we've got other rooms to check."

With the still incredulous Denny in the lead we crossed the corridor to a less imposing wooden door. This one swung open easily, but all that was revealed within was a towering heap of soiled garments and two circular tubs filled with water.

"An Evirian laundry room," I muttered in disgust.

Turning his back, Denny indicated the next door. "Here, let's give this one—"

"Wait a minute, the robes!" cried Adara suddenly, waving a finger at the dirty pile. "Those are apprentices' robes!"

Puzzled, I asked, "What do you mean?"

"Don't either of you see? The apprentices can walk any of the corridors in this house with impunity. If we put on—!"

"Of course!" Denny exclaimed. "We could walk right past that thing, or any others for that matter, unchallenged!"

They turned toward me, and I told them: "It's risky, but it sure is worth a try. Let's do it!"

We extracted three of the sweat-soaked garments from the pile, and we swallowed our revulsion as we donned them. Adara assured us that there were a number of female apprentices in the house of Kobuld, and I breathed a sigh of relief as I realized that it would not be necessary for us to conceal her identity by raising the hoods, something that was seldom done here. We returned to the corridor, where our initial steps were lengthy as we hastened to get the confrontation over with. But as we neared the turn we slowed, and I cannot say for certain if either of the taut pair chanced a breath, but I know that I did not.

Once again the horrik emerged in our path, its elongated arms entwined. For a few tense moments it stood there, and then, after nodding subserviently, it backed away. By the time we walked past the creature it had already resumed its position on the floor, and it barely afforded us a glance as we strode purposefully down the passage, our goal now even closer to being realized.

We were well past the humanoid sentry before we stopped. Perspiration flowed freely beneath the heavy robes, but we dared not remove them, for the corridor again turned sharply a few yards ahead of us, and it was not unreasonable to assume that another horrik awaited us there. However, this was not the case. In fact there was little left to guard, for the narrow passageway finally terminated at a bare wall about ten yards from where we stood. There were two sealed rooms on the wall to our left and one on the opposite side—the latter, unlike all the rest we had seen, displaying a pair of iron brackets and a heavy bolt.

"Our search is about over," stated the smiling Denny. "Take your pick!"

I indicated the first door on the left, and we cast it ajar with no more difficulty than the previous one. Almost immediately we were confronted with a huge, darkly pigmented horrik, but we managed to conceal our fear as we held our ground. Denny motioned the thing into the corridor, and it complied docilely. We then stepped inside, and I closed the barrier behind us.

"That devil just took a few more years off my life," Denny gasped, "and considering all that's happened I can hardly afford any more."

I nodded grimly, and we began to examine our surroundings. We were inside a laboratory—a small room containing stark tables and wooden shelves, all covered with tubes and beakers of various sizes. Some were empty, but the majority were at least half-full with a transparent, reddish-tinged liquid. On the back wall was a distilling apparatus, and it was currently functional—though its source of heat was not a flame, but rather a large chunk of the phosphorescent mineral that illuminated Kharith. At the end of the twisting coils small globules of the liquid dripped slowly into a broad-based beaker, one that had recently been placed there.

"Tirr oil!" Adara exclaimed triumphantly as we approached the complex still. "We need not look any further!"

"Indeed, young woman, your quest *has* come to an end!"

We whirled about at the sound of the unexpected voice, and our hearts sank as we observed the contingent now standing in the doorway. Foremost was the white-haired Kobuld, the Giver flanked by two of his acolytes. A pair of horriks were visible in the corridor behind them, and doubtless there were more—though this hardly seemed to matter, for any hope of escape was now shattered.

"How did you know we were here?" I growled.

Kobuld smiled beneficiently as he walked toward us. "The ways of this house are an enigma to those who have dwelt in Kharith for a lifetime, much less to you, who are newcomers. You did a very foolish and dangerous thing by coming down here." His tone was that of a scolding uncle.

"Are you planning to kill us?" asked Denny, his eyes darting from side to side in search of some desperate means of defense.

"I sense your futile thoughts, young man," said the Giver, "and I advise you against taking any action that you will later regret. No, you will not be destroyed, for this is not the Evirian way."

"It's not, huh?" I challenged, slanting my head upward.

Kobuld ignored the dig, and his smile broadened. "Ah, but you have so much to learn! What we do here . . . no, it is not for me to explain it to you, for my time is limited." He ordered his apprentices out of the room, and their places were taken by a pair of horriks. "Now, you must be imprisoned for your indiscretion." His tone was almost apologetic. "It will not be for long, perhaps a few days, because you are outsiders, and you did not know. Then you will be released to start life anew in Kharith, your home!"

Under the watchful gaze of the horriks we marched into the corridor—which was crammed with a dozen of the silent creatures, as well as those who controlled them. We were instructed to remove our pilfered garments, and to this we complied without a thought. Kobuld then motioned us to the room on the opposite wall, and one of the horriks hastened to open the bolted door. For a moment we paused on the threshold of the almost bare cubicle, which was about half the size of the laboratory. The closest horrik then responded to the command of an impatient Evirian, and we were thrust within. The door was slammed shut, the bolt reset; the echoing footfalls in the corridor receded, until an ominous silence reigned in the cell far beneath the house of the Giver of Wonders.

CHAPTER SEVENTEEN

THE GLOWING MINES

An hour passed, or perhaps five hours; we could not be certain. Adara reclined atop a small cot, the only piece of furniture in the room, while I sat cross-legged in a nearby corner. Denny, for perhaps the hundredth time since our internment, paced the floor along the base of the four walls; and when he again came to the door he lashed out at it with his heel, the ensuing noise rousing Adara from the brief moment of slumber that she had found.

"Damn it, damn it!" he bellowed. "How did we allow ourselves to get into this?"

"Will you shut up?" I snapped, rising. "I've had enough—"

"Stop it, the two of you!" cried Adara as she positioned herself between us. "With everything else that's befallen us must we fight among ourselves? We'll be out of this hole soon enough, and we'll then make new plans."

"Sure," I sulked.

"She's right," said Denny sheepishly. "I'm sorry pal, I really am."

"Me, too. You know, I've been thinking: since we're already prisoners in Kharith, what would you say this makes us now?"

"Prisoners in prison," Denny answered. "It sounds ludicrous."

"Everything about this damned city is ludicrous."

"Prisoners in prison," Adara repeated, the words falling off her tongue in a delighted singsong. Something about them struck her funny, and she sought vainly to suppress her laughter, which soon pealed forth. We could not help but be caught up in her amusement, and we began to laugh uproariously, until our breath was gone and our sides ached. But we did not care, for this outburst was a welcome reprieve from the ceaseless tension of the terrible day in the house of Kobuld, and we relished each moment of it.

Footsteps were soon audible in the corridor, each subsequent one growing louder, until finally they stopped. The bolt was lifted from its brackets, the door cast open, and with little formality Pahmun entered.

"Oh, of all the places to find you!" he snapped. "You have no idea how upset Deklus was when he heard of this. Why did you have to do it?"

"Pahmun, can you get us out of here?" I asked.

"I'm so angry!" he squeaked, shaking his fists. "So seldom have I ever been angry. This wouldn't have happened if I had stayed with you."

"Pahmun—"

"Yes, yes," he sighed. "Deklus has already spoken to Kobuld, and the Giver of Wonders has agreed to your release. But you can—"

"You mean we're free to walk out of here?" Denny exclaimed.

Pahmun nodded. "As I was saying, you can be sure that your activities will be more carefully scrutinized in days to come. And worse, it will be a long time before any of you are chosen to participate in the Pleasures. This foolishness of yours cannot go totally unpunished, you know."

We all but ignored his babbling as we pushed past him into the corridor, where we were immediately confronted by a giant horrik. "Pahmun!" I roared. "Didn't you say that we were free?"

"Of course. The purpose of this horrik was to remove the bolt from your door. You didn't expect *me* to do it, did you? Now stay close to me, please, lest you find yourselves in any more trouble!"

The energetic little apprentice guided us through the house of Kobuld, and I doubt whether he ceased his prattling for half a minute, though I could not recall even a fraction of what he said. We passed through the research halls, now empty, and by the door of the room in which the horriks were formed, the still bubbling vat standing unattended. Through the clinic, where a few injured Evirians still lingered, and out into the crisp air of Kharith—where we discovered, to our amazement, that it was dusk.

"Hurry, hurry!" Pahmun urged as he raced down the steps. "There is much to be done before the designated hour. I don't suppose you've eaten today, have you? Ah, the apprentices of Kobuld might have forgotten you for days, so engrossed are they in their Pleasures. Had I not been. . . ."

And so on, all the way back along the winding alleyway, which was not as well lit as Kharith's main thoroughfares. Darkness was total by the time we reached the house of Obbor, and the evening's gluttony was well under way, with the obese Giver of Sustenance himself leading the festivities. After gathering up what we required we returned to the street, and with a begrudging word of appreciation I dismissed the still chattering Pahmun, who was beginning to grate on my nerves.

"Remember now," he warned before departing, "do not make any more trouble for yourselves or it will reflect on both Deklus and myself. I would come for you tomorrow, but unfortunately I have other pressing duties."

"We'll keep our noses clean, Pahmun, I promise."

He scratched his head over my terminology as he walked away, and we breathed a conjoint sigh of relief as he disappeared into the crowd. We journeyed in the opposite direction for a few minutes, until we reached the steps of the house of Ralzon, and we welcomed the comparitive solitude there as we eagerly attacked our dinner.

"This night air sure feels good," said Denny, his words breaking a thoughtful silence that had dominated for a time. "After what we went through today I almost wish that I could sleep outside."

"Do you really?" the grinning Adara asked as she

motioned toward the house directly opposite where we sat. At the portal the sultry apprentice to Oghis, Giver of Lovemaking, was chancing reprimand for neglecting her duties as she gazed longingly at the now-flushed redhead. Naori, the sensual goddess of Kharith, summoned him to her den of ecstasy with a barely perceptible gesture; and there was no way that he could refuse her, even if he had wanted to.

Adara and I rose, and I clapped him on the shoulder as I said, "See you in the morning, pal, okay? Don't make it so early this time."

We hastened to Adara's cube, which we reached not long before the striking of the designated hour. As the night passed we continued to make up for the long months of empty yearning—the only blot on our joy being the brief periods in between, where the bleak visions of what we had seen in the chambers of Kobuld melded with those already housed in the recesses of our minds to wrest us again and again from our much needed slumber.

Dawn arrived, but we paid it little heed, and not until midmorning did we crawl groggily from the furs. We were dressed and scrubbed when Denny made his well-timed entrance, and we welcomed him eagerly in light of the fact that his arms were laden with food. As we ate I noticed his own haggard appearance, and I had little doubt that his night had been interrupted by similar unspeakable images. I wondered what Naori must have thought.

"What shall we do today?" Adara asked as we neared the end of our meal.

"Maybe it'd be best if we just sat tight," Denny

offered. "After what happened yesterday we ought to keep a low profile for a time."

Shaking my head I told them: "I want to see Kharith. I want to know everything there is to know about this place. There's no reason for us to be here now, and every day we waste is one day less that we have to do what must be done elsewhere. No one, not even Deklus or his blasted little apprentice, can find fault with us for sightseeing, can they?"

"I'll be happy to show you every square inch of Kharith," Adara offered. "I pray that one of you finds something I might have overlooked, though. . . ."

"Let's start with the mines you mentioned, where they dig up that glowing rock."

She nodded, and with renewed determination we quitted the cube for the streets of Kharith. If the populace knew of our previous day's transgression they chose not to show it, for we were greeted cheerfully by all who passed us, and upon Adara's advice we responded in kind. Then, as we reached the northern edge of the city, the lines of Evirians began to thin, and once beyond the outermost rim of houses we encountered none.

"The mines sit along the perimeter of the crater," Adara informed us as we strode atop the solidified lava floor. "There are three of them; two functional, the other closed."

I nodded. "We'll concentrate our initial efforts inside the bowl, which should probably take a couple of days. After that we'll work our way to the walls."

"Let's hope that we can come up with something before then," said Denny. "I heard talk in the house

265

of Obbor this morning that even more horriks have been placed at the gates and, worse, it's said that they're now patrolling along the base of the walls. We really shook these devils up yesterday."

Chagrined, I replied, "That's not the best news we could have heard. But in any case . . . hey, what's this?"

Four figures approached purposefully from the opposite direction—the dark quartet, obviously horriks, flanking a small, six-wheeled cart fabricated of iron. They did not pause as they drew nearer, nor did any look at us when they passed. Their eyes, tiny black beads quite unlike any of the others we had seen, remained transfixed on the city, their destination. I was unable to look into the makeshift mine car that they towed, though the glow emanating from inside the contrivance left little doubt regarding its contents.

"They must've had a bad day hunting for their rocks," I stated. "That cart doesn't look especially full."

"On the contrary, my love, they are returning to the city with just enough to fulfill the current needs of their masters. The walls of the shafts are lined with this mineral, so much so that one could be blinded from even brief exposure. Those horriks are nearly sightless out here, but they function well in the mines—this the purpose for which they were created."

Eventually we neared the base of the crater wall, though because of the terraced lava floor we did not see the first of the shafts until we stood within yards of it; for it was nothing more than a circular hole in

266

the rock surface, its diameter about four feet. The second opening, as indicated by Adara, was about thirty yards to our right, the last half again that distance in the other direction, this one covered with what appeared to be a slab of granite.

"All three descend vertically for an indeterminate distance before branching," Adara explained, "so say the indisputable records of Deklus."

"What do you mean?" I asked. "Haven't you explored all of them?"

"Just this one." She indicated the shaft before us with her toe. "I could not remove the stone from the old mine, and the other one was only recently dug."

"Maybe there's a chance here after all!" Denny exclaimed.

"All right, here's what we'll do," I stated. "Denny, you take this shaft, since Adara's already been through it. I'll take the one that's covered. Adara, the new one is yours. Now, is there some way of getting down them?"

"There are rope ladders: precarious, but negotiable."

"Even in the old shaft?"

"I believe so."

"Was it closed for reasons of safety?"

"No; it was because the mineral petered out, at least by Evirian standards. You must remember to keep your eyes averted as much as possible."

I kissed her firmly. "Be careful, love; you too, McVey. We'll meet back here as soon as we're done."

"What about the horriks?" Denny asked. "Will we run into any down there?"

"Even if we did they would prove harmless,"

Adara replied. "But there are no mine cars on the surface, hence no horriks."

I covered the distance to the sealed shaft quickly. Denny had already vanished below when I looked back, while Adara, just beginning her descent, waved vigorously. I responded in a like manner, until she too was gone, and I then turned my attention to the task at hand. The stone was indeed heavy, as she had indicated, but after much grunting and swearing I succeeded in shoving it to one side. With a bit of trepidation I began climbing down the thick hemp ladder, though my fears were quickly allayed as I realized that, despite its age, the sturdy thing had been constructed to withstand the weight of the immense horriks.

The shaft dropped far below the surface, until it became so dark that I could barely see the next rung. Then, at a depth that I approximated to be seventy-five feet, the walls began to exhibit narrow veins of the luminescent mineral. Before long the shaft below me was brightly lit, and I was forced to shut my eyes against its brilliance as I descended. If the Evirians considered this mine played out, then I could not begin to imagine how dangerous it must be for Adara and Denny in the more abundant pair.

It came as a bit of a surprise when I reached the bottom, for my eyes were still closed, and the rope ladder ended about two feet above, this nearly causing me to lose my footing. I lowered myself to the floor, and through the narrowest of slits I examined my immediate surroundings.

I stood at the junction of three tunnels, all of considerable size to accommodate the horriks who had once toiled here. For want of a better choice I entered the one nearest me, and not until I had penetrated a good few yards did I realize that, despite the loftiness of the smooth ceiling, instinct was causing me to walk stooped over. I quickly drew myself to my full height, and as I did I became aware of something else: the veins in the wall were decreasing, and it was becoming less difficult to see. In fact, the solid wall marking the end of the tunnel was only ten yards from where I stood, and it was devoid of the glowing mineral. It was not hard to understand why the excavation had been terminated at this point.

I returned to the ladder and chose another tunnel, this one far brighter than the first. I walked its entire twisting length, and I explored its two shorter branches, but the results never varied. As my frustration grew I lashed out at one of the barriers with my foot, and I discovered just how impassible it was. For a minute I thought that I had broken a toe, but I was able to walk it off, much to my relief.

The third tunnel and its single branch revealed nothing different. I returned to the ladder feeling both fatigued and defeated. The ascent seemed interminable, and on three separate occasions I nearly lost my footing. When Adara and Denny dragged me from the hole I could not even feel my arms; though moments after relinquishing my hold the life returned to them, and they throbbed painfully.

"Both of us climbed up some time ago," said Denny, "so we decided to wait for you here."

"I knew that the old mine was the largest," Adara added, "that exploring it would take longer, but this did not lessen the anxiety."

"Rollie, did you find anything?"

"No," I gasped. "What about you?"

Denny shook his head. "I drew a blank; but Adara thinks that she's got something."

I gazed hopefully at my dusty but beautiful mate, who said, "The new mine is by far the smallest, though the reason why is clear, for the main tunnel is carved entirely from the glowing rock. They've had no reason to dig any further."

"So?"

"This mineral is soft," Denny interjected, "and can easily be chipped away. Don't you see, Rollie? The mother lode might run for miles, and we could tunnel our way right under the wall!"

"Then again it could peter out after fifty yards. But let's say that it is the primary vein; if so, how can you be sure that it doesn't run right back toward Kharith?"

"I can't offer the precise direction," said Adara, "but I do know for sure that it leads away from the city."

"All right," I nodded, "we have an option now, not the best by any means, but at least it's something. However, there are too many intangibles that I see, and therefore I don't think that we should plan on exercising it until all else has been exhausted."

"That makes sense," said Denny. "Come on, let's get back to the city. I didn't expect this excursion to be as time-consuming and demanding as it was, particularly on you. Tomorrow—"

"Who said we were finished?" I snapped. "There's plenty of daylight left!"

270

"Ro-lan! For a change your friend is sensible, and you are the pigheaded one! Look at yourself, listen to your labored breathing, and then tell us that you wish to continue."

"Okay, you two," I laughed. "I surrender. No, on second thought I'll make you a deal. As long as we're out this far let's skirt the base of the crater and see if we can find anything. We'll head back to Kharith in an hour."

"A half-hour, no more," Adara insisted as she offered me her hand.

"That's reasonable, Rollie," added Denny as he also sought to assist me.

The doting pair pulled me to my feet, and we began walking along the crater wall. Our senses were alerted to anything that might prove of interest, but despite this we were afforded nothing out of the ordinary. When Adara announced that the time was up, a debatable point at best in light of our inability to accurately judge the passage of hours, I first argued against abandoning the quest. Then I thought better of it, and with a shrug I set off toward Kharith—my wife and friend, no less dejected, flanking me.

CHAPTER EIGHTEEN

THE GIVER OF ETERNAL REST

We walked in silence most of the way toward the city, each lost in thought, until we happened upon something most unusual about a hundred yards from the outermost building. A small hut stood alone in the midst of the empty lava plain; this darkly painted structure, although within our sphere of vision for some time, was invisible until now against the equally black landscape.

"Adara, do you know what this thing is?" I asked.

"Yes," was her hesitant reply. "This is the entrance to the house of Bhurz."

"A house? This little thing?" exclaimed Denny.

"The house, or more accurately the domain of Bhurz is directly below our feet. He is the Giver of Eternal Rest."

"What does that mean?" I asked guardedly.

Adara shuddered. "He accepts all of Kharith's

dead, and he dwells among them, like some ghoul!"

"I don't understand. Doesn't Kobuld get all the bodies for his experiments or his spare parts room?"

"Not the ones who die of illness or old age. Those belong to Bhurz."

"Sounds like a great place to spend an afternoon," Denny scowled.

"Adara, I assume you've been down there before."

"Yes, a couple of months ago, and it's not a visit that I would care to repeat."

"You saw nothing that might benefit us?"

"No. But I suppose you should see it, just to make sure. We can return in the morning—"

"What's the matter with right now?" I interrupted.

"Come on, Rollie, let's give it up for the day!" Denny exclaimed. "You know I'm as anxious as you are to get out of here, but for crying out loud, you barely made it out of that shaft!"

"I appreciate the concern, but as long as we're already here we might as well go down. Besides, how much time could it take?"

"On that point I must concur," Adara said dryly. "You will not wish to spend one second longer than necessary in the pits of Bhurz. Come, let's get it over with."

"Are you sure you'd rather not wait for us up here, or back in the city?" I asked.

She placed her hands on her hips and scowled at me. "We've already been through this once before in the arena of Ventoth, dear husband, and I'm not going to repeat myself. Now, follow me; watch your footing, for these steps are in need of repair."

With Denny and I vainly trying to suppress grins, the Homaru goddess strode haughtily to the door of the structure and pulled it open. We followed her into the dimly lit room, a few tentative steps carrying us to the top of a spiraling stairwell. An uncomfortable chill emanated from below, a startling contrast to the heat of the crater floor, and as we descended the crumbling stairs it became even more frigid. For more reasons than one it was apparent that we would not be expending a great deal of time in the house of Bhurz.

We had seen no Evirians within the sphere of the hut above, nor did we pass any as we plunged deeper into the rock, and this puzzled me. "Where are all the grinning fools?" I asked Adara. "Don't they flock to this house for whatever 'Pleasures' it may offer?"

She shook her head. "Though they wax ecstatic at the sight of their fellows being hacked to pieces, the Evirians shun this place like the plague, for they have an aversion to natural death. The preservation of the dead is a Pleasure that the Giver of Eternal Rest shares with only one, a young apprentice of questionable faculties. Our presence will be cause for rejoicing, as my visit was months ago." She shuddered uncontrollably, and not just from the increasing cold.

I soon became aware of a muffled sound from below—this growing in volume with each curving step. Finally the stairwell deposited us on the frost-covered floor of a domed cavern, and the source of the now deafening noise was revealed. An angry river dissected the icy chamber as it emerged from a small

274

opening on our right and then vanished in a froth through a slightly larger cavity that appeared to angle downward into the bowels of the mountain. The flow of the churning tributary, which measured about five feet across during its abbreviated journey through the cavern, was well controlled by barely sloping rock walls that had been worn smooth over the years.

"This river is formed by countless tiny streams that run below Kharith," Adara explained as we edged our way closer to the menacing torrent. "It is from them that the city's drinking water is drawn. When I first found out what transpires here on occasion I was glad that the house of Bhurz did not lie on the other side of Kharith, for I might not have drank another drop."

"What do you mean?" I asked.

"Bhurz deposits—corpses into the river at infrequent intervals," she stated, her lips curled in disgust. "I have no idea why he does this, but—"

"Rollie, those things at the base of the peak!" Denny exclaimed. "The body that they cannibalized must have come from here!"

"I had completely forgotten about that until now, though I can't see it as anything other than one more enigma about this place that I don't care to delve into. Let's—"

"Ah, so you were fortunate enough to see the kazos receive their offering! I must know all about it!"

We whirled about at the sound of the unexpected voice, and we were surprised to see the robed pair who stood less than five yards away, their approach concealed by the roaring stream. Foremost was a hunchbacked elder, an ancient, brown-toothed wretch with skin the hue and texture of animal hide. At his heels stood a gaunt figure, a towering fellow with sunken cheeks and a bulbous, malformed nose. Their leering expressions were nearly identical—although the latter, obviously possessed of limited mental abilities, absently stroked his narrow cranium as he studied us.

"Did I startle you?" the old man wheezed as he shuffled closer. "My apologies, but only once before in my life have I met anyone who has seen the kazos feed, so you can imagine my excitement. You must tell me everything—ah, but first things first. What brings you to the house of Bhurz?"

I glanced at Adara, who swallowed her disgust as she replied, "We have come to experience the Pleasures of your house. I have been here before, and now I wish my friends to see what I have seen."

"Otuma, did you hear that?" the wizened fellow crowed as he motioned his apprentice forward. "They have come to share our Pleasures with us!"

"I hear, Giver, I hear," the other replied in a snorting voice that was barely understandable; and he did not bother to check the foul mucus that dribbled from his tiny nostrils as he limped toward us.

"Yes, you must know all there is to know about the house of Bhurz," said the elder in gleeful anticipation. "Oh, I hardly know where to begin, for there is so much to tell!"

Motioning for us to remain still, Adara addressed

the Giver in an apologetic voice: "We cannot stay here too long, for we are poorly garbed against the cold. But a brief look about your house now will leave us anticipating our return, which will be within days, perhaps even tomorrow."

"Will you then tell us what it was like to witness the kazos as they partook of their offering?" he asked me, his eye cocked.

"We'll describe it down to the most intimate detail," I stated sarcastically.

This set the pair off into an ecstatic froth, and they struck one another repeatedly as they leaped up and down. Finally they regained some marginal control, and Bhurz motioned us forward with a gnarled finger.

"Let us begin with the principal storage rooms," he said. "Otuma, run on ahead and make certain that everything is in order."

"Everything in order, everything in order," the imbecile repeated as he limped away with surprising speed. We then set off in the wake of the ebullient Giver, our path paralleling the rushing tributary. As we walked I found myself curious about the previously forgotten creatures below, and despite my aversion to him I queried Bhurz about the link between the Evirians and the flesh-eating kazos.

"The kazos," began the Giver, "were first discovered by our ancestors during their ascent, and the toll of the encounter was high. Then, months after reaching the summit, Cuhram's people were again beset by the creatures, for their supply of flesh had dwindled, and their appetite for it was insatiable.

More Evirians perished, and the first Elite feared oblivion, for they did not yet have the means to create the horriks that might otherwise have protected them.

"Shortly thereafter an Evirian of advanced years died, and as an experiment his body was left along the edge of the crater. When the kazos next came they took it, and they did not trouble any of the others. Subsequent corpses were deposited near the top of the mountain trail, the end result being the same each time. Our ancestors had learned how to deal with the things from below, and they were never attacked again.

"The cavern in which we now stand was discovered during the early years by my own grandfather, who reasoned that the river he had once observed cascading down the side of the mountain was an extension of this torrent. Two days before the usual monthly offering was carried to the edge he consigned a corpse to the river. More than a week later he went himself to check on the offering, and he discovered that it was still there. Two, three more carcasses were piled along the rim of the plateau before Cuhram could be convinced that the effort was no longer necessary, that an even simpler means of satisfying the kazos had been found. As his reward my grandfather was entrusted with the responsibility, which of course he relished.

"After the walls were completed and Kharith sealed for all time it seemed unnecessary to feed the kazos, for they could not have penetrated the city. But my grandfather petitioned Cuhram to retain the ritual, and the Giver of Wonders made it official by written decree. It was subsequently passed on to my father, who during his time as Giver of Eternal Rest conceived of the signal that you must surely have heard, and finally to me. It is quite a responsibility, wouldn't you say?"

We nodded vaguely, and Bhurz beat his chest proudly as he guided us toward the first visible rift in the wall. Otuma stood before the narrow crevice, and he waved his arms excitedly as we neared.

"Everything in order, Giver, everything in order!" he exclaimed as he absently sucked in the gobs of mucus that now hung down.

"Otuma, what would I do without you?" he wheezed. "Here, show our guests the first storage room."

The tall cretin, beside himself with ecstasy over the duty entrusted him, squeezed through the opening, and he waved for us to follow. Passage proved more difficult for Denny and myself, but with Adara's help we soon found ourselves inside a small, circular chamber, its limited confines more than likely the cause of the heightened chill that penetrated to the marrow. Scores of perfectly preserved, frost-coated bodies were stacked as much as ten high along the walls, and about half that in two parallel rows near the center. Evirian men and women—both young and old, even a few small children—lay quietly in the natural freezer, none caring in the least about the unknown fate ordained for them by their ghoulish caretakers. It was an unnerving scene, and after making certain that there were no other exits, our sole purpose for going in, we returned to the waiting Bhurz.

"Was it not stimulating?" exclaimed the Giver. "Ah, but there is so much more to see! Come, come!"

With the snorting Otuma at our heels we followed Bhurz to the next room, a smaller one with identical contents, and no other adjoining passageways. The third storage chamber was larger than the first two combined, and the number of frozen corpses was staggering—though once again, despite our careful scrutiny, we were unable to discern any potential means of egress. Though I should have expected nothing more, I nonetheless found it difficult to restrain my growing frustration.

There were no more rifts in the wall, at least on this side, for we now stood within yards of where the river penetrated the stone barrier, and we were stunned by the devastating force of the foaming water as it disappeared into the heart of the mountain. Bhurz and Otuma stood near the edge of the foreboding tributary, though in light of the fact that they had negotiated this cavern countless times I doubted whether they were in any danger. After a brief conference Otuma scampered off, and when he returned a few minutes later he hefted a long, sturdy plank. He laid the timber across the angry stream, and despite his awkward manner he crossed to the far side with but three loping strides.

"If you think that you've seen anything yet, then just wait!" cried the Giver as he waved us toward the makeshift span. "You'll find it hard to stay away for long from the house of Bhurz; in fact, you might not even wish to go! Hurry, hurry!"

I crossed first, then Adara and Denny, with Bhurz close behind the redhead. Otuma bounded ahead of us like a happy cur as we followed the curvature of the wall, which remained unbroken for a considerable distance. Finally the apprentice paused before a circular opening, one so low to the ground that ingress necessitated crawling on his hands and knees. He disappeared inside, and with a conjoint shrug we followed suit.

"This is the most venerable of the special rooms," echoed the voice of Bhurz through the surprisingly long tunnel. "It was created by my grandfather, and in his honor neither myself or my father have seen fit to change a thing."

The large room into which we soon emerged was more brightly lit than any of the storage chambers, though this hardly lessened the chill. I was immediately aware of the fact that Adara, who had been here before, was discreetly staring at her sandals, and it did not take me long to discern the reason why.

Near the center of the room was a food-laden table, around which six frozen Evirians reclined in mock banquet. Others stood with formed smiles and gestured into infinity. Silent children sat on the floor and stared intently at an endlessly spinning top. In a bed along one wall a hoar-white man and woman made love, their ecstasy spread across an eternity.

Many other muted forms stood in the eerie room through which Bhurz and Otuma now pranced gaily, and I found it nearly impossible to concentrate on the task at hand. Denny was the first to tear his eyes away from the unimaginable sight, and he immediately noticed the large opening to our right.

"Where does that go?" he asked the Giver.

Bhurz winked one of his rheumy eyes. "Follow me,

and I'll show you."

The abbreviated corridor led into a similar room, where the obscene, suggestive poses of the unknowing participants more than hinted at the depravity of those who had toyed with them over the decades. Another low-ceilinged passage once again deposited us into the cavern, where for the moment I tried vainly to blot out what I had seen. Denny also sought to control his emotions, while Adara, who could not have helped but absorb some of what she already knew existed, dabbed at a bloodied lip with a piece of cloth.

It was not yet over: the two robed figures, both carried away by the degeneracy that they had helped to spawn, guided us through two more rooms, until it became impossible to withstand any more. I desired nothing other than to take their heads in my hands and grind them together, until they became part of the macabre scene that they had created, and I knew that the wishes of the seething Denny were no different. But as the thread began to unravel we again emerged into the cavern, and we were able to restrain ourselves before we jeopardized everything.

"We—we must go now, Giver," Adara gasped. "We'll be back soon, as I promised."

"Wait!" Otuma snorted. "They not see everything."

Bhurz grinned. "He's right; you've yet to see our own personal quarters."

"N-no!" she exclaimed, wide-eyed. "We have to—!"

I placed a finger over my lips to silence the agitated beauty, and I asked the Giver: "Is this the last of it?"

"It is."

"Then Denny and I will go. Adara, you remain here for the moment, and this time no arguments!"

She shuddered uncontrollably as she nodded her assent, while Bhurz said, "Ah, but the woman is indeed cold. Come then, let us show you our quarters, and then you can return to the surface."

The duo guided us through another tight crevice into a far less frigid chamber, where initially I sought to deny anything else there as I searched the walls in vain for any other passageways. But I could not ignore the odor that fouled the air, this emanating from one of a few partially decomposed bodies that lay scattered about the uncharacteristically ornate room. My disbelief mounting I gazed at the ashen-faced Denny, who had easily surmised the same thing.

"Won't you dine with us, honored guests?" the Giver hissed, while the salivating Otuma jumped up and down.

Without a word we staggered back to where Adara waited, and she quickly grabbed hold of our arms to steady us. Bhurz emerged from the crevice, but not so Otuma, the roar of the river marginally drowning out the slavering noises now audible from within. We backed away until they were inaudible, and only then did we pause to gather up the strands of our dwindling sanity.

"Was it not all that I said it would be?" the Giver beamed.

"All and more," Adara choked. "Now, is there another way we might reach the steps leading to the surface?"

"There's a bridge nearby. You won't have to go all the way to the other end. Follow me."

The plank that we soon traversed was wider than the first one, and this was fortunate, for our legs were wobbly. Once on the far side we hastened to the foot of the steps, while the Giver remained alongside the tributary. Before ascending we gazed across the cavern for the final time, and we all but ignored our erstwhile host as he waved vigorously.

"A dead end," Denny snarled.

"In more ways than one."

"All of you come back now, like you promised! Oh, you'll have hours of Pleasure here, and I'll get to hear of the kazos. Come soon, please!"

We began to climb, and the sound of the river, as well as the grating voice of Bhurz, Giver of Eternal Rest, faded below us. Chilled, fatigued beyond caring, we eventually emerged into the clouded daylight of the Borangan mountaintop. We had little breath with which to speak, and so we trudged our way silently into the city, which seemed to swallow us with a symbolic finality.

With Adara in the lead we wended our way along a number of unfamiliar streets, and not until we emerged before the house of Obbor did I have any idea of where we were. Even had I possessed an appetite, which I did not, I would have been sorely pressed to climb the mountain of steps; but I knew that we must have food for later, and so we reclined on the bottom three to regain our wind before challenging them.

All that had recently transpired flashed before me as I sat there, and I found myself unable to shake the feeling of total helplessness as I visualized the lofty, shrouded walls of Kharith that held us atop Boranga's crown. Once again I roamed the death cavern of Bhurz, the corridors of Kobuld. I descended the mines and I walked the perimeter of the crater, but nowhere in my journeys did I discover the path, either ill defined or clearly marked, that would lead us away from this mindless imprisonment.

The day waned. We slept the sleep of the dead in our cubes, and when the morning came we were still weary; but this did not matter, for we had things to do. We breakfasted on the remnants of what we had gathered the previous day, and we mulled over our new course of action.

I nearly bowled over the small table as I suddenly leaped to my feet and raced from the cube. I paused in the doorway, where I glanced at the incredulous pair that I had left behind. "Come on!" I cried, and I ran down the corridor.

They caught up to me in the street, Denny all but tackling me. "Rollie, what the devil's gotten into you?" he exclaimed.

"Nothing much; I just figured out how we're going to escape from here!"

"Oh Ro-lan, tell us!" Adara pleaded.

"Not now! We've got something more important to do first. Hurry!"

"But where are we going?"

"To the house of Deklus!"

Puzzled Evirians stared at us as we sped past, but we paid them little heed, for they did not matter. Eventually we reached the door of the Giver of Knowledge, and we elbowed our way disdainfully past those waiting in line outside. In the corridor I buttonholed Pahmun, the slight apprentice grinning broadly as he recognized us.

"We want to see Deklus, and I mean now!" I told him insistently.

"But that is impossible!" he protested. "He—!"

I lifted the mouse off the floor by his collar. "Tell him that I've come to make a trade!" I roared. "He'll know what that means."

"Very well, very well," he grumbled. "Come with me."

He led us to one of the heavily stocked libraries, where Deklus was in deep conversation with a pair of Evirians. After Pahmun whispered in his ear, the Giver dismissed the two and he waved us forth.

"Pahmun, bring some empty ledgers and two more apprentices," he ordered. "You'll have a lot of writing to do."

His instructions were carried out within seconds. The four Evirians sat on one side of a large table, while Adara and Denny flanked me on the other. For the next couple of hours we told the Giver of Knowledge everything, while he stared at us in dumbfounded silence. His acolytes were no less stunned, though not for a moment did they cease their frantic scribbling.

Finally we were done, and we sank breathless in our chairs for a few seconds. Now it was Deklus's turn to uphold his end of the agreement, and he proved as good as his word. The two other apprentices departed, while Pahmun, after extracting a dusty journal from amongst scores of others on a shelf nearby, walked back to the table and resumed his seat. The Giver of Knowledge opened the book to a premarked page, and in the hour that ensued the three of us learned the secret of Ras-ek Varano's powers.

EPILOGUE

The wind-propelled rain continued to lash out at the window as I tore my eyes away from the manuscript for a few moments. Two-thirty in the morning, the clock on the mantle said. I had already stacked a great deal of Roland's pages to one side, but there was at least a like number left to read. However, I had no intention of stopping until I learned the fate of Roland Summers, his wife Adara, and his best friend, Denny McVey. All I needed was a few minutes to rest.

Just a few . . . minutes . . . to . . . rest. . . .